FALCONS FEAR NO FRONTIER

FALCONS FEAR NO FRONTIER

Thankyou for caring
Richard Wood

Richard Wood

The Book Guild Ltd
Sussex, England

This book is a work of fiction. The characters and situations in this story are imaginary. No resemblance is intended between these characters and any real persons, either living or dead.

The Book Guild Ltd
25 High Street,
Lewes, Sussex

First published 1995

Set in Baskerville
Typesetting by Southern Reproductions (Sussex)
Crowborough, Sussex
Printed in Great Britain by
Antony Rowe Ltd.
Chippenham, Wiltshire.

A catalogue record for this book is
available from the British Library

ISBN 1 85776 018 2

1

Dirk flung himself down upon the springy turf beside the Echostones, his freckled face upturned to the vast blue expanse of the sky. He was gasping for breath after his long run along the field path which led obliquely along the shoulder of the ridge. A last turn through the fell-farm gate had angled him up a steeper slope, taxing his already bursting lungs to capacity. There he lay, sucking in long, deep gasps of cool clean air which the gentle summer zephyrs wafted over the crest behind. Gradually his overtaxed lungs slowed down to a more measured intake as his heartbeats became normal. His glazed eyes, until then closed, now stared unseeing at the vast blue vault until they focused upon a wheeling bird above. It hovered on vibrating wings, a dark blot against an azure heaven. Suddenly it plunged, its curved wings folded, plummeting earthwards. Dirk sat up to follow its course but in his lazy effort only succeeded in watching it rise with beating wings and trailing talons, which held tight to its prey. The bird veered away in a long sweeping curve, rising heavily and heading for the dark knoll of trees away to his right, where it must have an eyrie in the windswept beeches which guarded the crumbling remains of three Martello towers. Dirk inched back over the wiry turf to lean against the mottled lichen-covered rocks protruding a few feet above the peaty soil. The mellow afternoon sun was warm, drying the beads of perspiration which spangled his brow. The day had been ideal for his run, the grassworn tracks springy underfoot. The airs were so caressing that he lingered long before contemplating the easier downhill return. As he sat, knees pulled up to chin,

Dirk gazed fondly at the long familiar scene spread in panorama before his questing eyes.

To his right, where the ridge fell away westward, stood the black knoll of trees into which the kestrel hawk had flown. There the concealed towers overlooked the broadening plain, cleft by the confluences of three rivers. In his mind's eye he pictured the ancient Celtic scouts, obscured by moorland scrub, watching for the furtive advance of their dreaded enemies or other marauding tribesmen advancing along the well-worn tracks which crisscrossed the plain. In later times their progeny would spot the Roman legions as they left their walled camp of Ribchester to march eastward along the old Celtic escape road to Colne and Pontefract, along the tops of the wooded crest on the opposite side of the valley, and Dirk wondered if the Echostones against which he rested had been used to throw an early warning cry of danger. He imagined the bustle that would ensue, rounding up animals for hiding in the cloughs to disappear without trace into the scrubland which then covered those Pennine hills.

It was there, below him in the valley by the old stone bridge over the brook, that Prince Rupert's Royalist army had been ambushed by the Roundheads, hidden by scrub and ferns, and subsequently decimated. If only those slopes could speak, what a vast wealth of history they could unfold of battles, skirmishes and ruthless marauders and marching men!

Beyond the towers lay the ruins of Whalley Abbey, fondly built by Cistercian monks on the River Calder, then teeming with fish, where the flat meadowland yielded rich crops and fat cattle. From its stout walls which had in their day given shelter to the weary travellers, succour to the sick, sanctuary to the fugitive, the Abbot Paslew had fled before the avenging soldiery of Henry VIII, dealing out retribution and destruction to those religious orders which defied his avaricious decrees.

Dirk in his musings traced the route of the abbot's flight which led east along the hillside Dirk had just covered, along the rutted cart track which breasted the southern slope of the hill to the now disused barn which boasted Paslew's name. History has it that the abbot hid in that barn and to it the redcoats traced him, captured him and later, after a summary trial at Lancaster Castle, finding him guilty of treason, hanged him. They sacked the Abbey, evicted the monks, drove out the sick and maimed, and torched the timbers. Past the Abbey's ruins marched Cromwell to bombard and capture the keep at Clitheroe. In that one square mile the history of England had been written in blood. Dirk gazed at the scene and played with the thoughts thus dredged up from the confines of his mind.

Shifting his gaze to the spot where Cromwell was reputed to have spent the night in a cave which still bears his name, Dirk put two fingers to his mouth and gave a shrill whistle. Back came the echo after a second. He repeated it and chuckled as the diminished sound came floating back. The sheep, which had until then been peacefully grazing, became startled and restless and, with heads raised in defence against their natural enemy, the dog, they ceased cropping and moved to group and cluster in defence against the arrival of a collie. They now grazed fitfully with a twitching nervousness, gathering at a spot where a murderer had once been interred, at a point where three parishes met. There, at the convergence, Jack the Knave was buried. No churchyard would accept him but the grave had since been mutilated, the boundary stone removed. Only the indentations still betrayed the site, marked on maps, whilst embroidered tales survived of Jackanapes or Jack the Knappe and his exploits. The still wary sheep didn't seem to mind as they grouped, keeping a yellow eye on the whistler and a furtive surveillance for a collie.

Dirk stretched out his legs, turned face down and with a lithe movement, jumped to a crouch and stood erect. He walked across the intervening space to the field path, and deftly sidled down the steep slope to the farm. Reaching the cart road, he vaulted the five-barred gate and trotted down a tangent field path, timeworn with runnels of past rains and the passage of many feet. He reached the freshet which crossed the path, leaving sandy deposits and a fertile greensward, making for the wicket gate to the cultivated field of an adjacent farm where he followed a little-used diagonal footpath faintly discernible to the trained eye, thinking as he did so of the many clog-clad feet which had long aforetime imprinted their passage in their dawn and often pre-dawn trek to hillside quarry or distant factory in neighbouring Clitheroe.

Reaching the road, he sprinted past the dyeworks where his forebears had once toiled and sought the banks of the lodge which supplied that works. Under the tall trees which lined its verges, he sat and gazed at the expanse of water, the leaping fish, the scatter of ducks, the stately pair of swans and the red-beaked moorhens all busily rippling and furrowing the surface. Here, as a young lad he had fished with line and bent pin, watching the speckled trout and brown carp nibble the bait. Minnows he had netted there and watched the chicks of waterfowl develop. Removing his plimsolls and socks, he dangled his feet in the water, splashing occasionally, as the ducks, anticipating a customary titbit converged upon him.

In the new-mown meadow, across the short reach of water, the cows grazed peacefully. There, close to the bank was the unusually blue-coloured heifer called Cornflower which he had sometimes been allowed to milk for she was docile and indifferent to unpractised hands. Not so the big Ayrshire with the wicked-looking horns and her forefeet already in the shallows. She had kicked him off the three-legged stool as soon as he had touched her udder and everyone had laughed as he was sent sprawling on the rough cobbles of the shippon floor.

Dirk looked back down the lake at the field across which he had come. Sixty-odd years ago his great-grandmother as a girl had walked that same path along with many other girls of tender years to work the week-long in a spinning and weaving mill on the outskirts of Clitheroe, at Primrose Bridge. Each Sunday evening, come hail, rain or shine, the shawl-clad groups would leave the village for the week-long stay, sleeping in the top-storey of the many-floored building below which were the noisy weaving and spinning sheds with their crowded machines. Twelve hours a day they toiled with a half-day on

Saturday, when, at noon, they would start their trek, some four miles long, over the moor, past the Echostones and down that selfsame track which Dirk had followed. In his imagination he could picture them, their brass-bound clogs, their black woollen stockings, long skirts hitched up for ease of travel, shawl-clad, laughing and joking when fine, or head down and silent in the driving winter rain, clutching their hard-earned pittances and perhaps assessing the anticipated activities of the next thirty-six more hours ahead.

Times had changed. Now only two or three men trod the rapidly fading field path as they trudged to an occasional shift at the stone quarry as circumstances and the demand for dressed stone arose. Nature had healed her manmade scars, yet the ancient rights of way remained.

Casually, Dirk picked up a stone and threw it into the middle of the lodge. From the loud plop he watched the concentric ripples spread, growing fainter and fainter until finally merging into nothingness. Life, he mused, was very much like that . . . actions which caused ripples across the space of time and gradually faded into the faintest of recollections. As he proceeded to dry his feet with his socks and slip on his plimsolls, he pondered upon the relative brevity of the human span as compared with the trees under which he sat, the eternal greenery of grass and the permanence of the listening hills. He quickly tied his laces and left the watery scene, walking slowly along the footpath which lined the road until he reached his nearby home.

The terraced house he entered was the third of the first row in the village. As he passed through the dining room to the kitchen he greeted his widowed mother who was ironing by the fireside.

'How far did you get?' she asked.

'As far as Wiswell Moor and the Echostones,' he replied. 'It was lovely up there . . . very peaceful and quiet, like sitting on top of the world.'

'You've been a long time,' remarked his mother.

'Well, I sat up there for about an hour and came down to the Spring Lodge for another spell,' he proffered, adding, 'I need a good wash.'

Dirk passed into the kitchen where he picked up the ladling can and returning, lifted the iron lid of the side-boiler by the fire, dipping down into it to draw a can of hot water which he promptly conveyed to the enamel basin in the kitchen sink, returning again with an equivalent canful of cold tapwater to replace it. In the kitchen he stripped off and washed the dried sweat from his body, towelled and went upstairs to don his ordinary clothes, leaving his running vest and shorts on the window ledge to be washed through later. As he returned to the dining room he saw that his mother had finished ironing, so he folded the ironing board and stowed it away in its place under the stairs. He then sat down in the armchair by the fire to relax and read.

He was in his final year at the distant grammar school reading English, Latin, French and history, with economics as a subsidiary and religious knowledge as a voluntary optional subject. It had already been tacitly agreed that he should train for the teaching profession, but he realised that his prospects for being accepted for a college were rather remote. The year was 1932, the country in severe recession, the principle conversation and daily paper reading being of cuts and economies on every side and in every public sphere. The intake to colleges was to be minimal and the qualifications required were becoming highly competitive. Good results in Higher Certificate were essential and the amount of reading in his courses colossal.

Reaching for his attaché case, he extracted Hardy's *Dynasts* and prepared to engross himself in the text and its literary expression. Strangely, he could not bring himself to concentrate. His thoughts strayed back to Abbot Paslew and the Paslew Barn. 'If Paslew really meant to flee,' he mused, 'he would naturally need the wherewithal to sustain himself. His abbey was reputedly rich and money was what Henry VIII was anxious to lay his hands upon to sustain his ambitious European adventures and maintain his court and armies. Surely Paslew would take gold coin and, if he holed up in Paslew Barn as his first stop he would naturally secrete some for future use'.

Now, that was an intriguing conjecture. History reported no finds, no search upon his capture, so the probability might be a strong possibility. 'Still,' Dirk mused, 'others would have arrived at a similar conclusion and would have made more immediate subsequent searches.'

Here again, history had reported little. Maybe there was a cache there waiting to be discovered. 'What an intriguing thought,' murmured Dirk. He grimaced and forcibly switched his mind to *The Dynasts.* He scanned the printed pages where the author used an aerial view to describe the retreat of Napoleon's army from Russia. 'Vermicular' . . . the word stood out of the page. From the Echostones he too had imagined Prince Rupert's army winding down from Billington to Whalley and again twisting up and over to the Celtic escape road . . . a vermicular straggle of soldiery, shortly to be ambushed, mutilated and massacred. The comparison gave lifelike quality to the text . . . the winding column, the difficult terrain, the drooping spirits, the sagging morale. The Celts, the Romans, Prince Rupert, Paslew and Cromwell, Jacobite Scots, an ebb and flow down the years of human suffering, bitter strife and pain. The room felt warm from the heat of the low fire and his recent exertions and the printed page seemed to fade as, slowly, a soporific feeling descended upon him, causing fingers to relax, book to slip and Dirk to drift away into oblivion. His mother came in from the kitchen where she had been preparing the tea. She glanced across at the slumbering form of her son, smiled a wan, tired smile, then quietly, making the least sound, began to lay the table. Tea, such as it was, could wait.

Ten minutes later Dirk awoke with a start. A loud rat-tat-tat on the front door knocker shocked him back to consciousness.

'It's the postman, probably,' interjected his mother, coming through from the kitchen.

'I'll go, Mum,' said Dirk, hoisting himself to his feet. He reached the vestibule door and, on opening it, saw the letter, a long, white foolscap envelope lying on the mat between the two doors. He bent down to retrieve it. It was addressed to him. He turned it over out of curiosity and saw a green crest on the sealed flap which read Chester Diocesan Training College. Returning to the dining room, he lifted a small knife from the table and slit the flap, extracting the sheets which lay within, and glanced at the contents. He read it in disbelief and then read it through again to make sure that he had not made any mistake as to its message. It was an invitation to attend for interview with the college officials who were considering his application for a place in that college as his first choice. His heart seemed to race, then miss a beat as he slowly assimilated the implications. An interview . . . that was a step in the right direction, an opportunity beyond his wildest dreams. A door had suddenly opened and revealed a vista of uncharted opportunities.

Came a voice from the kitchen, 'Well, what was it?'

'You'll never believe it, Mum, it's a letter from a college for an interview,' cried Dirk excitedly, scarcely able to suppress his surge of emotion. His mother came through, wiping her hands on a towel, a smile of relief upon her face.

'When is it to be?' she asked.

Dirk handed her the letter. 'It's for Saturday week at half past ten in the morning at Manchester,' he breathed, smacking his fist into the palm of his hand. 'Isn't that great, Mum?' he blurted out.

'Don't count your chickens before they're hatched,' commented his mother as she perused the scripts. 'You'll have to get some advice on how to conduct yourself at an interview.' Then in a matter of fact, down-to-earth tone she remarked, 'Are you ready for tea?'

The question brought him out of cloud-cuckoo land and down to reality. 'Any time, Mum,' came the vague reply as his thoughts chased numerous ideas racing around in his brain.

'You'll have to find out what sort of questions they are likely to put to you,' broke in his mother. 'Why don't you go and ask your headmaster and get some advice on it?'

Dirk pondered on that remark, remembering some rather

unfortunate interviews with the head which he would rather forget.

'I'll think about it before I do that,' he murmured.

The letter was placed on the sideboard and they both set to to arrange the table settings and bring in the tea. His mother had prepared fish cakes in the Portuguese style, followed by scones which she had baked that morning, along with some bread and cakes.

'Where's Grandma?' asked Dirk, realising that she was missing.

'She's gone across to your aunt's. She may not be back until this evening,' his mother informed him.

Dirk looked at the clock. It registered a quarter to five.

'Janet will be on the five bus from school,' he remarked.

'Yes and she'll be ravenous too,' laughed his mother. 'Hockey today, so she said, and little to eat since this morning. She got up so late that she'd only just time to grab something before catching the bus.'

By the time they had finished their cooked meal, Janet has bustled in, dumping her case in the corridor, her hockey stick in the umbrella stand. She was tall and leggy with Titian blonde hair which fell about her shoulders in untidy waves, pinioned by an odd ribbon and slide.

'What's for tea?' she cried as she opened the room door, flopping into the nearest fireside armchair, legs full-sprawled across the hearth rug.

'Cold water sandwiches,' chortled Dirk. 'Here, you can have my place.'

'I could eat a horse,' she countered, pretending exhaustion.

Dirk rose, lifted his plate and cutlery and made for the kitchen, calling out, 'It's hungry, Mum. Got any more fish cakes for the starving blister?'

His mother entered, bearing a plate with several upon it, saying, 'Here, get these down, Janet, before you collapse, But go and wash first . . . your hands I mean.'

Janet, without replying gathered herself up, tottered through to the kitchen as though *in extremis* and returned to attack the fish cakes.

'Good show, Mum. Need this. Ravenous,' she jerked out between mouthfuls.

She ate hungrily whilst Dirk washed the dishes and pans in the kitchen. His mother sat down by the fire, knowing that all would be well. She had trained both of them in all the household chores and each knew what was expected. A widow, made so by the Great War, she had brought up her own two, and four more besides, assisted by her own mother, now quite elderly and also dependent. She had not succumbed to the pressures, dire though those sometimes had been. She was determined to surmount all difficulties and give her offspring the best that she could afford. As she gazed into the dying embers of the fire, she recalled her own childhood on the banks of the River Tagus on the outskirts of Lisbon and questioned the hand of cards that life had ultimately dealt out to her. The coals in the grate shuttered down. From the scuttle at the side of the hearth Janet rose to replenish the fire.

'Tired, Mum?' she queried gently, seeing the wistful look in her eyes.

'Yes, child,' was the reply. 'A heavy day. All the week's baking, some washing and ironing, shopping and the meals to make. It takes its toll.'

'Never mind, Mum, you sit still,' Janet murmured. 'Dirk and I will finish off. Have forty winks.'

This she tacitly accepted and as she gazed at the now blazing fire, her thoughts led her back down the years to her own happy childhood and youth.

2

Graeme Brothers of Glasgow, in the later nineteenth century decided to build a dyeworks in the village of Braça da Prata a few miles up river from Lisbon, the Portuguese capital. Labour there was comparatively cheap. The demand for printed cloth in the Portuguese colonies and elsewhere was good. The technical and mechanical processes were, however, their own prerogative. This was a venture which could not fail, if correctly managed. Good water in plentiful supply, sunshine in abundance for bleaching and drying, manpower readily available and technical knowhow which could be transferred there. How could they fail?

The factory almost complete, the machinery shipped out and installed, they cast about for a capable manager to run the enterprise. One of the brothers in charge of the labour force in their home factories suggested young Macdonald. They had taken him on as a lad from the crofts in the Isles where he had, from a child, been involved in cottage weaving and dyeing and who had been put through all the processes and was deemed efficient, keen and reliable. After much discussion they sent for him to the office. William Macdonald was duly summoned from the machine room. He arrived, cap in hand, and stood foursquare before his employers. There was in his eyes a certain aggressiveness, redolent of the cattle drovers and rustlers for which his clan had once been notorious. No servile hireling this. He approached the table where the four brothers sat and, with an enquiring air, began, 'Ye sent for me, whit's wrang nu?' in the vernacular of his clan.

'Nothing wrong, Macdonald. Tak a seat and listen tae whit we have tae say tae ye,' said the eldest. Willie brought up a chair to the far side of the table and sat down cap-on-lap, with an expectant yet suspicious air.

'Aye?' he queried as the brothers, looking at one another, paused. They smiled at him and the spokesman began, 'Wullie, we think a lot of you and the manner in which you have worked for us since ye came frae the Isles and we have a proposition tae pit tae ye.'

William nodded and sat silent waiting for the outcome and then the second brother piped in.

'Wullie, we're starting a new dyeworks in Portugal near the capital Lisbon and we're seeking a chap tae go out there and manage the place for us. We think you are the chap to fit the bill.'

Willie absorbed this slice of knowledge without batting an eyelid. He did not wish to betray his thoughts which were tumbling about in his head. 'Portugal,' he mused, silently, 'don't know much about the place.'

The ensuing silence was pregnant as they awaited his comment. Willie played for time. 'Is that plant the same as this one?' he queried.

'Oh yes,' came the reply, 'almost exactly, except that it is more modern with more refinements and better facilities.'

'Whit aboot the key men in the various departments?' Willie continued.

'Well,' began the youngest, 'we're in the process of appointing those and we're looking for highly skilled technicians from the length and breadth of the country. We are hoping to have it working within six months, when there will be a breaking-in period during which you and your technical staff will have to train the Portuguese workforce.'

'Aye! Weel,' parried Macdonald, 'I can see your drift, but how and when am I supposed to get there?'

The brothers realised that their task was half done and the third brother responsible for machinery chipped in, 'Oh, Wullie, that's easy. You'll go by boat in the Booth Line frae Greenock. It takes but three days, we'll pay your fare and we've arranged accommodation at the other end. There's a new house in the grounds, furnished forebye.'

Here the eldest chipped in to keep up the pressure, 'There's just one slight hitch from our point of view, Wullie, but we hope you can help us there.'

Macdonald raised an eyebrow and asked, 'What's that?'

Silence fell; each brother awaited the other. No flicker of assistance came from Willie. Eventually the eldest stated flatly, 'We would prefer a married man.'

A further pregnant silence ensued as Willie digested this latest sally. The brothers shifted a little in their chairs, awaiting the pronouncement from their chosen oracle. After a long pause, during which Macdonald sat, eyes closed, immobile, he stated flatly, 'I can't afford a wife on my present wage.'

The brothers relaxed and smiled at each other with relief. Here they were faced with a shrewd operative but they were prepared for this reaction. Up spoke the senior. 'How would you feel Willie, if we doubled your salary and paid you an annual commission on the success of the new plant?'

Willie remained impassive, his mind working furiously. Finally, after looking steadily into the eyes of each brother in turn, he spoke, 'I'll go. At least I'll gie it a go. If I dinna like what I find, I'll be back. I canna buy a pig in a poke.'

'What about the wife?' persisted the eldest, anxious to probe Willie's mind. 'That would be an essential part of our bargain, laddie.'

Without hesitation Willie broke in, 'Leave that tae me,' and added cryptically, 'it's no an insurmountable problem,' In fact, Willie had in his mind's eye a girl for whom he had long had a high regard. 'When would you require me to go?' he asked.

'Well, about August, in three months' time. That should give you time to readjust to the new situation,' came the reply. 'It all depends on the shipping and the installation delays.'

'Will that be all then?' Willie pursued, anxious to get back to his machines and as though this interview was all part of the day's work.

'Aye, Wullie, that's about all for the moment. We'll go over the details some other time. Now you're sure about what you're taking on?' anxiously pressed the eldest.

'Och aye,' said Willie, standing up to leave. 'I'll be giving it some thought myself forebye,' he added meaningfully.

Macdonald departed and the brothers exchanged glances. The second brother remarked, 'I think we have a good reliable man in Macdonald. You'll see.'

William Macdonald went back to his work deep in thought. He was flattered that his conscientious service to Graeme's was being rewarded. He was nineteen years old and had worked for them during the past ten years. Many's the time he had carried his younger brother on his back to work when barefoot and he well shod. He remembered the harsh days of his childhood, the harshness of the Highland crofts, the tenements of Glasgow, the child labour, his efforts to improve his lot and succeed. He welcomed the opportunity now presented to him. Marriage? Well, that was another entirely different prospect which had until then only touched upon the periphery of his mind. He knew a few girls at the church and Sunday School he regularly attended, a half-dozen at most, and the one who came easiest to his mind was Anne Briggs, whose family had come over from Northern Ireland and whose father worked in his section. She was small in stature, neat, sturdy, but always well turned-out and comely withal.

The more he thought about his problem and prospects the more his thoughts turned upon Anne Briggs. That evening, acting upon a sudden whim, he went to see her parents and, knocking on the tenement door, was bidden to enter. Without preamble, and to the astonishment of the family within, he explained the offer he had received from his employers and the conditions attached and ended by indicating that he would like Anne to accompany him upon his new venture. He realised when he had ended his peroration that the family was taken aback and not a little disconcerted, but with a tact born of long experience, he took his leave, asking them to consider the matter. Smiling expectantly at Anne, who had stayed silent throughout, he made his exit, saying he would call again in a few days time for an answer.

Willie was not one to let grass grow under his feet when important decisions had to be made. The days passed quickly. Willie knocked at the door again. The answer was 'Yes' and Anne and Willie were married on the third Saturday of the next month in the kirk they regularly attended. Anne was just sixteen years old. Adventure and the world stared them in the face.

They settled down in due time in the village of Braça da Prata on a curve of the river above Lisbon. There was nothing new in emigration. In fact scores of families were leaving Britain for the colonies and America to seek a better life. From the Clyde to the Tagus was but a short sea voyage in comparison to some, and they eventually settled down in their new environment on the other side of a railway which ran parallel to the river. The house was simply furnished with cane chairs and rugs, easily-cleaned tiled floors and really semi-luxury to what they both had hitherto experienced.

What was surprising to Anne was that there was someone to do the washing and the cleaning. Apart from the cooking and some entertaining of bachelor technicians sent out by the firm, Anne had never had life so comfortable. She set about putting a woman's touches to her new domain, whilst her husband immersed himself in the teething troubles of the plant and workforce. With help from native women, Anne learned to bake and cook new dishes, prepare new foods, adapt herself to new routines and natural difficulties. Ants were one problem overcome by placing table legs in tins of paraffin for the creatures marched in single file to larder and table wherever food was available. Snakes were new enemies and spiders prolific for they ate the plethora of flies which invaded the shaded rooms, making life unbearable as the summer heat stifled. All these and other difficulties were conquered or adapted to as the months rolled by and habits changed and the dyeworks flourished.

Life began to blossom for William and Anne. Came the children, one son and one, two, three girls in rapid succession, William, Isabel, Jean and Anne. They thrived with wetnurses ever to hand and childminders available. As these grew they became bilingual and what they lacked in formal education they gained in sporting pursuits and worldly knowledge. They flourished like tomboys, going barefoot, swimming, walking, learning musical instruments from tutors and housecraft from the native women; sewing, embroidery, the mandolin, the piano became part of their daily round and as they grew into teenage splendour, they attracted the attentions of detached males calling at the port and attending social functions arranged by the Embassy to which the British residents were customarily invited.

It was thus that Isabel met her ship's engineer and in a whirlwind romance was later whisked aboard and off to some river station up the Congo where she eventually died of yellow fever, leaving two young children to be brought back home. Graeme's meantine shipped out a young accountant, son of a prominent Glasgow doctor, who eventually married Jean and they in turn had two sons in quick succession. Only Anne remained at home now and she was courted by the younger dyeworks chemist, recently recruited from Lancashire. They married and lived in the family home, where tragedy soon struck with vicious ferocity.

A Portuguese workman had, by his carelessness, destroyed a batch of fabric prints and Willie Macdonald had sacked him. The following week this workman waylaid Willie as he left the works and shot him dead. He was buried in the grounds of the English church which had been erected and life naturally carried on. A son was born to Anne junior and she and her now widowed mother nursed and raised him.

Tragedy struck a third time. Roland, her husband, fell victim to typhoid fever, a result of his own folly and religious background. Reared in a strict Calvinistic code, he had, as a youth, been brainwashed into signing the Rechabite Pledge, never to touch strong drink. In Braça, where the well-water was suspect and had to be boiled and where wine was the common table fare, to drink the raw water was suicidal. The nature of his work, however, kept him in heated rooms with bleach and dyes. Thirst was a constant companion. The temptation to drink the well-water was inevitable, the result predictable. They nursed him, mother and daughter, but his heart was under strain and subsequently affected. They managed to snatch him from death, but the weakeness remained. Two years later the Great War began. The date coincided with the birth of their firstborn. Roland could have stayed and worked on but a letter from his brother in England that he was joining the Forces cancelled out all his plans and preparations were put in hand to return to the mother country and enrol. They sailed from Lisbon with a babe-in-arms, accompanied by the widowed mother and, in convoy because of the German submarines. They reached Liverpool and had a fond reunion with Roland's people. Roland became a soldier, fought and died, leaving widow, son and unborn daughter to the mercy of a less-than-grateful British Government.

The four survived with difficulty. From a life of semi-luxury the mother now went out to scrub floors, minded babies, did other folk's household chores whilst the government quibbled over the price of a soldier's sacrifice. Life was now hard but she stemmed from hardier stock. The grandmother was indispensable, helping in all the household chores and returning to her teenage love of knitting to provide stockings and socks, gloves and scarves, even the long forgotten tam-o'-shanter. Together they made rugs, towels, sewed curtains, embroidered blouses and tablecloths for the home and thus the grandmother paid her scot and lot, for she had no pension to replace her own murdered husband. To add to the difficulties, the other two sisters sent home to England their own offspring, so that the household became eight in number. True, their maintenance money was welcome, but it was erratic in arriving and in the case of the children of the eldest, who had died, it petered out altogether and no trace of the father was forthcoming.

'A land fit for heroes to live in,' said Lloyd George to the nation, whilst he himself was busy bedding strange women. There was no point in moaning. Roll up the sleeves. Instead of clogs to clogs in three generations, it was clogs to clogs in one, so fill the bucket and scrub. The family must survive and there were lots more in direr straits than those who had a small nest egg put by.

Thus Anne's thoughts revolved as she stared somnolently into the now glowing coals of the fire, whilst her own two children washed up the tea things, cleared the table and replenished the coal scuttle and side-boiler. No good dwelling upon the past. The good, carefree days were gone; so were father, husband, sister and possibly her brother-in-law. The Kaiser had seen to that. Life was unpredictable, evanescent and harsh. The present was all that mattered, the future was in the lap of the gods. Her constant problem was to provide for the uncertain tomorrow. Her middle sister had come home to claim her own sons, her dead sister's teenagers had gone out into the world and she was left with her own two and the matriarch of the family. Four souls had to be cared for, to be nurtured, clothed and fed. However, she had been more fortunate than some she knew. The government had relented and was about to grant her a pension proportionate to her late husband's civilian earnings which had been very good. The family, as such, would get by. Her immediate problem was that of her son's continued education.

Anne gazed on and reminisced until the coals shuttered once more and roused her to a consciousness of the life around her. She looked around, wondering at the uncanny silence. The table had been cleared. Her daughter was sitting in the armchair opposite, her homework books on her knee. Dirk was at the table, poring over his work. There was a muted hush, a glow of warmth, a sense of peacefulness which pervaded the room. Even the black and white cat on the hearth rug was curled up cosily in slumber, symbolic of the easing of the day's activities, a lethargy, a gradual descent into an oblivion of sleep which, as Shakespeare had so aptly written, 'Knit up the ravelled sleeve of care'. This was the quiet hour; this, the time for reflection and recuperation, the moments to pause and take stock. Soon she would be up again, dealing with the ever-recurring essentials of household chores. Here and now she savoured the brief respite before the next round of activities.

She heard the front door open, then the vestibule within. Dirk swivelled in his chair and reached to open the room door into the corridor to allow more light to penetrate. There was Grandmother Macdonald, all four foot ten of her, tiptoeing up to hang her coat on the hooks along the wall, pausing before the hallstand to adjust her greying locks and eventually turning to enter the dining room.

'Hiya Gran!' called Janet, 'had a good time?'

'Aye, that I have,' came the response, 'but glad to be home. I'm fair ferfuchin.'

They all laughed at the Scots dialect which she often used. She was indeed breathing rather heavily but seemed bright and lively. In any case she would be the last to complain for she suffered adversity with stoicism. Janet vacated the armchair and transferred to the sofa. The old lady looked across at her daughter and remarked, 'Jeannie's youngest has the measles.'

The announcement scarce caused a ripple of response. Jean now had four boys, ten years separating the eldest and the youngest. Gran continued, 'She says to keep away until the spots have gone. They won't be visiting either Friday or Sunday.'

These two evenings had always been the adult family get-together after the week's toil and after Sunday evening chapel, when village gossip, family problems and other titbits were chewed over, relished and swallowed or rejected as the case might be. It was then that the elders often spoke in Portguese if the subject was scandalous or the matters not for youthful ears, but Dirk had picked up enough of the language over the years to follow the general gist of things. He often picked up smatterings of scandal to relay to his friends when spicy. From these weekly sessions of overhearing Portuguese, he learned much of the philanderings of village life, the downfall of some hapless female, the desertion of some wife or what their opinions were about Mrs X at the chapel functions. Even the skeletons in the family cupboard were discussed in that medium, but Dirk never revealed the extent of his comprehension to his elders nor the facility he had in coping with the lingo. He listened in nevertheless, with an innocent bemused expression, belying the attention he secretly paid to the crosstalk. Homework had priority. The ingrained respect for education, inherent in the Scots, preceded all else. Study, piano practice, household chores, cleanliness, dress, and not necessarily in that order, were paramount. To fritter time in amusements was to interfere with the sound foundations for the future. So the old lady, after a few further informative remarks, lapsed into silence, retrieving her knitting from the shelf near at hand, and with the four steel needles began to turn the heel of the socks she was knitting for Dirk.

Eventually, Anne roused herself and turned to open the top drawer of the chest built into the alcove. The cat which had hitherto been slumbering contentedly, basking in the heat from the fire, bounded up at the sound and shot to the kitchen door. Dirk laughed and said, 'You see, even the cat remembers.'

They had brought the cat as a kitten from the farm some six years ago. It too had its vicissitudes, the most serious of which was to have one of its paws severed in the mowing machine in the meadow whilst stalking mice. It disappeared for days but eventually came limping home, its severed stump licked clean and healing. Dirk had mentioned the accident at the farm he frequented and the farmer remembered seeing it leap up in front of the blades and bound away into the long grass.

Dirk's loud laugh caused his mother to smile. She knew to what he referred. When there had been six children in the house, the tawse, that ubiquitous instrument of Scots discipline, had always been kept handy in that drawer and frequently used to effect, to maintain order and administer summary justice. These 'hammerings', as Grandma termed them, always scared the cat which either ran under the sideboard or shot into the kitchen to hide until the mayhem was over and peace restored. Indeed, Dirk could remember that when any of the children cried, the cat would come and put its paw on their knee in token of sympathy. The tawse, however, had long since disappeared. Dirk had taken it and thrown it into the dyeworks lodge. It had been temporarily replaced by a buckled belt, but as the family grew older and the inmates of the household fewer, the tawse had ceased to function. The cat, however, associated the opening of that drawer with turmoil, so much so that, when the time came to put it out at night where is had a cosy box in the out-house, Dirk need only open the drawer and the cat would automatically make for the kitchen and stand by the outer door.

'Aye,' interjected his gran, 'we nivver did ken what happened tae yon strap.'

Dirk smiled inwardly and bent his head to his books. He recalled the day he had been given a hiding for breaking a window with a ball. The next day he had taken the strap and whizzed it into the middle of the lodge from the bank where he often fished. There had been an exhaustive inquest over its sudden disappearance and its replacement by the buckled belt, but the latter was seldom in use as the tacit acceptance of the former's demise was condoned.

The pendulum clock on the wall struck six. It had assumed a flat tone due to its long travels o'er land and sea. Dirk arose, walked over to the ledge above the significant drawer and switched on the radio to listen to the news. The weather forecast was ending. The dry spell was to continue. 'Good,' he thought, 'tomorrow I'll have a run up to Paslew Barn.'

He could not get rid of the likely possibility in his mind that the building contained a mystery. He knew that until he satisfied himself of the futility of his conjectures he would have little peace and lack the necessary concentration for his essential studies.

3

The following day Dirk wakened early, long before the others were astir, in order to complete his run. He sluiced his face at the single cold tap in the kitchen, towelled and quietly left by the back door. As he loped along the semi-circular drive towards the two large residences which lay beyond the back meadow he heard the sound of the first factory whistle shrilly summoning the workforce of the village to their daily tasks. First, the high-pitched penetrating siren of the spinning mill which would awaken the dead, followed within seconds by the low monotone from the weaving sheds. 'As if one wasn't enough,' he thought. They sounded off at exactly five-thirty every morning of the working days and again at five-to-six as a final warning before the engines started up. The fireman had been on duty long before that, raking out the clinker ash from the overnight banked-up furnaces and coaxing the embers back into a forced-draught blaze, stoking up with coal as they quickened into active life, watching the gauges for an efficient head of steam to drive the shafting and keeping an eye upon the clock.

As Dirk turned the first bend to take the long rise up the hillside he looked back at the trailing cloud of black smoke belching out from the tall chimneys, scattering their outfall of soot over the roofs of the cottages to the east. Dirk passed in front of the red doors of the farm barn, through the swing gate and turned right up the field path where the old packhorse track led upwards. Here, small rounded cobbles, neatly set, were still visible where the grass had not yet overgrown them. It had ever been a source of curiosity and wonder guessing who had taken such infinite care to construct the short, steep stretch and from where had come those pebbles which formed the track. Only on the steep part were these laid down, presumably to assist the ponies or packhorses to grip on what otherwise would have been a quagmire. It was obvious that the path had been cut out of the irregular terrain for the ground to the left was man-high and the hedge on the right grew out of a low mound which fell away into a steep gully on the other side to the rear of the farmhouse. This steep bit was a killer for the runner, very steep and almost one-in-two in parts for some fifty yards.

Once out at the top and through the next field gate the terrain levelled out into gently rising ground. Dirk could see his goal, Paslew Barn, under the crest of the hill, with its walled enclosures on the valley side, useful for penning cattle and sheep. Twice the upward footpath criss-crossed a meandering stream and led up to the stone steps of the stile over the dry wall which brought him to the ling and heather of the open moor where the whinberries grew in profusion. Dirk slowed to a walk to see if the berries were ripe, making a mental note for the picking of them for future mouthwatering pies. Gradually he approached the cart road which passed in front of the barn and led across the highroad over the Nick o'Pendle.

Dirk approached the barn and examined the structure from all sides. It had become somewhat dilapidated from lack of use. He tried the doors and peered through the ventilation slits at the dim, partially flagged floors within before making a casual round of the walled-in folds adjoining. He laughed aloud at the crazy notion which had brought him here and after giving the building a further round he set off to jog along the cart track past Wilkin Hey Farm to the west and through the further gate to the pasture across which he had run the previous day. There had been a heavy dew and the long grasses through which he ran were heavily beaded with droplets glistening in the morning sun. They soaked through his plimsolls and socks as down he sidled from the steep escarpment, surefooted as a mountain goat, leaping the hollows, sidestepping the stone outcrops until he arrived at the lower footpath. Once there, he increased his speed by lengthening his stride, checked only by the field gates. Soon he was back at home where he quietly lifted the latch and entered the back door. No-one was yet astir. His sister had to catch the quarter past eight bus to the high school in Clitheroe. She was a heavy sleeper, difficult to rouse, and the drivers had been known to stop when she was not at the regulation stage. He called upstairs, 'Mum, it's seven o'clock.'

'Yes, I'm getting up,' came the reply.

He went into the kitchen and began his ablutions. As his mother came down, he began to rake out the cold ashes from the previous day's fire and lay it for future lighting. That chore completed, he went up to his room whilst his mother washed herself in the kitchen. There was no bathroom and everything had to be strictly timed to allow privacy. Gran had her bed in his room but she did not rise until all who were going out had departed. She was well past her three score and ten and visibly failing. He dressed in his school togs and made up his bed. Everyone had their daily round and he did his from force of habit. The house was coming alive. In one hour he would be catching the bus to Burnley and his final few weeks at the grammar school.

These last few weeks were vital. Much hung on the success or otherwise of his higher exams in three weeks' time. The pending interview for college presented many imponderables, besides being an unknown ordeal.

He descended the stairs. His mother was frying the bacon and eggs in the kitchen. The porridge would be on. He went to the sideboard and, extracting the tablecloth, set out the knives, forks, spoons and plates required. Passing through the kitchen, he opened the pantry door and from the big earthenware breadmug extracted a loaf which he then sliced, buttered and arranged on a large plate. He next picked up the jar of marmalade, one full of bacon fat, and the syrup tin. Surplus fat from the bacon had always been poured into a jar. Dirk seldom used butter, preferring to spread this fat on his bread and cover it with a smear of syrup. His morning diet of porridge, bacon and eggs and two slices of the former washed down with tea, had to suffice for the exertions of the approaching day. On schooldays it had to last until evening, apart from a midday snack, unless he went for a snack lunch at a commercial café in the distant town. This was usually pie, carrots and mash with a choice of dessert for a shilling. Otherwise it would be a few sandwiches and fruit which his mum prepared and wrapped in a table napkin which served as a tablecloth over a school desk. He would make tea over a Bunsen burner in the lab, and he once kept a cup in his locker for that very purpose.

Initiative was required by all pupils travelling in from outlying parts. There were some twenty from the periphery of the town. The headmaster had noted the problem of the boys from the outlying villages and was organising a luncheon club in the physics room where tea and the necessary crockery and cutlery would be provided for a penny a day subscription. The initial outlay was from the Head's own pocket with the condition that any profits were to go to pay off the debt. Dirk collected the coppers from those who stayed and kept the accounts. He ate his breakfast with relish, hungry from his morning exertions. He next packed his attaché case with the books required for that day, checked his bag of sports gear and set off to watch the morning sun at the top of the village. His sister, at the last minute as usual, was gulping her tea and breakfast with about ten minutes to spare before her bus came down the road.

'You'll miss it,' he jeered, 'and serve you right.'

She did not answer, her mouth full of food and not even sitting down to eat either.

As Dirk strolled up the road he noted the regulars coming out of houses and hurrying along to the main bus stop. Once there he joined the queue. Here came the solicitor's clerk in bowler hat, a few high school girls, together with an assorted collection of people, some on shopping bent, others with jobs in neighbouring towns *en route.* He knew them all and casually passed the time of day with those who spoke. Just after eight a bus pulled in round the corner on the opposite side of the road which would pick up the Clitheroe contingent on its way down, his sister amongst them, he hoped. His own bus arrived in the opposite direction and began to unload and load. He noted that it was one of the new and much talked about Leyland Lions, more comfortable, more powerful and more spacious. The people boarded it. He always sat near the rear. It was a source of amusement to him to note that the more elderly kept to the forward end whilst the younger, in descending order of age, always gravitated to the rear. Being now in his late teens, Dirk had moved forward from the rear seats to one just in front of the rear wheel arch. What prompted this psychological advance he could never quite understand or explain. Maybe it was some change in chemical make-up or a subconscious mutation in mental attitudes.

At the last minute before the conductor rang the bell for departure, a girl in her mid-teens boarded, out of breath from unaccustomed exertion. She sat on the seat opposite after a gasped 'Hello' to Dirk. She was a year or so younger than he, and for some obscure reason had started high school at a later age than most. He was conscious that a few years before she had posted to him a Valentine in the form of a large playing card of the King of Hearts, which had embarrassed him unduly, so much so that he had, on the homeward-bound bus, demanded to know which of the group of girls was the instigator. She had admitted being the sender and apologised for causing him anger. Now, having a little more sense and less sensitivity he realised that he had been rude and grossly at fault and had, on occasions, tacitly tried to redress his crudeness. They chatted across the aisle about the interests they had in common and it relieved Dirk to feel that perhaps she had forgotten the former episode and his gaucheness.

The bus picked up passengers at various other stops, filling the seats, and conversation was cut off. Dirk resorted to his books as the chap who had sat down next to him opened a newspaper and began to read. Dirk casually glanced at the headlines: 'Economy Axe' in bold type stared out from the page. He reverted to his notes about 'Diminishing Returns'. His economics exam was imminent. Someone had laughingly said, 'Economics is the subject where the questions are always the same and the answers are different.' Dirk was beginning to think that this was manifestly true. There were several schools of thought about economics. The basic principles were laid down but the reality never matched the pattern which was supposed to follow. The country was going through a sticky patch. There were many people unemployed. The word 'dole' was on everyone's lips and a new phrase was stalking the cheerless streets: 'The Means Test'. People were angry, frustrated, desperate, or anxious or resigned. A dismal pall of depression had settled down upon the cotton towns and it wasn't from belching mill chimneys; many of which were idle. As the bus reached Gannow Top and began its gradual descent into Burnley he could count the dozens of tall black chimneys denuded of smoke, like gaunt, swart fingers menacing the grey sky. Even the Government was nonplussed as to how to alleviate the widespread distress. This law of Supply and Demand which Dirk was reading-up was all right in the theory of the printed page but very unpredictable in practical terms. There was no demand for goods because money was tight so the supply had dried up. Prices fell left, right and centre and so did manufacturers who went bankrupt by the score. So, where did the human element enter the scheme of things? How reliable were the dry bones of theory?

The bus reached the Cattle Market terminus, no longer a cattle market but a vast cobbled open space which served as a bus station, once a year as a fairground and where occasionally, marquees could be seen housing faith-healers, quacks, evangelists and various eccentric organisations. Dirk began to walk the last half-mile to school, across the centre where the trams rattled out their dying years to make way for the new generations of buses, polluting the air with the fumes from their highly toxic Russian oil products or 'ROP' as they were familiarly known. Past the brewery he strode with its aroma of pungent hops, past the row of dingy shops to St Peter's Parish Church which time and industrial soot had blackened, up School Lane to enter the yard, where a football game was in full flow. Soon he would be turning his back on this familiar scene to a future which was doubtful and a destiny unknown. Somehow everything revolved around the forthcoming exams and the laws of supply and demand. He propped his cases by the school wall and joined in the game. This was more to his liking.

Rooms 1, 2 and 3 were the oldest part of the school, separated from each other by folding shutters, glass-panelled. At morning assembly and exam times these were folded back to make a large hall. The whole school assembled there for morning prayers in descending order from the Sixth to the Second forms, the staff arranged along the west wall, begowned and, in the main, predatory; that is, all except the few Roman Catholics who considered themselves a race apart and who entered later for the 'Notices'. Last would come the Head on a podium just inside the heavy iron-studded door, take off his tasselled mortar board and bid 'Good morning' to the assembled throng. He was a martinet whose word was law and whose law was strict, backed up by a bevy of prefects, punitive detentions and, *in extremis,* two, four or six of the best. He would announce the hymn and Bentley, on the recently acquired two-manual organ, would play the opening chorus, after ensuring with a muttered whisper that Alderson or some other first-year sixth former was pumping away at the side to supply the vital wind. It had been occasionally known for these muscle-men to go on strike, especially when it was a long hymn and the verses were short-counted. *For all the saints* was one which had been sabotaged and the 'from their labours rest' took on a significant meaning. Few of the first year sixth were saints or ever likely to qualify. Normally the singing was lusty and raucously harmonised except by the tone deaf and broken-voiced who frequently got a kick as a reminder of their unwelcome incompetence. Next came prayers, ending in an over-enthusiastic 'Amen', followed by the Lord's Prayer and the notices. Dispersal to classes would follow and the day's grind begin.

Give the Head his due; a brilliant classical scholar, he ran a tight school but treated his Sixth Form with some affability, regarding them as adults and, as such, to have a mature approach to life and a similar response to their duties about the school. Seldom was this trust betrayed, but when it was, and some lapse from standard decorum was discovered, his retribution was immediate and dire. So much so that when Dirk was filing out from assembly that morning he was singled out by the Head, who stood at the foot of the staircase, and motioned him to proceed to the Sanctum Sanctorum adjacent. Dirk's adrenalin surged through his body. With the panelled door to the Sanctum closed and a disrobing silence by the Head ensuing, he eventually turned and addressed Dirk.

'You will recall that earlier in the year you were asked to take over as Pendle House secretary in place of Blaydon?'

'Yes sir,' replied Dirk, wondering what was coming next.

The Head continued, 'No explanation was given you as to why this change took place, but, no doubt, you suspect, as did the others, that he had sullied his escutcheon. I realise that the end of term is near and you will be involved in important exams, so I am taking this opportunity of complimenting you on the manner in which you assumed that vital role. As a double *Victor Ludorum* of the school and from the reports I am receiving from your subject masters regarding your . . . er . . . shall I delicately say . . . unexpected, yet most timely improvement in your academic work, I am sincerely hoping that you are not going to let me down in *my* subject. I refer of course to your Latin compositions which you will have observed from my marks and remarks are, to put it kindly, a little below par. It may be too late for me to expect a miracle but you must realise that in three weeks' time your fate in that subject will be sealed and my informed guess is that unless you can pull a rabbit out from under your school cap you will not be able to say, *Exegi monumentum aere perennius quid non imbris edax neque arcu.* Do you understand me, Mr Waldron?'

'Perfectly sir,' answered Dirk, realising that Latin was his Achilles heel. 'I shall try not to let you down, sir.'

'Quite so, young man. Just a word in season, which I'm sure you will act upon!'

'Yes sir, thank you, sir,' responded Dirk, relieved that some misdemeanour was not the cause of this unsolicited interview.

Along the corridor in the Sixth Form room Dirk reflected on what had been said. It was typical of the boss to mix compliment with warning, especially to his Sixth, whom he seldom denigrated or made to feel small, but he left one in no doubt that he had his finger on the pulse of every prefect.

The school day passed in very much the usual pattern. The Modern Sixth class was relatively small in number and sat on stools around two heavy deal tables which were ideal for table tennis. There were fifteen at most except when the Classical Sixth, much less in number, for they were considered to be the 'swots', joined them for Latin with the Head. At morning break, noon and afternoon break table tennis and shove-ha'penny were played on these tables, non-participants resorting to football in the yard until required to answer to a 'challenge' in the ladder-table posted on the classroom notice-board. The rule was that anyone could challenge someone not more than three higher in the ladder and success caused the names to be interchanged. Naturally those who stayed to lunch were the most efficient due to constant practise. They were halcyon days, with the Chess Club on Friday evenings, football and cricket in season, inter-school matches all over the county, and Wednesday afternoon set apart for house matches, each house fielding four teams in descending age groups.

Dirk was proud of his First XI Soccer tie, his prefect's badge, his name signed at the bottom of the weekly posted house teams. Pendle House, which had been in the doldrums when he joined the school, was now in the ascendancy and had been popular for the past three years, beginning to win most of the trophies on offer except that for swimming which they never seemed to be able to capture. The wheel of fortune had changed so that the red flashes on his cap which advertised his house allegience was proudly worn. These matters were important to the hour, vital to the participants, but, on sober thought, were ephemeral, somewhat accidental, if sufficient to the day, the week and the year. Apart from the names on the Honours boards, who would put face to name in twenty years' time?

Looking at the many Honours boards in Assembly, the names of the different houses appeared and faded. Once it was all Ribblesdale, then Brun, now Pendle was having its run of luck. Only Calder, which seemed to monopolise the swimming trophy, lacked athletic prowess of late. Maybe in twenty years' time a new generation of youth would assemble and, waiting, eye those boards and read the names as a passing occupation, unable to put face to name.

'Think not the struggle naught availeth,' thought Dirk. The homilies that the boss churned out were perhaps apt and had a permanency . . . character building, playing the game, organisation, duty observance, selection on merit, discipline, regulations, uniform, smartness of turnout, clean shoes, collar, smart appearance with neatly pressed trousers, no slouching, orderliness, collective responsibility . . . all these phrases passed through Dirk's mind as he leaned his elbows on the window-cill overlooking the yard to watch the usual soccer game in progress at noon, his eye cocked for likely talent, wearing the red flashes and demonstrating extra skills and ball control. There was young Illingsworth from Pendle, known as 'Tuppence', for his older brother had been dubbed 'Shillingsworth', wading in and being knocked about by Fourth Form bustlers, yet not giving ground. He turned as Landon, the head prefect entered the room to post up the following week's duty roster. Dirk went over to peruse it, searching out his name and allocations. He read, 'Top corridor Tuesday, bottom corridor Thursday, yard duty Friday.'

He didn't like the bottom corridor stint. That was where the lower forms hung out. They had to be taught manners and school rules in no uncertain fashion. Some prefects would administer a cuff or a side kick to a roistering bully, but Dirk had his own excrutiating response . . . the slack of the pin-stripes hitched up and a painful ten-yard march along the corridor accompanied by groans of agony. Seldom was it necessary to repeat the dose. To any boy who came through the yard door with cap flat-aback or on his bonce at all, Dirk would remove it and drop it on the floor for the culprit to pick up. Other prefects at this juncture would administer a side kick to the rump, whereas Dirk preferred a flat-hander. They had all been through the same procedure and now appreciated the rationale behind it all; the standing, when a master entered the room, the measured walking along corridors, no elbowing past, no rush, keeping to the right in single file, etc. There was the occasional horseplay but it was rare and brief for the threat of a hundred lines would quench the erupting ardours. Experience dictated whom to watch and from what source trouble might arise.

Dirk realised that he was privileged and being, as it were, groomed for the world outside and the next stage of his physical and spiritual journey. School would leave its mark. They said the the Battle of Waterloo was won on the playing fields of Eton. That might have some basic truth in it, mused Dirk, but he was certain that the next spot of bother in which Britain would become embroiled would be won or lost on the *esprit de corps* established in the grammar schools. The corridor bells sounded. Joey, the janitor, had his finger on the button, his eye removed from the clock. History followed French, English Literature followed Latin. Thus at four-thirty p.m. ended another school day, another school week, interrupted only by yesterday's holiday for Founder's Day.

Dirk caught the bus back home after sprinting down Bridge Street and across the centre of the Cattle Market. Today the bus left on time. It was one of the old rattle-trap Daimlers, hard tubular framed seating, sit-up-and-beg rexine-covered benches. Its clapped out engine crackled into life, vibrating the whole loosened-up structure. The conductor jumped aboard, pulled the cord which ran roof-high along the length of the bus. Ting-ting went the cracked bell and after several coughs and a jerk the clutch connected and it departed, trailing a cloud of blue pungent exhaust gases.

A voice over his shoulder pleaded, 'Could you help me with this?'

He turned and there was Maureen, who had moved up from farther back and was poring over her books, as usual.

'What's the trouble?' asked Dirk as kindly as possible, remembering the Valentine.

'It's some Latin translation,' she responded.

Dirk chuckled, recalling his morning session with the Head. 'It's the blind leading the blind, I think,' laughed Dirk, 'but let's have a look.'

He wasn't too bad at translation. It was the grammar which foxed him. She passed the book over. It was old Horace again to which he had said goodbye in the Fourths. He remembered well the terminal exam when faced with an unseen translation. He had baulked at the phrase, *Volvens in mente* and was chewing the end of his pen contemplatively when Toddy, the supervising master paced along the aisle. Toddy, who taught French, raised his eyebrows, his hands behind his back, under his tatty gown. Dirk pointed to the question paper and underlined the phrase. He came alongside, peered at the paper, took one hand from under his gown and placing it at his forehead closed his eyes and twirled it round and round as though mixing up his brains. He looked at Dirk again and repeated the movements. It dawned on him what Toddy was striving to convey, namely, 'turning over in his mind'. The dawn of recognition on Dirk's face caused Toddy to smile and continue on his way, brushing his clipped ginger moustache. Dirk wrote on. 'Good old Toddy Shaw,' he mused, 'fancy him knowing Latin. Thanks Toddy.'

Dirk snatched himself back from his fleeting reminiscing and looked at the page of Horace that had been handed to him by Maureen. Again he had to smile for there it was: *Exegi monumentum aere perennius,* etc. Without pausing, Dirk translated, 'I have raised a monument more lasting than brass which neither the rains nor the arrows can destroy.'

Maureen raised her eyes to his in admiration at the facility with which he reeled off the prose. He completed the poem's translation, not disclosing that it was mostly from memory for he had once learnt it by heart. He remembered his own difficulty at her stage and how he had sent for a crib for the text. The poem was burnt into his brain. Ending, he casually flipped over the once familiar pages. Yes, there was *O fons Bandusiae splendidor vitro* . . . and the one about Danae immured in her tower and he thought what a far cry it was from that to Cicero and Juvenal's satires with which he was currently wrestling. He wondered whether a girls' school would be allowed to study Juvenal's pungent and bawdy lines in depth for Higher Certificate and what the ingenuous Maureen would think about them.

As he returned the book and turned away, he recalled with a wry smile the day when the headmaster, seated on one of the stools in the Sixth Form with copies of Juvenal in front of everyone, suddenly ejaculated, 'Stop, I shall translate the next bit,' and chortled secretively as he gazed around. Dirk had looked at Mitch and then at Conroy as much as to say, 'What's got into the boss?' They had not long to wait as he began, 'He carried his peacock to his bath . . . and returning to his couch retrieved the golden bowl and quaffed it off with a mighty sup. Ha! Ha! Ha!' He tipped back the stool to guffaw. Joey had recently oiled the deck and the stool shot from under him and gown, book, specs and the boss landed in a heap upon the floor. Had it been one of the lads they would have laughed loudly and long, but a silence reigned as he picked himself up, adjusted himself and in great humour cried, 'My old and mouldy bowler . . . that was a near squeak!'

'What's amusing you?' enquired Maureen.

'Oh, nothing in particular,' chipped in Dirk, 'just something that occurred in school which the Latin brought back to me.'

By this time the bus was grinding its turgid way up the steep incline towards the valley in which the village lay. As the driver crashed in the bottom gear there followed a few kangaroo jumps and then a dead stop. The brakes went on to arrest the reverse roll. Clutch in, a horrible grating noise ensued, followed by a jerky start and a slow grinding climb to the summit of the gradient and a cautious dropping into the valley below. Two stops to allow the descent of passengers and finally the terminus and the general dispersal of occupants. As Dirk paced down the street towards home he saw one of his friends at the factory window waving and calling to him, 'Don't forget tonight!' Dirk gave a thumbs up sign for he knew the other could not hear over the cacophony of the looms. 'I could do well without any evening commitments,' Dirk thought. The midnight oil would have to be burnt and there was tomorrow's early run to come. He progressed further down the road, acknowledging people as he passed until he reached home. He left his attaché case of books and his Gladstone bag with sports gear in the corridor and sniffed the air for the cooking smells. He suddenly felt hungry and opening the door to the dining room he noted the table already set. There was no fire in the grate. It had been a hot day.

'You'll have to boil a kettle on the gas,' called his mother, 'if you want to wash.'

'Oh, cold water will do today, Mum,' he replied, 'what's for tea?'

'It's fish and chips,' responded his mother, 'the fish cart called today. I bought some fillets so we'll have to wait for your sister off the other bus.'

'OK Mum,' said Dirk, 'I'll wash and change then.'

He was always glad to shed his school uniform, black jacket and pinstripes, into something less formal. He bounded upstairs to disrobe before using the kitchen to wash off the town grime. Open neck shirt, pullover and flannels would suffice, ready for the evening relaxations. No homework tonight. Tomorrow would be soon enough. He'd had a surfeit of books.

4

The following Saturday saw Dirk seated in a bus, Manchester-bound, to attend the much dreaded yet anticipated interview for college. He had humorously subjected himself to a final inspection by his parent, been made to put a high polish on his shoes, trim his finger nails, wash, comb and subdue his unruly auburn locks and put on a neat matching tie. His suit was fairly new, made to measure by a tailor who called at the house annually to seek commissions for ladies and gents tailoring. In contrast to his school uniform, this was a light fawn tweed, smartly cut and up to the minute fashion-wise.

Hatless, for he seldom wore a hat, except as school rules demanded, raincoat over arm, Dirk had caught the various bus connections and was now gazing at the passing scene. The rugged Pennine valleys rose sheer on either side of the road which meandered along the winding ravines of the cotton towns en route, stopping frequently to set down and pick up a motley array of passengers bent upon their several weekend duties. This last stage would take at least an hour and he had bought a *Manchester Guardian* and settled down to read the main items of news and attempt the crossword. He had been schooled in the *Guardian* crossword on his frequent visits to his paternal grandmother's where the solving of it was a daily ritual.

It was a second home, with an ever cheerful welcome as first-born grandson, where housework was a religion almost and rigid routines firmly followed. Friday evening, however, was regarded as a respite from the long week's toil. His grandfather, a heavily-built, muscular, wheelwright-cum-handyman, bushy eyebrowed and bewhiskered, would be seated in the twin rocking-chair to the left of the hearth, his pipe of twist alight and the fire blazing merrily sending reflected gleams from the highly polished surrounds. The chimney breast spoke of blacklead, elbow grease and burnished steel. One aunt would be ironing on the scrubbed-topped table, another in the kitchen attending to the chores. His grandmother would occupy the right hand chair and be poring intently over the page, pencil in hand.

Dirk fondly visualised the scene in his mind's eye as he too scanned the clues for inspiration. The excessive vibration of the wheels over the uneven cobblestones blurred the page as they trundled along. He found his concentration fading and abandoned the task after filling in a few easier answers. Even glancing at the headlines was depressing as the bus rolled through the Manchester streest and eventually came to a stop at its terminus. Dirk descended and strolled the quarter mile back towards the hotel where in half an hour he was scheduled to appear. He entered the foyer to check with the receptionist and was given instructions as to which room to proceed. Glancing at his watch, he pondered whether to take a stroll along Deansgate to give the shops the once-over, but rejected the temptation. Finding the lounge, he reopened the crossword and filled in some more squares. After some twenty minutes he made his way to the designated room where already three youths were seated around a large table occupying stand chairs.

These youths he greeted formally, and was at once engaged in intimate conversation. They came from grammar schools against which he had played soccer, mostly from surrounding towns. A door opened from what he presumed would be the interview room and out came another youth, followed by a man who called out a name, at which another arose and disappeared behind the closed door. Those remaining questioned the newcomer as to how he had fared, what had been asked, in an effort to improve their own chances when summoned. He seemed non-commital, naturally, and collecting a coat from a side chair he left on his way out. Dirk calculated that each session lasted about ten minutes and at precisely eleven-thirty his name was called.

Immediately there was the usual rush of adrenalin as he paced towards the open door and entered the room. There were two interviewers and he was directed to the far one. Dirk had been advised not to sit down unless invited so to do. Approaching the table he stood and said, 'Good morning sir,' to which the reply came, 'Good morning Mr Waldron, please be seated.'

Dirk first straightened the chair which had been left askew by the previous interviewee. He then sat down, adjusting his well-creased trousers and eased the chair forward to the table, folding his hands and placing them on the table's edge. He noticed that the interviewer glanced at his hands and Dirk felt a glow of satisfaction that he had always been trained to keep his nails well-maintained and maincured. There followed the customary introductions and a series of questions about his curriculum vitae, his school, the offices he held there, his hobbies, his extra-mural interests and his background. Then followed an unexpected question about the payment of fees, having elicited that his mother was a war widow and assuming that there might be difficulty. Dirk knew that this was the problem which had given his mother much concern, but he had been recently apprised that his paternal grandfather had insured him from birth against such a contingency and that a sum equivalent to the first year's fees was now available and that a grant from the county in the form of an interest-free repayable loan had been promised. Dirk therefore stated that there was no difficulty on those grounds, without disclosing any unnecessary details. The questions petered out and Dirk rose to leave with an assurance that he would be informed in due course of the conclusions arrived at. In the outer room he was assailed by a couple still awaiting interview. Giving a rough, brief outline of the procedures and collecting his gear he departed.

Walking along Deansgate, he found a suitable café, where he ordered Welsh rarebit and tea to stave off the hunger which was beginning to gnaw at his vitals and to help him on his return journey. Back in the village he marshalled his thoughts as to the pending inquisition from his parent and other concerned relatives. That evening there was a dance at the Anglican church school. He had saved two shillings on his weekday lunch allowances so he would, with luck, be able to attend and trip the light fantastic along with his friends.

He was noncommittal when quizzed by his mother. He did not wish to raise false hopes for either of them. As a nonconformist he was up against severe competition for the small proportion of places awarded to non-Anglicans as a condition of the Government grant. The College was accepting only a few over forty that year as compared to three and four times that number in former years. This piece of information he imparted first before speaking casually of the interview. Tight-lipped, his mother listened to it without comment and Dirk ended his brief peroration by stating that there might be other options open. To terminate the monologue he smiled and mentioned that he was quite hungry, so the subject was abandoned for the preparation of a meal.

5

The second week in September found Dirk walking through the side gates of Chester College along a footpath flanked by dense shrubbery, with what appeared to him to be a chapel to the right. Down two short flights of broad steps he dropped to reveal a terrace some sixty yards long below which were two tennis courts, and beyond, a vista of extensive playing fields with soccer, hockey, rugger and cricket pitches extending into the far distance. Dirk stopped and lowered his suitcase to take in the scene. An iron rail fence skirted the periphery of the grounds outside which was a red-grit footpath hugged by low sparse shrubberies and a high red brick wall overhung by tall trees. With a critical eye he measured the perimeter and concluded that the distance round would be something like half a mile. As his eye ranged round, he spotted a pavilion abutting the cricket pitch and about a score of sheep grazing busily in the foreground. Retrieving his case once more he made for the centre of the terrace where stood a large modern brick-built structure with a Georgian façade in stark contrast to the red sandstone edifices with mullioned windows which towered to flank and rear. A narrow cobbled alley led to the older buildings with a footbridge crossing it overhead. Up this, Dirk ambled, eventually arriving at a small quadrangle tiled underfoot. From what appeared to be a house opposite emerged a figure in flannels and sweater sporting a green and white striped college scarf, who, seeing Dirk, turned and came across to meet him saying, 'Can I be of any help?'

'Thank you,' replied Dirk. 'I'm one of the new intake. Where do I go?'

'I guessed as much,' countered the other, 'by your suitcase and the fact that your face is unfamiliar. I'm a third year student. My name is Robinson. If you go up the steps, ahead on the left you will enter a classroom. You should find someone there to give you instructions.'

'I'm obliged to you,' said Dirk, 'my name's Waldron.'

'You'll soon find your way about,' replied Robinson. 'I'll see you around, no doubt.'

With that Dirk walked towards the steps where a heavy door opened outwards. Entering the room he noted a small group of students sitting at desks and being addressed by an elderly man with a sheaf of papers in his hand. As Dirk closed the door the man broke off his peroration and, looking towards Dirk, remarked, 'Ah, another one, and what is your name?'

'Waldron, sir,' responded Dirk, 'initial "D".'

The man glanced at his list, his eyes coming to rest near the bottom.

'Ah, yes,' he murmured, 'Dirk Waldron, you are assigned to Top John. Can you remember that? Top John dormitory, that is. Now if you will all follow me I will show you the way to the dorms where you will find your names on a card inserted in a metal slot on the middle of the sliding doors. You may all leave your cases here for the time being and you can collect them later after you have found your bearings.'

The group filed after him towards a corridor where there was a small square about the size of a house room. On one side Dirk saw a notice board and opposite on the other side shelves and pigeon holes for letters, all initialled. An open door on the far side led down some steps to another classroom at a lower level. Following the group they came to a winding stone staircase totally enclosed, which, when negotiated, emerged on to a second floor.

'This is Bottom John dormitory,' announced the guide. 'Those of you assigned to this floor find your cubicles. The rest follow me please.'

Up the spiral stone staircase, the treads of which were hollowed out by countless feet down the ages, went the remaining five, shortly to emerge upon a third floor identical to the one below.

'This is Top John to which you are all assigned,' stated the guide. 'Down there,' he said, pointing behind him down a short flight of steps, 'is Rooks dormitory. Find your own cubicle. Your trunk will probably be there if you forwarded it by rail. Have a scout around. Find your bearings and return to B Room in half an hour. By the way, your trunks must be emptied and carried down to the square by tomorrow afternoon at the latest.'

Dirk wandered along the dormitory, glancing left and right at the names in the metal slots on the doors. One sliding door was already open, revealing a bed, a chest of drawers, a row of hooks fixed to the wooden partition some seven feet high and across the angle of the far corner, let into a triangular fixed board with a circular hole, was a metal basin and in it an enamel jug. The floor was bare boards, the bed of the truckle type. The corridors were in the form of a cross, four facing cubicles in each arm, meeting together in a central square, in the four corners of which were four brass cold water taps over fixed basins with drainage. 'Dotheboys Hall,' muttered Dirk to himself half-aloud as he went on scanning the names upon the doors. He registered the fact that the names were in roughly alphabetical order: Stanley, Thompson, Underwood, Vance, Watcham, Wood. Eventually he spotted his own on the opposite side and slid back the door to see his trunk inside the entrance and an identical interior to that which he had seen before. He entered and sat upon the bed, which creaked metalically as it sagged beneath his eleven stone ten. Two deep drawers in the dressing table cum chest of drawers, two smaller ones at the top, with a small mirror attached to the wall above it. A tall, narrow window gave light to the room, a louvred hopper at its base for adjustment of fresh air, and below the ewer, a chamber pot.

Dirk divested himself of his coat. 'No hangers,' he remarked aloud with a shrug. 'None in the drawers either, I bet,' he surmised, as he opened them one by one. 'Good thing I put some in the trunk,' he mused as he stood to hang up his coat by the tab on one of the four wall hooks. The face of one of the chaps who had come up with him appeared round the door.

'My name's Windle,' he proffered, 'what's your first impressions of this lot?' he enquired archly.

Dirk held out his hand in greeting with, 'Mine's Waldron. It looks pretty spartan, don't you think?'

'Spartan?' laughed Windle. 'It's grim and stark . . . not much to commend it, what?'

Dirk sighed, 'Well,' he remarked, 'for better or worse we're here for the next two years, off and on. We'll have to make the best of it.'

He dropped back on the creaking bed. 'Musical beds too. You don't get that even in the best hotels. Take a pew. No chairs. It's obvious we're not expected to loiter or spend time here.'

'Just so,' agreed Windle. 'Where are we supposed to study?'

'That remains to be seen,' countered Dirk. 'Let's see what's cooking down below in er . . . B Room, I think he said.'

Quitting the cubicle, they strolled down the corridor, negotiated the winding staircase, ducking to avoid the jutting stonework at head height, and returned to B Room where other recent arrivals were gathered as well as others from the earlier groups. They were all shapes and sizes. A blackboard had been erected on which in chalk was an instruction: 'All first-year students to assemble here at 4 p.m.'

Dirk looked at his wristlet watch, which said two-thirty. He felt hungry. Picking up his case from the ruck in the corner, he returned to his cubicle in Top John where, opening first this, then the trunk, he proceeded to transfer their contents neatly into the available drawers. The travelling rug from the trunk he placed folded at the foot of the bed. Toiletries were arranged on top of the drawers; suits in cotton covers he placed on hangers on the wall hooks alongside his dressing gown, similarly draped. Books he placed on the window ledge. The spartan cell began to look lived in.

A face appeared round the door. It was Windle's,

grinning.

'Found the bogs yet?' was his arch query.

'Not yet,' laughed Dirk, 'but could do with them. Any ideas?'

'Yeah,' came the response. 'Turn right at the crossroads and it's right of the window at the end. And it's pretty spartan too, mate,' he added. 'Twenty four cubicles, four taps, one bog and what appears to be a tutor's room at the end of the left spur,' he concluded, raising his eyes to heaven.

'You've been busy,' laughed Dirk, locking his trunk and upending it, 'have you done any unpacking?'

'Not yet,' sighed Windle. 'Can't seem to summon up any enthusiasm for the job yet.'

'Well, you'd better get a move on, hadn't you?' Looking at his watch, Dirk chided him. 'Fifteen to go before the next assembly and cases and trunks to be down in the main square by noon tomorrow.'

So saying, he picked up the trunk and placed it in the corridor, sliding to the door.

'No locks,' he ventured to Windle.

'No nothing!' echoed Windle disconsolately.

'Cheer up,' encouraged Dirk, 'there's worse things happen at sea.'

'Here, I'll give you a hand with that,' offered Windle.

They negotiated the winding stairs awkwardly, placed the trunk in the corner of the square outside B Room and entered, selecting adjoining desks amongst the rapidly assembling throng, the noise growing minute by minute as each small group discussed their lot with mixed feelings. Dead on four o'clock, a gowned figure entered, mounted the rostrum behind the desk where the wall blackboards were and silently and severely scanned the melée spread out before him. He had a hawk-like expression, a pair of pince-nez clipped to his nose at a rakish angle, over which he glared intently at the assembly before him. Rapidly, a hushed silence fell as, one by one, those with their backs to him realised that the noise was abating. Each student made for an empty desk and gazed at the tight-lipped tutor, motionlessly awaiting a total subsidence of noise. After what appeared to Dirk to be thirty seconds of pause, broken only by an occasional shuffle or cough, the mask spoke through clenched teeth.

'Welcome to Chester College, gentlemen. Please respond when your name is called with the word "Adsum".'

He then called a roll of some forty-odd names, pausing to place a mark against those from whom no reply was forthcoming. That operation concluded, he outlined the general rules and regulations governing the college, ending with, 'The second year students will be arriving from approximately five p.m. onwards. Supper will be served in the refectory at seven-thirty p.m. Until then you may familiarise yourselves with your new surroundings and the various buildings and environment of the college. The senior prefect will now address you.'

Without more ado he descended from the dais, walked through the door and disappeared. Was it a sigh of relief that rippled the rows or was it a relaxation from the tense atmosphere which that awesome tutor created? A heavily-built fellow then mounted the rostrum and announced: 'That was Mr Morell, the Vice Principal of the college and the education tutor. You will see more of him anon. Meanwhile you must remember that you must all meet in the common room at eight-thirty this evening. I shall now take you to the refectory room where you will be allotted places at the various tables. Please follow me.'

He led the way to the refectory where, again in alphabetical order, each student was given a place at one of some twelve tables down the main hall and two more in a side alcove. To the last table in the side alcove were assigned Waldron, Watcham, Williamson and Wood, after which the senior prefect departed and the first years gradually drifted out into the square to go their several ways, bent upon exploring the various venues.

Dirk stayed on, talking to the three at his table and exchanging first impressions with them. They were eventually asked to leave by a flunky, apron-clad, who appeared from behind a screen, no doubt leading to the kitchens, offside which was a serving-hatch. The four then discovered the changing rooms for sports, the outside toilets consisting of troughs down which water flowed to the lower end. Handy for floating lit-paper down, Williamson laughingly remarked. Thence they walked to the gymnasium, the lecture theatre with its tiered seating, the common room, the junior block with the art room above, the library, the various classrooms, the chemistry room, the woodwork and metalwork rooms, the lounge and billiard room and finally the chapel.

Despite the novelty of new faces, fresh surroundings, strange routines, a deepening depression was assailing Dirk. Austerity was writ large everywhere. Nowhere was there any sign of comfort or places to relax. He retired to the dorm to finish his unpacking from the suitcase and make a final rearrangement of his clothes, then went down to supper in the refectory where the whole college complement was now assembled.

A grace was intoned before the meal: *Non nobis domine, sed nomine tu da gloria : non nobis nomine non nobis.* Supper consisted of bread hacked from a loaf, a block of butter divided fairly evenly between twelve men by the prefect in charge of table – Winterbottom by name – earthenware jugs of tepid tea, quite weak, and hunks of cheese carved from a lump in the centre of the table on a wooden platter. The cheese had seen better days. Dirk's spirits sagged still further. He was plagued by a gnawing hunger which such fare would scarce assuage, but brightened when some senior mentioned that the canteen would open after the meal for half an hour where biscuits, chocolate, cigarettes, sweets, etc. were on sale. Dirk bought a bar of chocolate and some biscuits with the meagre reserve of money he had brought and reckoned that it would not last long if this were to be the pattern of life. He then made for the dormitory, only to be stopped from ascending by a senior student, who informed him that students were not allowed in dorms before nine-thirty. His depression returned. Back he went to the common room to discover a milling crowd of students talking and calling out excitedly. About eight-thirty a hefty senior student jumped on the large table near the fireplace at the farther end and bellowed for silence. Some drifted to the seating around the walls whilst others lounged in a half dozen armchairs with cushions or sat astride stand chairs in nonchalant pose. Gradually the noise subsided. The student on the table began to address his audience in flamboyant tones.

'Fellow students,' he began, gazing around the hushed throng, 'I must acquaint our newly arrived junior year students with the unwritten laws governing this common room. New students, note the white line drawn on the floor from the entrance door to the right hand side of the fireplace. No junior year student is allowed to cross it at any time except by invitation. The armchairs are for prefects, the stand chairs for seniors and the small room by the exit door for prefects. Down in the open square, juniors may use only the right hand side of the walkway. They may not pass through the gate which connects the junior and senior changing rooms, nor use the approach to the senior changing rooms. The figure on the plinth over there is the college mascot. His name is Colonel Heezaliar. All junior students will now stand up and do obesiance to him, first raising their arms above their heads. Up, up, up on your feet, you louts. Face the mascot. Come on now, jump to it! Get those arms up high. Now you will all bow three times to Colonel Heezaliar.'

Every new student present stood, amid catcalls from the esconced seniors who called words of derision or encouragement such as: 'Down lower,' or 'Get 'em up higher,' or 'Touch the floor with your paws,' or 'Take that smirk off your face.'

A stentorian voice from a window seat roared, 'One chap there only bowed twice. Seize him, chaps,' at which he crossed over the white line, singling one out and leading him to the table. The student on the table demanded the student's name,

'Dawson,' came the response.

'Very well, Dawson. Up on this table with you.' And up climbed Dawson, a slightly-built youth.

'Esteemed seniors, here we have Dawson who bowed only

twice to our revered mascot. Have you any suggestions as to the penalty he shall pay?'

'Let him sing a song,' called one.

'Recite a poem,' called another.

'Make a speech,' roared a voice amid other somewhat ribald suggestions.

The student on the table with the victim called for silence. 'This first year lout will first of all bow the regulation three times. Then he will make a speech on the benison of sleep.'

With that he jumped down from the table, leaving Dawson in splendid isolation.

'Go on! Get on with it,' came the chorus of senior voices. 'Speak up too!'

Dawson hesitated somewhat and then began an extempore peroration on the subject of sleep, which was punctuated from time to time by ribald remarks, humorous interjections and sarcastic comments from beyond the white line. He was eventually stopped in mid-sentence and made to kneel facing the Colonel. The student-in-charge jumped up beside him. 'From henceforth your college name will be Sleep. Anyone not using that name will be fined or fatigued.'

Sleep was then permitted to get down and retire to his window seat.

Another senior crossed the line and, singling out a junior, called out, 'This oaf was smoking when he bowed to the Colonel. Teach him some manners.'

He was duly led to the table and mounted it.

'What is your name?' asked the leader of the rag.

'Coleman,' came the audible reply.

'How do you spell Coleman?' was then asked. The student spelt it.

'But C O A L spells coal,' came the retort amid laughter, 'and coal burns and makes the chimney smoke and you were smoking Coleman, weren't you?'

'Yes,' acknowledged Coleman.

'Then you too will make obesiance three times to the Colonel whilst kneeling.'

This he did, after which the rag leader pronounced, 'From henceforth your college name shall be Smokey. You will now sing *Old King Cole was a Merry Old Soul.'*

He began to sing after which the seniors and then the juniors joined in with a will, adding malicious verses from the old rugger repertoires.

During the next twenty minutes three more new students were 'christened', each performing a task peculiar to the name conferred. C.A. Burton became Cabby from his initials. A chap named Wood was made to sing *The Tree Grew in the Wood,* and when all the repetitions were exhausted and the song got down to the twig and the bud, they had christened him 'Bud'. Dirk sensed that this would go on every night in the recreation hour until all were named or the seniors tired of the game. Meanwhile a bell shrilled out from the top of the stairway and the majority spilled out to the evening vespers at college chapel. Not so the dozen and a half nonconformists who stayed on in the common room where seniors arranged chairs either side of the table, which now became a lectern. Hymn books appeared miraculously from a window ledge behind the piano and, following a short explanation of this morning and nightly routine, a senior whom Dirk adjudged to be a prefect, emerged from the anteroom and took charge. A portion of scripture was read, a hymn sung to the accompaniment of the pianist and a few short prayers were said in an atmosphere vastly in contrast to what had preceded. The benediction followed and after returning hymn books to the ledge the chairs were again scattered and normal conversation renewed.

The seniors then crossed the white line and made themselves known to the newcomers, informing them as to the many pitfalls they would be likely to encounter, and urging them to join in the fun unresistingly. Dirk learned that the prefect who took the service was known as the 'Non-Con-Bish' in college vernacular and that he had an assistant, also a prefect, and that from time to time others would be asked to participate in the proceedings. Some fifteen minutes later the anglicans debouched from the chapel and the atmosphere of the common room changed to one of wary silence.

Dirk decided that his first day had been long enough so he headed for the dorm and sleep. Just as he was dozing off, a loud voice called from the double cubicle at the entrance to the dorm, 'Ten minutes to lights!' adding, 'All juniors may place their shoes in the corridor to be cleaned by the bootboy.' Then followed a noise of sliding doors as some complied, but Dirk had already attended to his and drawn water for morning. Again the voice roared, 'Five to Lights!' rousing Dirk from descending oblivion once more, until finally, the last call came – 'Lights Top,' and total darkness prevailed.

Dirk slept heavily. He was jolted awake by the shrill, vibrant tones of an electric bell. He looked at his watch. It was seven-twenty. Roll call at seven-thirty. Ten minutes to wash and dress. Up he jumped to a rapid routine, carrying the basin to the sluice and noting on the way that a pile of whitewashed shoes lay in the centre of the square. Leaving his bed unmade, he shot off down the winding staircase amidst a headlong flight of motley students. Standing at the bottom of the stairs was the tutor who had addressed them the previous afternoon, his pince-nez askew, grey, wiry-haired head tilted, fixing each student with his beady eye. He stopped one in front of Dirk, a dark-haired senior youth, and through clenched teeth jerked out, 'Yees, Grainger, no shave, no shave, go back and stand nearer the razor and afterward report to me!'

Dirk sidled past, thankful for his Titian locks and that his fair beard did not show, thinking, 'It's worse than Sing-Sing', and registering that he would not rise late again. Down in C Room a prefect called the roll at exactly seven-thirty: Bailey, Bradshaw, Bradbrook, Brennan . . . and the Adsum rang out from students busy adjusting ties, buttoning shirts in a last desperate effort to appear shipshape and tidy. Three late arrivals were booked for fatigues. Roll call over, they dispersed and wandered back, chatting, to the main square, to await the opening of the refectory doors for breakfast. For Dirk it could not come soon enough. He was starving, his intestines rumbling and registering a distinct sinking feeling at the pit of his stomach.

He noted that a large proportion of the students were smoking cigarettes whilst chatting in small selective groups; that others were pacing up and down the approaches to the changing rooms behind. Some wandered up the stairs to the common room while others leant against walls scanning notebooks and folders. He perched himself on the third stone step leading to the common room and, head in hands, absorbed the scene before him.

When breakfast arrived it consisted of a heavy oatmeal porridge, which wasn't so bad except that the milk provided was a watery blue. He noticed that the seniors on his table had brought with them pots of jam or syrup or honey to augment their diet. Next came a salver with sausages and curly bacon which the prefect in charge, Winterbottom, doled out equally to the best of his ability. The sausages were not all the same size and ran to about one per man, whilst the bacon was sparse and rather underdone and greasy. A loaf of bread in the centre of the table beside the usual block of butter was cut and distributed, as was the appropriate pat of 'slide'. Tea came in a metal pot, quite large, the tea plentiful, if weak and that was it. The *Non nobis domine* took on a new meaning for Dirk as he wondered if he would last out until one o'clock. On completion, the senior prefect from Table One went to the rostrum where breakfasted three tutors and, extracting a list from his inside pocket, announced, 'The following will be required for trunks-fatigue after breakfast.' There followed a list of defaulters from roll call in alphabetical order, six in number. Asking the senior student next to him what 'fatigues' involved, Dirk was given a graphic rundown of the various tasks it might be his lot to 'cop-out' on, such as:

1. Picking up fag ends in the square
2. Removing sheep droppings from the various pitches in use
3. Sweeping the common room, laying the fire and filling the coal scuttle
4. Marking out pitches, or sweeping the terrace clean of fallen

leaves etc, etc.

One chore no-one escaped and that occurred twice a week, usually Tuesdays and Thursdays, and that was 'The Chain Gang on the Alps'. Any students who contravened rules, flouted accepted customs, were late on parade, or adrift from town, were automatically put on fatigues of one sort or another. There was, however, a permanent fatigue which excused a junior from all others unless he was guilty of a misdemeanour and that was the laundry fatigue. All students put their laundry in a special personal bag and dumped it every Friday in large wicker baskets placed in the inside square by B Room. These were taken down to the cellars at a given time after supper and Matron supplied cocoa and cakes to the three selected. On Tuesdays the laundry came back from 'The House of Mercy' where nuns dealt with it and was redistributed to the various classrooms in individual parcels. Dirk was informed that this was a 'cushy' job which only involved a day on the Chain Gang. Enquiring what the Chain Gang consisted of, he was informed that they were levelling a sloping field behind the pavilion and groups of four had to fill two jinny-wagons with earth and push them down lines to the bottom of the field where they were emptied and brought back. It involved roughly an hour's hard work, less if rushed and sweated labour. Anyone guilty of a major misdemeanour was given the task of clearing up sheep droppings with his bare hands and a bucket.

Dirk, still hungry, digested all this gratuitous information and much else besides, gleaned minute by minute from obliging seniors who, no doubt, embellished the facts. There were other pitfalls to avoid. For instance, no junior was allowed to be seen speaking to a female in the city or he could be 'jammed'. Any senior spotting a junior in the act, be it in a shop, on the street or in a café, could steal up, put his hand on the junior's shoulder and say, 'You're jammed', which entailed the junior providing a pot of whatever conserve for the said senior's table. Nor was a junior allowed to bring a female within 200 yards of the college without special permission from the Guild Council, which consisted of tutors and selected prefects. This precluded visits from females of the family. Dirk brooded on the multifarious restrictions applicable to him and the melancholy of the previous day returned.

After lunch the afternoons were free to any student not otherwise kept occupied by fatigues or the chain gang, or in the time after fulfilling a chain gang session. Saturdays were free from lunch to seven-thirty, most weeks, with one Saturday per half term allowing an extension until nine-thirty. On Sunday the deadline was five for Anglicans, who had to attend college chapel, whereas the nonconformists were allowed to attend Sunday services at chapel in the city. A senior confided in Dirk that he always signed-in that he had attended Green Fields Mission, which at least raised a laugh. Every weekday evening there was an hour between eight-thirty and nine-thirty set aside for private study in the classroom, seated at one's desk and supervised by a prefect who insisted on total silence. The whole smacked of monasticism and the more Dirk contemplated his lot, the less enamoured he became of college life. His original aspiration concerning it had long ago evaporated. It was a case of grin-and-bear-it. Fortunately the reaction to all this restrictive discipline was the energy put into ragging, sports, the various societies and the enforced humour.

It was with a huge sense of relief that Dirk was selected for the laundry fatigue. Provided he walked the straight and narrow and did his stints on the chain gangs he was excused all else in the way of fatigues. For this perk he had to thank a senior who had attended his grammar school and with whom he had played cricket and soccer. He had a friend at court. Rowing and soccer filled three of his afternoons and Saturdays, and he gradually settled down to a recognisable routine.

Inevitably the time arrived for his 'christening'. He was made to recite 'The boy stood on the burning deck' amid catcalls and corrections to the bawdier versions. They then played about with rhymes to his surname: Waldron, Cauldron, Witch, Wizard, Merlin and after a deal of argument Merlin it became and stayed henceforth.

6

One fine afternoon early in October the whole junior year were summoned to appear on the terrace after lunch at two clad in PE gear and plimsolls. Dirk sensed some rag was afoot when he saw the turn-out of seniors foregathered. Sure enough, they were made to group around and a prefect explained that it was the custom before half-term for the junior year to race around the close roughly half-a-mile distance. A whistle started the race from the near end of the terrace to allow stringing-out before passing through the gate to the narrow periphery path. Dirk covered the distance with ease, but delayed arriving first for he suspected that something might happen to the first or the last. Sure enough, it was the last they picked upon. The Colonel had been brought out from his plinth in the common room and placed upon the terrace wall and MacClellan was made to kneel and do obesiance, after which he was christened Nurmi after the world famous Finnish miler, amid laughter all round. That accomplished, the crowd dispersed. Dirk was beginning to see that there was some logic about the creation of these diversions to relieve the tensions of the harsh disciplines to which they were being subjected. He noted that the tutors were always otherwise engaged when ragging took place.

That night in the dorms there was 'jerry' racing. The corridors were covered with polished brown linoleum and two chamber pots, or 'jerries', as they were referred to, were placed side by side, full of what looked like coloured water but what could have been the real thing. Juniors in each dorm were matched against each other, the loser having to compete again, until the ultimate loser was found, to match against the ultimate loser of the other four dorms, and so on, until the Champion Loser was singled out. The idea was to tie the hands of the competitors behind their backs and they pushed the jerries with their forehead as far as the square. Obviously it paid to be first but speed caused the contents to slop over the brim on to the head and neck and finish on the floor, through which knees had to travel, feet following. A senior stood by with a squeegee and mop and bucket to clean the floor between bouts and one was posted on the stairway to warn of the approach of tutors, for this rag was very much frowned upon in high places. It took place surreptitiously nevertheless and relieved the tensions more than somewhat. There was no escaping the rigours, the lack of privacy, the strict time-tabling and the routines.

Week followed week with monotonous repetition. Escape was hard to come by. An odd afternoon by the river, strolls through the parks, visits to the interesting places in the city, compensated in a way. Even the racecourse was out of bounds. Far from home, deprived of creature comforts, in a bed that sagged and creaked, denied even the benison of hot water save once a week on bath roster when the juniors were last and the water tepid, reduced to low diet and the most unappetising food, Dirk marked the days and crossed off each one on the small calendar he had brought. Add to that the fact that there was no heating in the dorms and the weather was becoming markedly colder and Dirk counted the days to half-term.

During lectures his gaze would wander to where he could see the white clouds drifting by through the tall Georgian windows. In his mind's eye he could conjure up pictures of the landscape at home, with its wild flowers, its rich autumn tints, the twittering birds and the home-flying rooks. A shrilling bell would announce the end of the session and the five minute break before another followed. When the fifteen minute mid-morning break came, there was the usual mad dash for the canteen where the smokers would light up their fag-ends with, 'Gis a light, please,' for matches were scarce and lighters, few and far between, had long ago run out of fuel. Dirk had never before smoked but the hunger gnawing at his vitals induced him to try the habit, believing it would allay the pangs. In a way, it did, but the cost was a drain on his resources. He wrote home as often as he could but told them nothing of the situation as it really was, except tentatively to suggest that a parcel of food might not go amiss. As if in answer, the parcels began to arrive, but at irregular intervals. These he shared with his equally hungry friends, Mike, Windy and Liz. These were supplemented by kind-hearted invitations to tea by local nonconformist families who welcomed him to their Sunday evening services and seemed to know the conditions obtaining in the college.

The subject matter of many of the college lectures was 'old hat' to Dirk. Nature study, an optional subject, he had pursued since childhood. Rural science was inbred. The compulsory religious knowledge was repetitious from chapel and Sunday school. He could help students from the cities with snippets of country lore that even the tutors were unaware of. This left him free to spend more time, such as he got, on the professional subjects and his selected advanced courses. One irksome chore was that when seniors were out on school practice they would break in upon the evening study sessions of their junior year and commandeer someone to draw, paint or sketch the illustrations they required for their lessons. They too were under intense pressures and it was sympathetically, if reluctantly, that Dirk had occasionally to comply, spending valuable time upon that chore. One student of Dirk's acquaintance had already absconded, unable to withstand the pressures and the phrase 'Do a Thomas-John,' was bandied about when chaps felt uptight, for these were the Christian names of the departed one.

Tuesday of the third week in October plunged Dirk into a renewed abyss of depression. He made for the square to inspect the postal pigeon holes marked W to Z to see if any letters had come for him. An unusual yellow envelope lay flat in the slot with his name on it. He picked it up and scanned the front. There was no indication from where it had come. It dawned upon him that it was a telegram which, when opened, read, 'Grandfather died Monday. Funeral delayed Saturday. Come. Mother.'

Dirk glanced around. The square was unusually deserted. He read the print a second time, with a sense of numbness. The raw words penetrated his brain. His grandfather had been to him protector confidant, father figure and friend, whose foresight and generosity had ensured his college fees for one year at least. When he had suffered a seizure some eighteen months ago, it was Dirk who had taken charge of the allotment on which, upon his retirement, his grandfather had spent much time and money. As he slowly recovered from the paralysis, Dirk, on daily visits, had assisted him to walk again. Their roles had then, in a way, changed. Even before he had left for college in September, Dirk had cleared the garden of most of its vegetables and stored them, picked the fruit in season and arranged for another tenant to take possession. It was the middle allotment of nine, some fifty yards long and eight yards wide, with apple, plum and pear trees down the centre, the sides lined with blackcurrant and redcurrant bushes half way, raspberry canes at the bottom, rhubarb at the top and a screen of brambles separating the plot from the stream beyond. The first half was down to vegetables and in dry season he had carried hundreds of cans of water from the brook to nourish the seedlings.

In his mind's eye he could see his grandfather seated on the form by the toolshed and butt of liquid fertiliser, chatting to his cronies on warm summer evenings when Dirk himself was an infant. He would seek him out and his grandfather would go and pick an apple, peel it with his clasp knife and slice it up for Dirk, later plunging his hand into the fob pocket of a moleskin waistcoat to produce a penny or two for sweets, or marbles or whatever happened to be in season. Together they had wandered the countryside, attended cattle auctions, eaten from market stalls, called at friendly inns, visited distant relations, watched processions, wandered round county shows, joined in galas, pigeon racing, sports events and picnics, helped at haytimes and harvests and he had taught

Dirk about the flora and fauna of the district. A carpenter and wheelwright, he had taken Dirk to the houses of the landed gentry to inspect and repair carriages, to Stoneyhurst College to do repairs, taught him to recognise trees, their shapes and peculiarities. The debt of gratitude for his forebear was immense. He owed him much.

This reverie was crudely interrupted by 'Windy' Fairweather who had been sent to summon him to a junior students' meeting. He was snatched back to reality.

'Where is it?' he asked rather listlessly.

'In the art room,' came the reply, 'come on, we've started.'

'What's it all about? Why the hurry? Is it that important?'

'Course it is . . . it's about the concert that the juniors have to put on at Christmas before we go down.'

'Oh! That's it! I remember now. I said I'd offer a few suggestions.'

Dirk gathered his scattered wits, thrust the telegram into his inside jacket pocket and followed Fairweather at a smart trot. They were discussing the form of the proposed entertainment. The affair was to take place in the lecture theatre. Dirk eventually proffered a suggestion. 'What about two one-act plays. They would involve about a dozen people and be easier on the individual participants.'

'Can you suggest some, Merlin?' asked the student in the chair. Two came to mind that he had done at home. '*Campbell of Kilmohr* would go down well I think, and there is another called *The Purple Bedroom* which might be an innovation. There's a bedroom scene but if we get the PE lecturer's wife to take a part, the Prinny's wife would scarcely veto it. The bedroom scene is a bit near the bone, but funny.'

The discussion rumbled on. It was eventually decided that everyone connected with the show would give the suggestions deep thought and meet again to finalise arrangements.

As the bodies began to drift away, Dirk walked over to his friend 'Sonny' Bailey and, extending the telegram said, 'Take a look at this.'

Sonny read it and read it again quizzically. 'Genuine or doing a runner?' he asked.

'Genuine! You twit!' came the response.

Sonny expressed sympathy and concern.

'What's the drill?' asked Dirk. 'I have to go, but will they wear it?'

'Well, you'll have to get an "exeat" from Morrell first. Sooner you than me.'

'I'd rather go direct to the Prinny. He might be more sympathetic. After all, he's a canon of the church and should understand.'

Prinny's away this week in London seeing the Education Minister. They're threatening to close the college, you know.'

'Yeah, I heard from Quids, my Advanced English tute. Perhaps I could have a word with him?'

'Might as well bite the bullet and see Morrell. He's sure to be in the refectory to inspect lunch and cast his eagle eye on the layout.'

'OK, will do, but I have a feeling that there'll be difficulties. I'll beard the lion in his den.'

Without hesitation, having made up his mind, he made a beeline for Morrell's Sanctum Sanctorum just beyond the square. He knocked upon the door.

'Come in!' growled the voice from beyond the green baize door.

Dirk entered and closed the door behind him, then approached the desk.

'Well, Waldron, isn't it? What do you want? I'm busy.'

'I need an "exeat" to go home to attend my grandfather's funeral, sir.'

There was an ominous pause as Morrell digested the information, which seemed to stick in his craw. He eyed Dirk up and down and fixed him with his customary penetrating stare, calculated to disarm any student.

'How do I know your relative has died, Waldron?'

'A telegram, sir. Arrived this morning.'

Another pause and the same long searching stare over the

pince-nez, ever askew.

'I'd like to see it, Waldron.'

Dirk extracted the flimsy from his inside jacket pocket and placed it firmly upon the edge of the desk, from where it was picked up and examined in great detail. For want of other remark, after a further long perusal, came: 'Where is it you live?'

'A village outside Burnley, sir.'

Placing the telegram on one side, Morrell opened a drawer and extracted what appeared to be a rail timetable, scanning its pages. Eventually, after a careful search he remarked in clipped tones: 'Mm . . . . Mm . . . . Yes. There's a train at five-thirty to Manchester. I believe you can bus it from there to Burnley. The funeral should be over by four. There's a train back to Manchester at six-thirty with a connection to Chester. I want you back here about nine-thirty or just after, on Saturday. Understood?'

'Thank you, sir. May I have my telegram?'

'No, you may not. I'll hold on to it for the time being.'

Dirk made his exit, anger churning up inside. 'Not a word of sympathy expressed. The minimum of assistance granted. He could have given me till Sunday. The sadistic bastard!'

He reached the fresh air, breathed in deeply, straightened his shoulders and made for the footpath around the close. There he could be alone with his grief.

The melancholy appointment with the funeral rites was duly effected. He shouldered his grandfather's coffin along with his uncles and cousins and bore it into chapel and then to its final resting place. He listened with emotion to the orations, cast his quota of soil upon the coffin and retired to foregather with family and friends for the customary meal laid out in the Sunday school. There wasn't even time for him to mingle with the many who attended before he was catching a bus on his return to the college grind. It was ten in the evening before he arrived in college. The Vice Principal, Morrell, had gone home so Dirk reported to the duty tutor, 'Ranzo' the history man. The following morning, in the rush down the stone staircase to prayers in the common room, he encountered Morrell in his usual inspection place at the bottom.

'Yees, Waldron,' he called between his clenched teeth, 'I see you made it back!'

'Yes, sir,' replied Dirk, looking the Vice Principal straight in the eye, 'I'd like my telegram back sir,' and moved away down the corridor, briskly, without waiting for a reply.

'Polly' Winterbottom the table prefect at breakfast handed the telegram to Dirk before the salver of greasy sausages and bacon were served out with difficulty to the ten occupants. Dirk murmured his thanks, slowly and silently downing the unappetising food, after which he retired to the solitude of the close once more.

Half term gave Dirk the opportunity to eat wholesome food. His mother remarked upon his now taciturn and uncommunicative attitude, so he related the funny episodes which had occurred and avoided describing the rigours with which he was constantly faced, locking them up in his mind so as to unburden them on his friends, to disillusion them as to his fate in a sort of catharsis of confession. Thus relieved, he returned after three days to the spartan ambience once more. Christmas came and went. The spring term brought school practice. He was assigned to College School, next door almost, and spared the dawn risings and bus rides into Liverpool, the Wirral, Birkenhead or Warrington. There were demonstration lessons by seniors, a taste of things to come in the following year.

In conversation over the refectory table, regarding current affairs, he was trapped into participating in a full college debate. The Oxford Movement was enjoying a widespread vogue as reaction from the Great War and the recession was fully exploited. 'That this House will not fight for King and Country' was the subject of debate up and down the land. Dirk's views had always been radically opposed to this attitude and he had been provoked into expressing them. The Non-Con-Bish, who was an ardent pacifist, then challenged him to a public debate in the common room. Dirk scented a public brawl but could not avoid the challenge. The affair was arranged with much publicity and the principal of the college was invited to attend, as were various tutors. He knew himself to be in the minority for he had already debated the same subject the previous year in the Young Men's Sunday School class and been heavily defeated. Came the night and the common room was packed as for a Roman holiday. Dirk scented that he was to be the victim for the slaughter. For once he was allowed to cross the white line and sit at the common room table with the participants.

First the proposer spoke. His speech was emotive and well delivered for he had considerable practise as a local preacher and Dirk had twice listened to him in the city Methodist chapels. When Dirk's turn to address the assembly was announced he rose to a tense silence. He described what was going on in Germany and Italy with the rising National Socialist parties, the military uniforms, the marching, the Jew-baiting, the summary arrests of vocal opponents, the glorification of the German race, their demands for *Lebensraum,* etc. etc. He then briefly gave a rundown on the Prussian character through history, and, in a highly emotive challenge, asked his audience about their reaction should such drunken, brawling, goose-stepping Huns ever invade our shores, the effect they would have as they plundered, raped and carried off into continental slavery the flower of our nation – our womenfolk, our fiancées, our sisters. Carried away on the tide of his own oratory, he ended by declaiming, 'And you cowardly lot would be prepared to stand idly by and watch the cruelty, the rape, the deflowering of our maidens, the sack of your towns and villages.' Then, with an inspired further prophetic utterance, Dirk dropped his voice to a sibilant whisper and said, 'The day is not far distant when you will be called upon to face up to that challenge. Now is the time to tell the world that you will stand in that evil day.'

He sat down amid a muted applause. He felt he had at least stirred them, provoked them, made them think, but it was to no avail. As expected, in the climate of opinion enveloping the country at large, they endorsed the proposition by a large majority. The only satisfaction which Dirk and his seconder got was a word of congratulation from a tutor on retiring. His reward came later in the year, when the Non-Con-Bishop invited him to become his successor in that office for the ensuing year.

The spring term merged into the summer term. Athletics now occupied Dirk's leisure time. His ability was quickly noted by the second year men and he was selected to represent the College Athletic Team in the annual match against Sealand Aerodrome for which a cup was the coveted trophy. Dirk trained hard on the tracks. The college had never yet won the trophy, largely because they were disadvantaged in the field events, whereas they were a match for them on the tracks. It was a case of late teenagers against mature men in their middle and late twenties, who had an advantage in events such as the javelin, the shot-putt, the tug o'war, the hammer, not to mention the pole vault, for which latter event the college had no facilities. Thus, the outcome was almost predictable. Nevertheless, Dirk intended to give a good account of himself in the four events to which he was assigned. The meeting was a lighthearted affair with the RAF personnel very affable. Matched against a Flight Lieutenant Lightbown, he soon struck up an affable accord, exchanging information about their differing lifestyles. Lightbown was obviously from a well-to-do family whose influence had gained him a commission. He spoke about training corps attached to colleges as a front door entry into RAF training for commissions and painted a more than glowing picture of their lifestyle. Lightbown suggested that Dirk might be interested in coming to Sealand to learn to fly in a private aircraft which he could hire there. The offer was tempting but Dirk's circumstances precluded such a venture, and he said so. They chatted over the meal, subsequent upon the competitions, which the college narrowly lost by the smallest margin of all time and Dirk promised to keep in touch. They shook hands, having established a bond of athletic ability, and Dirk returned to college in very deep thought.

The first year exams brought mid-July and the welcome respite of eight weeks at home with a pile of vacation work to get through. Dirk phoned an old school friend, now a trainee accountant with the local authority, and they agreed upon a trip to Liverpool Docks to visit the ships currently in port. They went by train and boarded two large freighters as well as a liner moored alongside the inner docks. With permission they were given *carte-blanche* to wander at will down ladders, through engine rooms, up to bridge and chart rooms and chatted with duty officers regarding voyages, destinations, cargoes and life in the Merchant Service in general. The germ of a thought was beginning to stir to life in Dirk's subconscious for he felt that the air or the sea held some attraction for him. He recognised that he was not too happy with his present vocation and that his mind was questing other possible outlets for his developing talents.

He returned to college in September, now a senior, having been appointed jointly with his friend as a prefect in charge of Top John. He wrily contemplated the ragging that would stun the unsuspecting junior intake. Remembering his own reactions, Dirk resolved to temper the wind to the lambs about to be shorn. The weeks passed too quickly as he adapted to the daily round of duties, responsibilities, amusements, relaxations, and the modicum of increased comfort now prevailing. Spartan diet, paucity of cash and sleep, soccer, rowing and the ceaseless round of lectures, school practice, stage productions, all took on a fresher aspect, viewed from the other side of the white line. Autumn merged into spring with an all-too-brief Christmas respite; Easter followed and summer blazed and with it the regattas, the swimming and athletics and the dreaded Final School Practice with the awards of Colours and the ultimate examinations, buoyed up by the award of three Colours in soccer, athletics and rowing, he faced the subject question papers at stated times. The last was Advanced Latin after most students had departed and but four of his colleagues remained. The rooms and corridors seemed empty, the corridors echoing with sombre vacuity. The summer heat permeated the classroom with oppressive lethargy. Dirk loosened his tie and removed his jacket after perusing the questions, which were not easy. One two hour paper followed by a break then a one and a half hour essay to follow. The sweat trickled down his forehead, his handkerchief worked overtime. He had already dispatched his trunk and his suitcase was ready, so, with a final check of his papers, a further glance at the instructions, a silent prayer for the outcome, he handed in the scripts, collected his gear and made for the door.

The fresher air was like a benison to his fevered brow, which he mopped with the already dank handkerchief. The final bell shrilled out as he waited for the last few to appear. They all wearily shook hands, a little sadly, for amidst the adversity there had been a camaraderie which had overcome the harshness of the spartan discipline. Commiserations exchanged, Dirk made an exit through the side door, carrying his case, went from thence to the station and home to await the result of his two year incarceration and labours.

His worst fears were unjustified, for in the week just prior to his twentieth birthday, a college envelope revealed his fate. He slid his eyes down the alphabetical role to the bottom. A pause to read, a missed heartbeat and a sigh of intense relief. Another hurdle had been cleared. The world was his oyster.

What a world! Unemployment, dole queues, protest marchers, depression, a falling birthrate: which augured badly for his profession inauspicious, in fact . . . and jobs to be had were few and far between. Locally there was only supply work, which tided him over. He would have to 'get on his bike' as the saying went. He filled in endless application forms and dispatched them. December approached and with it two interviews in the Home Counties. He attended and drew a blank. Shuttling back by train two more interviews awaited him. He had hardly time to grab a change of clothes and he was off again. Again he drew a blank. Eventually on Christmas Eve, by registered post, came the offer of an appointment at a school in North London from which interview he had recently returned. He immediately phoned his acceptance and confirmed the date for his reappearance to finalise the necessary paperwork. The wheel of fortune had finally turned in his favour, or so he thought.

7

Dirk received a letter from the Head of the school to which he had been assigned. It contained local newspaper cuttings and information as to the types of accommodation available within a reasonable distance from the school. This too he acknowleged and within the brief period before he took up his appointment, he wrote to three likely people, finally accepting one which offered a bedsit with dinner, breakfast and a light tea at weekends for 35s. per week with a 10s. retaining fee for extended terminal vacations. Dirk had already calculated that his starting salary would be slightly over £3 per week after the customary deductions for superannuation and income tax, and considering that his mother had managed to feed four on about the same amount, he had little cause for complaint. His contemporaries in the factories of the North were mainly on half that amount and they had been employed for over six years already.

Dirk presented himself at the school the day prior to opening, at the express request of the Head. He was greeted by an elderly headmaster some three inches taller than himself, with a rather stern and unbending presence. Following a few introductory exchanges of general information, the Head got down to the essential part of Dirk's visit.

'Now Mr Waldron,' he remarked, 'I'm going to assign you as the form master of 2c' . . . adding with matter-of-fact tone, 'you can't do much harm there.'

Dirk gave a wry smile of acknowledgement at the sting in the tail, but nodding in acquiescence, accepted the implied stricture with equanimity. After all, he thought, it was necessary to prove himself before being wholly accepted. He was then given the timetable and syllabus for each of the various subjects he had to teach and was informed that he was expected to take boys' PE throughout the school. That was somewhat of a bonus anyway. He was then taken along to meet the rest of the male staff who were also in school arranging their classrooms for the morrow and finally shown the classroom from which he was to operate as form master. Later the male staff had foregathered in a staffroom up a short flight of stairs at the end of the corridor and he was apprised by them as to the other 'extra' duties which would now fall to his lot, such as corridor supervision at break, Saturday games fixtures, the ordering of PE and games kit, playground duties, etc. His future colleagues seemed affable enough, one of the elderly ones evincing a friendly and almost paternal interest in him. He learned that this was the Deputy Head, who confided that the school had recently received a whole set of gymnastic equipment, as yet untouched, and that Dirk was expected to put it to immediate use to justify its acquisition and to augment it in due course. The new surge in physical education promulgated in college was to be implemented in the school and that was the main reason, amongst others, for his appointment.

Dirk set about his tasks the following day with a will, determined to make his mark. Form 2c was a tough proposition, consisting of children of families rehoused from the East End of London and placed in a new council housing estate built on some spare land in the middle of commuter suburbia, and it was patently evident that there were two distinct types of pupil attending the school. The physique and general appearance of the majority of the pupils in 2c, not to mention the deportment and behaviour of many, left a lot to be desired. Dirk, however, soon established his disciplines, which had been totally lacking in the classroom of 1c where they had been the previous year. The academic attainments in the three Rs were low and this had to be remedied too. All in all, Dirk had an uphill task, a task relieved somewhat by the PE, the art and the craftwork to which he had been assigned in other more able groupings elsewhere in the school.

Came the end of January and the first pay-day. He received a summons to the Head's room where piles of notes and silver had been counted out and placed in chalked squares on the Head's table, each square having the initials of the appropriate teacher chalked in white. Dirk appeared to be the first to collect. The Head pointed to the appropriate square at the top end with the monition, 'You had better check that, Mr Waldron. There doesn't seem to me to be much money there.' He seemed genuinely concerned. Indeed, compared to some of the other stacks of notes and coinage, Dirk's seemed quite insignificant. He counted it, '£11. 3s. 6d.,' he said to the Head and accepted it as a correct amount as he had no idea of its accuracy, it having been a short month for him. With a 'Thank you, Mr Scott,' Dirk made his exit as others arrived to collect theirs. He had calculated that he should be paid net some £14 and a few shillings per month after deductions.

Dirk soldiered on undeterred. February, around the third week brought a short spell of beautiful sunny weather. That morning's PE session involved 2a and 2b boys who, when stripped off down to shorts and vests, he led outside the school into the spacious playground, himself resplendent in white flannels and sleeveless vest. They doubled round the yard and eventually formed four lines for the routine exercises before team games. A well-used footpath skirted the school play area and the chain link fencing gave people an excellent view. This open air PE was an innovation and people stopped to stare. There appeared to be animated conversation amongst the elderly at the sparse clothing worn by the boys who, to all intents and purposes, appeared to be enjoying themselves in the non-stop activities. The lesson ended with a smart trot back to the upper cloakroom to wash and change. Dirk received a summons to the Head's room where an irate complaining grandmother had just left, after giving the Head a piece of her mind regarding her grandson being made to do PE in February clad in next to nothing.

'Well,' said Dirk, smiling, 'you wanted me to introduce the

new PE. That is part of it. On suitable days we shall be out and eventually when they become better organised the apparatus will go out too. It's the fresh air treatment and it will do them good.'

Dirk could see the Head was in somewhat of a quandry, caught between innovation and parental concern, so he added, 'I can cut it out if you so wish and operate indoors.'

'Oh no!' chipped in the Head, 'carry on as you think fit, but just use a bit of discretion for my sake, what?'

Dirk, anxious to make his mark, was saved from further controversy by a further setback in the weather, and not until the summer term arrived could he repeat the tactic. Meanwhile, on the corridor, an elderly female teacher who operated at the other end of the corridor from him, and whom he had observed taking her class for games clad in fur coat with handbag clutched under her arm, accosted him in mid-corridor and in very high dudgeon remarked haughtily, 'I don't know what educational advantage you get from displaying your body in such a fashion when taking PE.'

Dirk was taken aback and rendered almost speechless but managed to recover sufficiently to remark, 'I'm sorry if you find it offensive, but that is what I was appointed to innovate . . . the new style PE.'

The bell, ending break, shrilled out and cut the encounter short and Dirk wondered what sort of remark she had made to the new PE mistress, his opposite number, who strode the corridors in a skirt scarcely touching her well-developed thighs and a blouse which seemed to point at one and which attracted much spectator attention when playing netball in the girls' yard and in the adjacent field, at hockey. The atmosphere must be a bit tense in the women's staffroom with three elderly ladies and three comparative youngsters recently arrived. As for the senior men, they thought it hilarious and urged Dirk to keep up the good work. They agreed that the PE was doing the lads a world of good, making them more alert and less lethargic in class. Edwards, a King's Scout, a little older than Dirk, who taught handicrafts, clapped Dirk on the back and said, 'Don't let that old fuddy-duddy alarm you. She's anti-everything . . . smoking, drinking, enjoyment and she's a vegetarian too – belongs to the Quaker Movement.'

The senior master introduced Dirk to Saturday morning inter-school football and the arrangement of inter-school matches in the leagues, prior to handing over responsibility for them. Dirk didn't mind the extra-mural work. It filled his leisure weekends, which palled at times. A master from the junior school on the floor below who also used the staffroom, gave Dirk's name to the local football club and eventually he received a card to play at Catford in the Southern Amateur League.

He first had to find out where Catford was and how to get there. The day of the match in mid-March was bitterly cold. A raw easterly wind of a searing Force Eight was driving sleet across a frozen pitch. He entered the green wooden hutment which served as a dressing room and found men already in process of stripping. Making himself known, he was assigned a place with a locker and wall-hook and set to to strip down. The chap next to him was lacing up his soccer boots and without stopping remarked to Dirk in broad Lancashire dialect, 'We're lakin'up-hill today; it's fleein'cowld innit?'

Dirk laughed as his own tension was relieved. 'Aye, ah'm frozzen awready afoore wi start,' he countered.

'My name's Hirst,' said the other as he held out a hand. 'You're playing outside left aren't you, and I'm left half so we'll be seeing a good bit of each other today.'

'I doubt that,' remarked Dirk, 'you can't see the length of the pitch just now,' pointing through the windows. 'My name's Waldron.'

'Aye, it's bad, lad,' continued Hirst in the vernacular, 'tha wants to put thi ganzy unner thi shirt.'

It turned out that Hirst was at Edmonton Grammar School and came from Accrington so they had much in common. The match got under way. Dirk was given little to do and to save himself from freezing-up, ran around just for the heck of it when feasible. The sleet, driving almost level with the ground, was blinding and when the match was finally ended,

Dirk had to thaw out under the showers, which gave him excrutiating pains in his arm and leg muscles. He had not acquitted himself well and they had lost.

'Ne'er mind,' said Hirst, 'there'll allus be another time.'

'That depends if I get selected,' replied Dirk.

'Tha will,' assured Hirst, 'there's noan sa many Southerners as'll turn out i' this weather, tha'll see. They're noan used to it like us.'

It was heartening to hear the dialect spoken and after exchanging a few snippets of things in common, they both lapsed into the King's English again for the benefit of the rest, who were fascinated by their chatter.

The summer term brought cricket, athletics and swimming with the appropriate inter-house, inter-schools and county meetings. Quite early in the term Dirk had been instructed by the Head to demonstrate to the whole school and staff the use of the newly acquired PE equipment, now fully delivered and in use. This, and the thought of it, overawed Dirk for a time but after devising an interesting routine with a selected team of thirty boys whom he trained in off-duty hours, his initial apprehension subsided. The demonstration went like clockwork and the non-stop routines in the forty minutes at his disposal passed quickly. The staff looked on, non-committally, Dirk thought, especially the older women teachers, but when the senior master slapped him on the back and complimented him on the whole performance, he felt that he had made his mark, been accepted and arrived.

Came the swimming gala and athletics competitions on the adjacent club cricket field. During the gala at the open-air baths, in the high-board diving contest, one of the boy competitors hit the water awkwardly and came up gasping for breath, obviously stunned and distressed. Dirk dived in, clothed in his PE gear, to keep the lad afloat until he recovered sufficiently to make for the side and haul himself out. This incident and others in the gym and on the playing fields established Dirk's reputation amongst the boys, some of whom stayed on until their sixteenth year to take RSA exams.

On the last day of term the Head sent for him. 'Now, Mr Waldron,' he began, 'I'm going to take a risk with you next school year. I'm going to give you Form 1a, which is the pick of the new intake.'

Dirk's emotions soared. This was more than he expected as a newcomer. A move up to a 'B' form he had anticipated, but an 'A' form was a challenge indeed. The Head gave him the syllabus and lists and a thorough briefing as to what he expected, ending with the monition, 'Don't let me down, now, will you?'

Dirk assured him of his full cooperation and of his intent to justify the confidence placed in him and departed for the summer vacation a happy man.

He returned to his northern hills with a sense of pleasant exhaustion, for he had been thoroughly drained of energy, both physical and mental. He renewed his former acquaintances, played the occasional game of friendly cricket, went to dances at the Tower Ballroom, Blackpool, rambled over the familiar hills in congenial company and slept in his own familiar bed. The five weeks flew by as he laid the plans for his future academic work with the school's new entrants Form 1a. Using all the Lancashire skills and knowledge of weaving, and with some assistance from an uncle and friends in the trade, he built a miniature loom for his hand work classes, collecting surplus yarns with which to set it up. This, he felt, would be an innovation for the Home Counties and a variation on other more familiar routines.

8

When the autumn term started Dirk faced a class of mixed twelve-year-olds all anxious to have a second crack at the Grammar Schools Entrance Exam, held in the late spring of the succeeding year. Walking into his new classroom the day previous to opening the school he noted, already in place, twenty four dual desks in six lines of four. Both the floor and the furniture had been scrubbed, the walls repainted and the wall-boards blackened. The following day, after a brief morning assembly in the corridor, he ushered his new charges into the classroom, assigning them temporarily to desks in alphabetical order, the better to be able to pinpoint their names, yet taking care to pair up boys and girls in separate desks. Calling the roll for the first time, he used their full names but subsequently decided, as was the custom, to address the boys by their surnames to mark the transition to seniority and to use both Christian and surnames for the girls, to avoid the inevitable duplications. The challenge facing Dirk was to distinguish those who were keen to transfer to grammar education and to afford them all the best opportunity of so doing. Several, after the first day's settling in process, applied for homework, an additional chore. Dirk still had his role of PE master throughout the school, together with craftwork and art in the lower forms. By constant preparatory work, Dirk kept his class fully occupied with the rigours of the three Rs. Within the first few weeks the Head summoned Dirk to his room after afternoon school had ended.

'Ah, Mr Waldron, would you be interested in privately coaching one of the girls in your class for, say, two evenings a week?' he ventured.

'Which girl?' asked Dirk.

'Miriam Lishman,' announced the Head. 'Her mother is a widow and she is very keen to have her daughter brought up to the required standard for transfer. Before, she was at a small private school and she thinks she needs coaching.'

'Well,' countered Dirk, 'my early impressions of her are that she is a very tentative type, evincing little initiative as yet, and much slower than her classmates.'

'Yes, I gathered that from the parent. Now will you take the job on?' persisted the Head. 'I'm giving you the first chance. The mother is willing to pay the going rates. It's up to you.'

'I've never coached before,' responded Dirk, discounting the fact that he had, back home, coached a policeman friend for his sergeant's exam. 'What is the professional rate to charge?'

'Mostly it runs out at 5s. or more an hour. It will be for two hours on agreed evenings. What do you say?'

Dirk cast about in his mind for two vacant evenings. He was involved with a youth group at a local Baptist church on Mondays and he had been roped in for their choir with practices on Fridays. Wednesday he had been going to the Odeon for a few hours' escape from the pressures of the job.

'You have her address in your register,' prompted the Head, 'why don't you either phone or go and see the mother? Their house is in Palmers Green.'

'May I come back to you on this, sir?' asked Dirk.

'Let me know your decision by tomorrow at the latest then,' concluded the Head.

Dirk left in deep thought. He did not want to become too involved in his work. He needed time for leisure to recoup his expended energies, but on mulling it over he decided he could do with the cash.

The first few coaching lessons went well. He noted that the girl, whilst being subdued at school, was very precocious at home, as if she had been cossetted a good deal, but she responded to encouragement and Dirk's patient tuition, whilst the mother busied herself about the house or listened with earphones to the radio by the fire, whilst knitting or sewing. As the hour's end approached, Mrs Lishman would disappear into the kitchen area and prepare her daughter's supper, always including a beaker of cocoa for herself and for Dirk. Whilst her daughter supped, and Dirk gathered his papers and books, she engaged in small talk to round off the session. On Dirk rising, she would accompany him to the door and each Thursday pay him the requisite agreed-on fee, at the same time ordering her daughter to bed.

About the sixth week, Mrs Lishman held Dirk in conversation for a longer period than usual and, with her hand on the knob of the vestibule door, asked Dirk if he had ever thought of changing his digs, as she was prepared to take in a paying guest. Dirk was quite happy where he was, except that the meals could be a bit erratic as to time and Dirk liked to know when, and at what hour, he could guarantee to go out.

'Think it over, Mr Waldron. You would be made very welcome. Miriam seems to respond to your teaching,' she concluded.

Dirk said he would give it some thought and took his leave. The following week he arrived on the doorstep for the hour's tuition, was ushered in and immediately got on with his task. Mouthwatering odours of cooking and baking wafted in from the kitchen as from time to time the door to that department opened and shut. Dirk had already eaten at six at his digs, but the amount of physical energy he expended during the school day always left him with a feeling of hunger. Even after his weekly session at the cinema, he would always call at the nearby chippy to assuage the pangs. The hands of the travelling clock on the sideboard crept towards eight-thirty when Mrs Lishman entered with Miriam's supper. Dirk gathered his things to stow away in his briefcase. He noticed that she had not brought in the customary beaker for him. Instead she engaged Dirk in lively conversation whilst Miriam downed her frugal nightcap. Eventually she turned to her daughter and said, 'Off you go now. I'll come up and see you in a few minutes.'

Her daughter was reluctant to depart. Dirk didn't blame her for he had often as a child been in the same predicament. Nevertheless, with Dirk, her form master there, she could not prevaricate as Dirk suspected she might have done. The mother was taking advantage of his authority.

Miriam came round the table and kissed her mother, bidding them both good night, and made for the stairs. Dirk rose to depart, but Mrs Lishman interjected with, 'Don't go yet. I've been cooking and baking. Won't you join me at supper?'

Dirk hesitated. He thought of all the things he ought to be doing before tomorrow. He had two piles of books to mark which would take the best part of an hour, but the appetising smell percolating through the room was too much for his salivary glands. He agreed to stay. Mrs Lishman opened a cupboard in the sideboard and extracted a bottle of wine. From a drawer she spread an embroidered cloth and place-mats with napkins. Cutlery and condiments followed in quick succession and after a brief interval in the kitchen during which she kept up a desultory flow of conversation, she produced two steaming bowls of soup, inviting Dirk to open the wine and pour. This he did and carefully decanted the ruby liquid into two crystal glasses standing on coasters. The soup was very hot and delicious. Dirk could not christen it but the croutons had the faintest hint of garlic. This was followed by a concoction of chicken and rice with chopped French beans and other mysterious ingredients which baffled Dirk. He did not venture to ask the recipe but commented on the deliciousness of the plate. Conversation ranged from topical news to international affairs, to hobbies, sports and entertainment. Mrs Lishman was quite knowledgeable about most subjects and conversed brightly and intelligently with a vivacity no doubt enhanced by the wine. Dirk too felt his tongue had loosened as he laughed and joked about the humorous incidents at school. There came coffee and liqueurs and Dirk felt a glow of satisfaction pervade him.

Sitting with his back to the fire, he began to perspire slightly. The room felt over-warm for him. Without appearing to be ungrateful he steered the conversation around to returning to his digs. She questioned him about them and the facilities he had and asked if he had thought any more about her previous offer. Dirk had, but remained undecided as he had contracted to stay for the year at least as a trial period.

He looked at the clock. It said ten-thirty and he rose to depart, expressing the while his gratitude for her hospitality. She preceded him to the vestibule door, holding him in running conversation and Dirk sensed that she was about to make advances towards him. He had already judged her to be about ten years older than himself and quite attractive and smartly dressed. She wore an array of jewellery which was by no means cosmetic and which was interchanged with each differing item of dress. She placed a gentle hand on his arm, insisting once more that he give her offer some thought and almost inadvertently she raised her free arm to place it about his neck, tiptoeing up to kiss his lips. Dirk's heart missed a beat and accelerated noticeably. He was taken aback, but her approach was so gentle, and he found himself inadvertently drawing her towards him in a tender yielding embrace. Then suddenly, without hesitation, he turned and, opening the vestibule door, made to depart. He sensed the abruptness of his move and, turning again, placed a hand of consolation against her cheek.

He noted the tears start from her eyes, their brown orbs round with anxiety, so Dirk took her in his arms once more and kissed her passionately, caressing her firm, rounded breasts. He then released her and, without speaking, opened the outer door. As he left she whispered hoarsely, 'You'll come again on Thursday?'

'Yes,' said Dirk, anxious to depart and calm the tumult of his brain with the cool night air. She watched him close the garden gate. Dirk raised a valedictory hand and, turning, paced down the street to catch the trolley bus back to his digs.

Thursday evening saw Dirk knocking as usual on Mrs

Lishman's door for a further coaching session. Miriam opened it and ushered him in. He placed his books and papers on the table as usual and straightway plunged into his lesson. After ten minutes or so, Miriam's mother came in from the kitchen, apron-clad, obviously cooking or baking. She greeted Dirk with a quizzical smile, excusing her absence from the room. Dirk reciprocated, appropriately resuming his work with Miriam. Sixty minutes passed quickly and in came Miriam's customary nightcap. Casual conversation followed while the girl lingered over her drink. They discussed the weather, local news, and Miriam's progress, and eventually Miriam was ushered off to bed. Delaying her customary payment, Mrs Lishman once more invited Dirk to supper. He readily assented and she set the table as before, producing the customary bottle of red wine. She then disappeared into the kitchen for a spell and emerged saying, 'I'll just see to Miriam. I won't be long. Pour yourself some wine in the meantime.'

Dirk picked up the corkscrew and slowly opened the bottle, wondering the while how he was going to deal with the impending situation. He was in a quandary and resolved to meet it as it developed. Mrs Lishman had gone to more trouble to dress, discarding her customary array of jewellery. She was eminently an attractive person, well-read, cultured in manner and deportment as well as accomplished domestically, for he had noted the room was tastefully furbished and immaculate as to decor. As he poured out the first glass of wine Mrs Lishman returned. 'Make yourself comfortable,' she ventured. 'I will not be long serving supper.'

She then lit two candles in silver sconces on the sideboard and, placing them on the table, switched off the bright electric lights in the central chandelier. A mellow glow pervaded the room and supper was served. The conversation flagged at first but, as the wine loosened their tongues, it flowed.

'Have you thought any more about my offer of accommodation, Mr Waldron?' she ventured.

'I have, Mrs Lishman,' admitted Dirk, 'and I couldn't very well leave until term-end and I should have to give a month's notice as agreed.'

'Call me Naomi, please,' said Mrs Lishman, switching the theme. 'Your name is Dirk, is it not?' she asked.

'Yes, that's right. I suppose Miriam told you.' he responded.

'No, I saw it on the envelope you were using as a bookmark,' she laughed.

'I like it,' responded Dirk, 'it could have been worse. There are Naomis in my family too. I had a great aunt once so named. She was a twin and the other died in childbirth along with the mother and the eldest sister, my great grandmother, then aged fourteen, brought up the whole family. In fact Naomi thought she was her mother, but that was nearly a century ago when times were hard, even harder than at present.'

The conversation turned on ancestry as the meal proceeded at a leisurely pace, interrupted by the occasional visits to the kitchen. Came the coffee and liqueurs, as before. Dirk was invited to sit by the fire in a most comfortable, yielding armchair. There followed an extended period of relaxation as the glowing warmth of the fire and the lambent glow of the candles irradiated peace. Naomi rose and sat upon the arm of Dirk's chair. His arm encircled her waist and he drew her ever so gently down upon his knee. As Dirk eased himself into a more comfortable position the conversation flagged. Eventually the room fell silent as they held each other in close embrace, each awaiting some movement, some signal from the other. Finally Naomi sat up and in the gloaming of the candles' light, gazed into Dirk's eyes with enquiring, questing intensity. She slowly eased herself erect, grasping Dirk's hands and asserting an insistent pull, raised him from the comfort of his chair. He responded and, standing tall, drew her more closely towards himself. Clasping her freed hands around his neck, she raised herself on tiptoe, seeking out Dirk's lips, at the same time nuzzling her slim body close to him. The fire had died to a suffused glow. The two candles wavered in the disturbed air. In the yielding pressures of her parted lips, Dirk sensed the quickening of her breathing and the heightened throbbing of her pulse. He realised that he was too tense, his muscles too taut. He could not hold her for long for she was clinging and insistent. One candle guttered and died and their static pose was broken. Naomi now held back her tousled head, her face suffused with the firelight's glow, and murmured, 'Dirk, it's been a long long time since I did this.'

There followed an extensive pause whilst Dirk sought an appropriate reply. Finally he found his voice and whispered, 'Naomi, we're playing with fire!'

She did not respond but laid her head against his shoulder, averting her gaze. Dirk caressed her ruffled hair which now tumbled about her oval face and, tilting her chin, bent his head to press his lips gently upon hers. The remaining candle guttered and expired. Naomi drew herself apart with a long shuddering sigh, emotive with suppressed desire and tinged with heartache. She extended her hands to Dirk and clasping his, drew him down to kneel upon the soft deep pile of the hearthrug. There she gazed solemnly into his eyes. Nought but the insistent tick of the clock upon the farther sideboard intruded upon their muted reverie. Each awaited the other's prompting. The coals in the grate suddenly shuttered, sending sparks upwards, momentarily lighting up the scene. Dirk thereupon broke the spell and whispered hoarsely and with suppressed emotions, 'What's the time, Naomi?'

She did not move, remaining mute and listless for a few moments, then turning slowly and kneeling up to peer over the table towards the clock murmured as though in a trance, 'About eleven, I think.'

Dirk released her hands and holding her head in his, said, 'I really must be going.'

As he leaned away, preparatory to rising, Naomi held his arm and sadly murmured, 'Must you?' There was a wistfulness about her tone which Dirk detected and he waited a while before replying. Eventually he insisted. 'Needs must, my dear, needs must,' and grasping her by the arms he raised her up, kissing her damp forehead. She leaned limply against his chest. Gently he released her imprisoning arms,and moving away, he proceeded to collect his books and case, then, passing a comb through his disarranged unruly locks, he said, 'Don't come, I'll let myself out. Goodnight Naomi! *Shalom!*'

Statuesque and placid, her emotions now drained, she placed two fingers to her lips and with a faint, wan smile, extended them, palm outwards, a fleeting figurative gesture which she then imprinted upon Dirk's lips.

'*Shalom!*' she breathed.

Dirk turned slowly, walked to the inner door and down the corridor and let himself out, closing the outer door quietly behind him until its lock clicked home. He paused at the outer gate, took in three deep breaths of the cool night air, then swiftly strode off along the avenue towards the garish glaze of the main highway.

9

Dirk considered this new and radical development in his life. It was not that he was unfamiliar with the relationships between the sexes. He was well-read on the subject and had during the course of his life had many encounters of an ephemeral nature with females. His first rather passionate love affair, apart from boy-girl attractions at his elementary school, was when attending grammar school, but she proved to be as flighty as a butterfly, more interested in conquests than constancy. There followed another, more serious, with a girl who travelled on the same bus. They had dated frequently and dallied on and off when opportunity presented, but they were both rather diffident and undemonstrative and the affair gradually fizzled out from apathy rather than mutual consent.

Dirk was seventeen when he met his Waterloo on the field of romance. She had overwhelmed him with her attention and advances, waylaid him often in awkward situations, tried to isolate him from his friends and thrown herself unreservedly at him in an emotional and physical sense. She made all the running and Dirk thought it high time to run faster, which he did, absenting himself from likely ambush and keeping a very low and distant profile where she was concerned. She soon transferred her fervid attentions elsewhere and Dirk breathed freely once more. Following her, he developed a crush on a dancing partner with whom he paired to enter competitions, for, despite her robust figure and firm build, she moved gracefully, was as light as a feather when circling the dance floor on which they moved as one, her suppleness and perfect balance had thrilled him, whilst their frequent physical proximity had aroused his deeper sexual emotions, but she did not reciprocate the advances he made towards her. Only on the dance floor would she signal him, for they were perfectly matched physically and complementary in all their timing.

All these encounters had taught him much about the opposite sex, so that out of the sum total of his somewhat peripheral experiences of romance, he had learned how to recognise the differing approaches, how to interpret body language and how to respond in any given situation. Contemplating his amours of the past, Dirk had never experienced any sensation like the one he had responded to with Naomi. But she, unlike the others, was experienced as none before. He knew the old cliché, that 'the way to a man's heart is through his stomach', and yet he had condoned this well-rehearsed trick of Eve, and accepted it unresistingly and unreservedly. Naomi had quite imperceptibly broken down his innate reserve; had, with a naturalness born of grace, gently demolished his defences without affecting his male self-esteem. Neither had made the running in their natural attraction. In the cold light of day, he knew that they were completely at one in mind, body and spirit. He could not imagine Naomi to be possessive, monopolising his time, a trait he had long deplored. Their recent total uncompromising commitment had been so natural, and her surrender so trustworthy, that Dirk felt that Fate for once had dealt him a Queen of Hearts. Yet his conscience prodded him into a vague suspicion that he was a Knave who might be there only for the jam tarts. He had already pushed to the back of his mind the fact of her race and any likely reactions, if any, from his or her family. She might have the same problem with him, for he had not yet enquired into her relatives nor her antecedents. The accusation could be levelled at him that he was taking on a ready-made home and family, but that was mere coincidence. Fate had thrown them together by a quirk of circumstance, and the commitment naturally followed.

It was the year of the Olympic Games. They were scheduled

to take place in Berlin. Dirk had resolved to go but discovered the expense involved too great. He had had his attention directed to a holiday in the Black Forest, which was much more in line with his financial situation, and he discussed the matter with Naomi. She was horrified. She informed Dirk of all the stories which were coming out of Germany concerning members of her race, many of whom were selling up and coming to Britain or emigrating to America and how their religious leaders were collecting monies to aid the less fortunately placed. Dirk had read his fill about the recurrent pogroms throughout history, but he could scarcely credit what he now heard. Nevertheless, he was resolved to go and assess the situation for himself. In no way could he persuade Naomi to accompany him, such was her aversion to the idea. On the contrary, she urged him to go and see for himself and this he put in hand by booking a holiday in advance through the International Friendship League in Tavistock Square, a holiday which was most reasonably priced in his opinion. Travel was by rail and covered the first two weeks in August. He would by then be twenty two years old. Dirk sent off the booking fee and promptly dismissed it from his mind.

Mid-February saw the grammar schools entrance exam, after which the homework chore. ceased and some of the pressures were off. Even the pupils relaxed and began to direct their abilities to other diversions, such as art and craft exhibitions, music festivals, plays and a school concert. He even organised a special PE demonstration for the Parents-and-Staff Association of which he was secretary, largely to win their cooperation and confidence in the work he was pioneering. This led to a 'Dads and Lads' soccer match, which was a huge success, for the Lads walloped the Dads, Dirk playing for the Dads. It was as though a weight was lifted from his shoulders and a new-found freedom to organise and promote new departures presented itself.

It was short-lived. The Board of Education were advocating the setting up of Government keep-fit classes to counter the accusation that we were a C3 nation healthwise. Dirk was roped in to organise classes for unemployed girls, of which there were many. As a keep-fit instructor he met with colleagues in surrounding schools to agree on method and content. Dirk had his own ideas. They were referred to as 'routines for "unenjoyed" girls' by the wags. Dirk's classes were over-subscribed numerically. Many women already attended eurythmic classes in private dance halls where they paid a fee. Dirk's was free and many transferred, despite the fact that it involved gymnastics and apparatus work. He could have been occupied four nights a week but that was too much and he settled for two nights with the same group. Now, in place of coaching Miriam, he was expending his surplus energies on what little was left after the school day as a Government keep-fit instructor. Naomi and he had to reorganise their lifestyle.

The first keep-fit session was hilarious. Many arrived tentatively wondering what they were up against. Dirk directed them to a changing room which was the school projection-room fitted with curtains for black-out. When they emerged, shyly, into the large hall, the variety of rig was, to say the least, comical. Swimming costumes, leotards, beach shorts, multi-coloured knickers and a plethora of hand-knitted jumpers. Figure-wise there were the brash, the eager, the tentative, the shy, the long and the short and the tall, the slim, the plump and the gorgeous hussies as well as the querulous queenies. Dirk trotted them round the hall to get the shyness out of their systems, changing to a slip-step sideways, demonstrating with them all the time and changing directions on the whistle. He had already made the requisite number of chalk marks on the floor, to which, on command, without stopping, he ordered them to move and continue skip-jumping. Some were beginning to blow, so he changed to simple eurythmic arms swinging with variations until they got back their breath. Next into trunk movements and the prone abdominal leg-lifts and press-ups which produced some groans and collapses. They were C3 all right and he was really tempering the wind to these shorn lambs about to be put through the hoop in the next few weeks. He gave them a breather every twenty minutes, during which he made suggestions regarding correct rig, the wearing of jewellery, follow-ups at home, etc. He knew they would feel stiff the following day and said so. His aim was to build up the routines gradually so as not to scare them off. Next, he had them handling and placing apparatus to form eight groups of five, demonstrating beginners' agility work with 'catchers' ready to assist the timid and the stumblers. The safety factor was high in his mind. Changing round the groups, they all had freedom to express themselves on box, horse, mats, beams according to their several capabilities. The hour passed quickly and Dirk could tell by the sounds of their voices at the end of the session that they had enjoyed the novelty of it all. He had already picked out likely group leaders from among the crowd knowing that almost all would come again.

The following morning, as he ascended the staircase to the staffroom in company with Edwards, he was asked, 'How did you get on with your "unenjoyed" girls?'

Dirk laughed and proceeded to describe to Edwards what had occurred.

'You lucky blighter,' countered Edwards, 'come across any likely talent?'

'Oh yes!' laughed Dirk, 'never seen so much bare pulchritude in one place in all my life.'

'Why didn't I take up PE instead of woodwork and metalwork?' groaned Edwards.

'That's your bad luck,' answered Dirk, laughing. 'Why don't you start a female woodwork class? I bet it would go like a house on fire.'

'That's an idea!' exclaimed Edwards eagerly, 'I'll remember that.'

Discussion in the staffroom regarding this new keep-fit craze caused the senior master to remark, 'This is the start of the preparation for the next world war.'

Two others, both of whom had experiences in the First World War, were inclined to agree. They pointed out the signs which internationally were looming up to confirm the observation. The Maginot Line, Hitler's sabre-rattling speeches, Mussolini's stage-strutting harangues of Italian crowds, German brownshirts goosestepping, the Danzig corridor and the National Socialist movements in every country, not forgetting Oswald Moseley who had jumped on to the jackbooted bandwagon. They were scathing in their condemnation of the scenes both at home and abroad. Dirk listened attentively, keeping his counsel, unwilling to chip in. There was a good deal of truth in their remarks. The situation was more ominous than it had at first appeared to him. Dirk began to read the press more seriously, especially *The New Statesman,* which Burton had brought weekly and left lying around in the staffroom and *The Observer,* which carried articles on the international panorama. It suddenly struck him that Naomi was better informed than he, and although they now met only at weekends, usually travelling up to the West End to view selected entertainments and sight-see, they kept up their liaison with ever increasing respect and affection. Dirk had explained his family commitments at home in the North and Naomi understood the dilemma he was in. Their mutual trust and growing confidence in their bonding placed a timely brake upon an otherwise unfettered devotion. They filled a vacuum in each others' lives and were serenely content to nurture and protect their position, and not to react unfairly to each other.

By the middle of the summer term the grammar schools' transfers were published. The Head summoned Dirk to his room and handed him a list of the successful pupils. The list was long. Dirk scanned it slowly, searching for Miriam's name amongst the thirty five of his class appearing. It was there. He breathed a mental sigh of relief. Thirty five out of forty eight. This was fantastic, better than his wildest hopes. His spirits soared as he looked up from his perusal to meet the grey, unwinking eyes of the boss.

'Well, Mr Waldron, what have you to say?' he began.

'I'm overwhelmed,' said Dirk. 'I can't believe it!'

'Well,' continued the Head, 'it's all there . . . all thirty five of them. I hope you realise that when we lose those at the end of the year, the reduction in school numbers will bring my salary down a grade, and that my pension, which I had hoped to qualify for next year, will be proportionately reduced.'

This pronouncement took the gilt off the gingerbread. Dirk had not taken that into consideration, so involved had he been in making his mark. Dirk looked at him, not knowing quite what to say. Then, with a candour typical of him, he said, 'Last year you said you were taking a risk by giving me Form 1a. I tried to do my best for the class despite your stricture.'

'You did,' said the Head, 'in no uncertain terms. You are right to be proud of yourself, but it has given me food for much thought.'

The boss did not enlighten Dirk as to what might be passing through his mind, so Dirk handed back the paper, expressing his thanks for the information. Thinking that the least said at the moment the soonest mended, he turned to leave. As a Parthian shot, the Head called out, 'You can keep 1a next year, Mr Waldron, with my blessing.'

'Thank you sir,' said Dirk, his wilting confidence returning, and as he closed the door he thought he detected the faintest beginning of a smile on that stern countenance.

To celebrate the successes Miriam, Naomi and Dirk spent a pleasant Whitsuntide break in a cabin cruiser on the Upper Thames. They sailed as far as Abingdon, negotiating the locks and mooring each night at conveniently placed riverside hotels. It was Naomi who suggested the idea, saying that, the cruiser was on loan to her from a relative. Dirk did not query this, nor did he enquire too closely into its ownership. Dirk regarded it as a splendid opportunity to get to know Miriam better, away from the academic routines. They swam, they fished, they picnicked at chosen sites and visited the riparian countryside where there were villages of architectural interests and local fairs. Dirk was in his element once he had learned to handle the boat. It was obvious to him that Naomi was no landlubber either, but she tactfully confined her energies to the cooking, whilst Miriam and Dirk attended to the many chores. By the time they had completed the round trip, Miriam was treating him as one of the family. Her initial diffidence had gone and she reacted naturally to Dirk's more relaxed attentions. Dirk saw the light of satisfaction in

Naomi's eyes at this longed-for reaction on the part of her daughter. They were slowly but surely spinning themselves a cocoon of unbreakable strands, of invisible cords, silken yet durable, slender at first, yet daily more powerfully binding. Their cup was full and brimming over.

10

As the summer vacation approached the news coming out of Spain was disturbing, if not ominous. The elected government of Largo Caballero was being assailed on all sides. Propped up as it was by the vocal Communist Party, their support was suddenly withdrawn. Outside the Cortes, the army generals of whom there were many, and who, throughout Spanish history, had always been a powerful force, were plotting along with the Catholic clergy to undermine the Socialist government's power base. An ambitious and aspiring young general, Franco by name, commanding a ready-made mercenary army in Morocco, was chosen by his peers to head the revolt. Crossing the straits with his troops, Franco was marching on Madrid, raising support as he progressed. The Government, unable to rely on the loyalty of their senior army officers, fell back upon the support of the conscript army, mainly from the north and east of the country. The Civil War was joined. Fascist states in Europe came down on the side of Franco and were neither tardy nor secretive about lending him their aid. Democratic countries, though sympathetic towards the elected government, preferred to keep aloof, rendering only moral support through press and radio for the hard-pressed Cortes. The mood in England was such that open practical assistance was politically naïve, any diplomacy vocal but ineffective. Britain's upper-class hierarchy was divided on the issues at stake. It was left to the radical elements of the middle classes, together with liberal-minded elements, who were protagonists of democracy, to fill the vacuum thus created by their respective governments' inactivity. For the first time in history an International Brigade was formed to resist dictatorship.

Serious-minded academics, headstrong students, unemployed seeking adventure, ex-professional soldiery converged like iron filings towards a powerful magnet and sponsored a cause. Skippers of dirty British coasters, scenting a lucrative trade, directed their salt-caked smoke-stacks towards Spain, and, with the dark stirrings of Elizabethan mariners' ancestry surfacing in their brain, they ran the blockade with the Jolly Roger at the masthead and the tattered Red Duster on the Jackstaff, ferrying the mercenaries, carrying supplies and ploughing dark furrows through the Biscayan Main.

The press had a field day. Daily they pinpointed new heroes rallying to the cause, highlighting their exploits, exaggerating the risks, for a readership deep in depression, avid for adventure. Something began to rouse itself and stir in the atrophying soul of Britain as the climate of opinion slowly changed. The spirit of Drake and of Wellesley revived. The hitherto much vaunted Oxford Movement suffered a sea-change. This was not King and Country: this was a principle at stake. Here was a fraudulent violation of fair play, something which wasn't quite 'cricket'. Here was an entirely new banner to rally around, a new crusade to adopt, which was fanned into a burning zeal by journalist and freelance reporter alike.

Dirk devoured the daily bulletins eagerly. He had no radio in his bedsit but the cinemas were quick to latch on to the public's craze for sensation, for thrills and glamour. *Pathé Gazette* pandered to this zeal for real life drama, presenting to the public eye scenes from the Front, supposedly objective in theme, but in reality geared to arouse sympathy for the hard-pressed victims of the Franco advance. It was in this fever of international uncertainty that Dirk left for his holiday in Germany, the participants in the scheme convening one Saturday at the concourse in Victoria Station preparatory to boarding the train for the first leg of the journey. The group mustering there seemed fairly young and enthusiastic, leavened by a sprinkling of middle-aged eccentrics equipped with rucksacks and standard continental walking gear. Dirk had dressed casually, in flannels and loose sweater, preferring to travel light rather than lug a heavy case across half of Europe. In the reserved carriage to which Dirk eventually gravitated, a friendly, voluble, relaxed bunch were gathered. He managed a corner seat and before the train departed a young lady entered and occupied the only vacant seat next to him. Gallantly, but more as an opening gambit than a gesture, Dirk offered to place the lady's suitcase on the rack, readjusting his Bergen rucksack to make room. She thanked him shyly and they struck up a conversation, introducing themselves. Catriona Watson was a nurse anticipating with some anxiety and misgiving her first continental holiday and had plumped for group travel for safety. Dirk held her in conversation, extending it to take in the rest of the fellow travellers heading for a common destination, and soon a congenial and lively atmosphere developed.

'No good sitting like Christmas cards waiting for greetings,' laughed Dirk, 'we're all bound for Gernsbach, I presume,' he added, scanning the eight occupants. 'Let's make the most of what may prove to be a tedious journey.'

The talk flowed freely as the relative barriers of reserve were flattened. The group consisted of a shop assistant, a stenographer, a motor mechanic, a civil servant, a lorry driver and a waitress, a total of eight with Catriona and Dirk. Most were in their early and mid-twenties and from differing counties. Catriona, the nurse, was a native of Perth, but working in London in a private clinic. The accents were distinct and varied and fascinating to Dirk, who studied regional dialects. By using some of his Grandmother Macdonald's quaint phraseology and imitating her accent he amused Catriona who seemed to respond to him.

They were in Dover before they realised how time had flown. Catriona attached herself to Dirk as a travelling companion and he gave her his lighter case to carry in place of her seemingly heavier one, shouldering his rucksack and heading for the boat alongside the marshalling yards. The summer sun had declined towards the west. The straits appeared calm. It would be a smooth night crossing. They headed for a couple of seats at a table on the main deck opposite the bar, and after securing their luggage, settled down to relax and maybe get a little shut-eye before departure. Dirk could sleep at the drop of a hat when necessary and was in oblivion in no time at all. He came to a couple of hours later to find a weight upon his shoulder. It was Catriona's head. She too had dozed off, and slumped sideways to lean upon him. Dirk shifted his cramped position slightly so as not to disturb her and sat on with stoic calm. They were finally aroused by the ship's siren emitting three loud blasts on entering harbour. Dirk glanced at his watch. It was well after midnight. They docked and passed through the Belgian customs.

The night train left at two a.m. for Frankfurt. There was an hour's wait and it was chilly. Dirk suggested they search for a buffet. The found it closed. Glancing at the departures board he noticed that a train was about to leave for Aachen. He suggested that rather than become cold waiting, they board it and wait for the following train there. Catriona agreed. There was no time to advise the others so they dashed down the platform to the train about to depart. Dirk knew they were travelling on the cheap, but he did not bargain for wooden seating, no matter how cleverly they were shaped to allow maximum ease. Moreover, it was a stopping train which precluded continuous slumber. Dirk curled up on the double seat on his side of the divide and Catriona followed his example on the other. Conversation wilted as the train clanked on through the night. So they remained, cramped but undisturbed, until in a pale dawn, with a squeal of brakes and much extrusion of steam, they jerked to a stop at Aachen. Rousing themselves, they collected their gear, revived their numbed wits and debouched on to the platform in a grey, unwelcoming dawn. Neither could speak German, but Dirk had made a cursory study of a Hugo's phrase book which he had acquired. An approaching official pointed them in the direction of the customs barrier way down the length of an extensive platform. Inside the room, funnelled along by barriers, they had their passports stamped and returned. They examined Dirk's rucksack, riffled through Catriona's suitcase and closing it, waved them through without comment. 'So far, so good,' thought Dirk. Two trains were stationary in the sidings, with a guard outside one, flag in hand, gazing at the approaching sprinkle of passengers filtering through Customs. Dirk approached him and asked, *'Nach Franfurt, bitte?'* The guard pointed to the other train on the other siding down the platform and, extracting his pocket watch remarked, *'Eine uhr'* or so it sounded and confirmed it by raising one finger. *'Danke schön,'* said Dirk and turning to Catriona remarked, 'It leaves in an hour. Let's see if we can find some grub. I'm starving, I don't know about you.'

She submitted that she had a raging thirst and could do with a long, hot drink to slake it. They scoured the station buildings, eventually discovering a sort of kitchen where a station food trolley was being prepared. It sported a large metal urn, trays of buns and sandwiches with soft drinks, cartons of milk and an assortment of sweets and confectionery. Dirk mimed the drinking bit and pretended to shiver at which the stout lady in charge of the operation poured out two large beakers of steaming black coffee from a pot on an electric ring upon a sideboard, lacing them with sugar. They took the mugs, Catriona warming her hands as she clutched hers. Dirk pointed to various appetising-looking sandwiches and *Kuchen,* offering German money. Consulting Catriona he managed to get the lady to fill a paper bag with food and then asked, *'Wieviel Mark?'* and paid the requisite amount.

'You managed that well,' remarked Catriona, giving a little shiver as the hot drink thawed her out, 'do you know German?'

'Not a bit,' laughed Dirk. 'I studied the phrase book before leaving and fortunately a lady who works with me is a fluent German linguist. She gave me a few basic essential phrases for common situations. That's my limit.'

They found a waiting room where a group of people were standing, clustered around a central stove. It was considerably warmer in there and they sat in a corner to eat.

'I'm glad I came with you,' admitted Catriona, 'I wonder

what the next train's seating will be?'

'No better,' ventured Dirk. 'We shall get what we paid for and that's the cheapest form of travel. I should have brought an air-cushion. I'm not too well upholstered in the rear,' he continued.

They munched on, glad of the warmth and the food. Dirk eventually went back to the kitchen place and bought two cartons of skimmed milk. Returning with his purchase he remarked, 'It'll do for the next leg to Frankfurt.'

They then strolled down to the waiting train and selected a suitable carriage. An engine had been attached and was blowing steam at the carriage linkages. Dirk was wrong in his conjectures for these carriages had upholstery. 'With luck, we may be able to stretch out and have forty winks,' smiled Dirk. The train pulled out with a fussy amount of steam. Much later, at Frankfurt, they arrived to noise, bustle, clanking, steam and milling crowds. Luggage and baggage trolleys rattled past, trundling over serrated pavings, adding to the din. The shouts of the guards were unintelligible, but Dirk discovered that a train left for Mannheim in half an hour and connected with one to Karisruhe, where they were instructed to change and await a train to Gernsbach, their ultimate destination.

They were weary of trains. Catriona was flagging and seemed visibly dejected, so Dirk commandeered a small trolley for their luggage and pushed it along down subways to the platform indicated. Fortunately the buffets were open and food available, so more sustenance was bought to rouse the weary bodies. Noon found them boarding a diminutive mountain train, chugging along a single track up the gentle slopes from the river at Karlsruhe through farming country and wooded pasturelands towards Gernsbach. They squealed to a tired halt at a picturesque railway station and tumbled out to a sunlit wooded landscape with the heady scent of pines in the crisper air. Dirk drew in long breaths of it. 'This is more like it,' he said, 'let's see if we can find another of those trolleys.' He wandered outside the little rail-fence where a ticket collector punched their tickets. Some four-wheeled little dog-carts stood alongside a wall. Dirk secured one and turning back to the ticket man he said, *'Was is der weg nach Hotel Badhoff?'* The fellow gabbled unintelligibly but pointed a directive finger which was sufficient for Dirk and they set off. It was good to stretch the legs after the interminable sittings.

At the hotel they were surprised to see them so early and bustled about to find someone to deal with them. It appeared they were to be boarded out in houses in the village and eat in the hotel. Off they went again with the trolley across the river bridge and up the village street towards the forest, passing lovely wooden chalets with window boxes dripping with gay flowers and sporting tidy lawns and gardens. A porter from the hotel accompanied them, who knocked at the door of the next to last house and announced them to the lady owner. She waved them in cheerfully. She took them up a wide wooden staircase to a long attic room which spanned the whole house and in which were two beds, one at either end, with settees and wooden furniture scattered tastefully in between. The floor was highly polished with brightly coloured rugs matching the antimacassars over the chair backs. The view from two corner windows was superb. Dirk look at Catriona, who was non-plussed. The *hausfrau* noted the hesitation, probably thinking that they did not like her rooms. She adopted a puzzled expression which Dirk quickly changed to one of alarm. He pointed to his signet ring and mimed that they were not married. He caught hold of Catriona's hand to display a bare third finger. The truth dawned upon the *hausfrau,* who lapsed into a spatter of German. They retreated downstairs to the door to leave. The porter had taken the dog-cart so they trekked the half mile back to the hotel, running the gauntlet of peering faces behind chintz curtains from people who, no doubt, were likewise awaiting guests. From the *hausfrau*'s comments Dirk had learnt that *stringen* was a word which meant marriage, so that back at the hotel he used the word to explain their predicament. Stage whispers followed. Asides were indulged in. A consultation ensued. From the sidelong glances cast in their direction Dirk knew that they were unused to two single people travelling together. It ended with the receptionist showing them to adjoining rooms on an upper floor of the hotel which were spartan by comparison with what they had left. She left and they emerged to examine each other's quarters. Dirk then dissolved into laughter at the situation they had encountered and created. It subsequently became a *cause célèbre* in the village. Once more they were out of luck. They had just missed *Mittagessen* but Dirk managed to convince the landlord, a portly chap, that they were hungry and food was eventually laid on.

It was five in the afternoon before the rest of the party arrived and had been allocated around the village; some joining them in the hotel rooms along a series of corridors. Before the evening meal there was an official welcome with glasses of wine and pretzels at which an English-speaking courier introduced herself. It appeared that there were Germans of both sexes included in the party too. The muster count was well over fifty so far, with stragglers yet to arrive. An itinerary for the ten days was posted on the assembly room notice board which listed hikes around the vicinity, excursions to Freudenstadt, through the Black Forest villages, the city of Freibourg, a couple of *Schlosser,* swimming in open air baths and a soccer match against a village team with sundry entertainments to while away the evenings.

Early in the week, one evening, a visit was paid to the village hall where folk singing, drinking and dancing were on the menu. They sat at long, scrubbed tables where wine or beer was served. The place was full of brownshirts, portly men of the village and its environs who became brash and truculent as the night wore on. On the dance floor the English girls came in for some rough handling in the fast German waltzes and folk dances which were being demonstrated. Even the German women in the party remonstrated with the cruder rustic types.

Dirk was sitting beside a German woman teacher of English who was anxious to converse with him to improve her accent and style. She too commented on the crudities of the evening, almost apologetic for her countrymen. Dirk was particularly observant and what he saw was little to his liking. This was a glimpse behind the scenes and his thoughts turned to what Naomi had said to him. He was glad for her sake that she had not consented to come. During conversation with his neighbour, he learned a variety of phrases suitable for the scene before them. He sensed the Fraülein teacher was monopolising him and he panned around to see if he could locate Catriona. She was with a group near the stage at the far end of the room from which most of the boisterous horseplay was coming. The teacher insisted that he call her Anna and in her national garb of embroidered draw-string blouse and dirndl skirt she was in a curious way attractive, if a bit of a pouter pigeon, a fact which the blouse did nothing to hide. Nevertheless, apart from engaging in a few folk dances which she tried to teach him, hand and thigh slapping and all, Dirk was determined not to become involved.

That she had singled him out was evident, for she had knocked at the door of his room on the pretext of informing him of all the activities and diversions available, and lingered a little longer than was necessary, while he dressed. She plied him with the local wine, which was slightly sour to his palate so that he sipped it casually to avoid offence. Near the stage some of the brownshirts who had imbibed too many steins of beer, had forced their unwelcome attentions upon the guests, the females in particular, and the makings of a brawl were brewing. The 'oompah' band struck up to drown the noise of the fracas and divert attention to the dance floor but Dirk noticed Catriona, who was in that vicinity, standing on a chair and looking wildly around in mute appeal. He rose quickly and elbowed his way down the dance floor towards her calling her by name. As he approached, she heard him above the din and jumped down into his extended arms, where he shielded her from the milling crowd. He suggested it was time to go and they left the hall to return under a full moon, down the unlit street, towards the hotel, Dirk talking quietly and calmly until the tremors in her voice had subsided. As they reached the corridor to their rooms Dirk could sense her ragged nervousness, as she turned and threw her arms about him clutching him tightly in a reaction from fear.

'Thank you, Dirk,' she murmured, 'I was really scared back there.'

Dirk could feel her trembling and allowed her to hold. With a loose hand he opened her bedroom door, took her by the shoulders and said, 'You'll be all right now.'

'I'm still scared,' she said, looking appealingly at him.

'If you can't sleep give a knock on the wall. It's made of wood. I'll hear it,' Dirk said soothingly. 'Sleep well, you'll be all right.'

She snatched a fleeting kiss as Dirk released her. Her eyes were those of a frightened animal. She was truly distraught.

'Look,' said Dirk, 'there is a connecting door between all the rooms with bolts on both sides. I'll undo my side and if you feel uptight and strung-up you can always open it and call me. I'm a sound sleeper but I wake at the slightest unusual noise.'

With that, he ushered her reluctant frame within her room and slowly closed the door, retreating to his own and noisily drawing the bolts as he had promised. He stripped and washed in cold water for his head was throbbing slightly from the noise and the wine. Beneath the feathery duvet he speedily fell asleep, a deep, wine-drugged sleep. He dreamt he was lying on the hills of home in the heather with the warm sun pouring down, with the moor-birds wheeling overhead and the sheep cropping close by. He was awakened in the total darkness by a sensation which penetrated his subconscious. Slowly his conscious mind assumed control and instinctively he pushed his hand under the pillow where his wallet was nightly placed. His hand met an object before it reached the pillow. He stopped, listened, his senses now keen, his heartbeats pumping adrenalin into his veins. Slowly he reached up to where he thought the light cord should be and with a sudden jerk switched it on, at the same time sitting up. He was momentarily blinded but half-closing his eyes, he became aware of Catriona sitting on the edge of his bed, the connecting door open.

'What's up?' asked Dirk.

The reply came low and clear. 'Someone's been trying my

door and there's been a brawl down the corridor so I came through just in case. I didn't want to waken you. I'm sorry.'

Sitting up in bed, dressed as he was in his shorts, Dirk thought he must have made a curious picture. Catriona still had her back to him and was clutching the bulky duvet around her for warmth. She reminded him of his sister with her auburn hair all tousled. Then he remembered that Catriona was a nurse and accustomed to nudity in all its forms so he drew his own duvet to the side away from her and said, 'You may as well lie down on the bed as sit there like that.'

Slowly she turned and swivelled round until she could stretch out upon the bed. In the harsh tungsten lighting they looked like two mummified corpses, each in a sarcophagus. Dirk laughed quietly as he commented upon the fact and raised a wan smile from her. As they talked, she gradually relaxed and Dirk reached up to switch off the light, which was harsh to his eyes. He heard Catriona adjust her duvet in the darkness and, as each moved to ease their tension, their hands touched and held. There was a pause, a few seconds of suspended immobility, each listening for the other's reaction. It came by mutual consent as they both rolled inwards. Catriona began to sob. Dirk hushed her, drawing her close.

'Don't cry,' he murmured, 'you're safe here.' Was she? thought Dirk.

They lay there motionless until her tremors had subsided and he adjusted his arm, trapped awkwardly under her waist. She brought her free arm down from around Dirk's neck to lie between them, now only separated by the double thicknesses of the duvets. They lay silent for what seemed an interminable time until she slowly raised her tear-stained face to his, seeking out his lips with hers in a mute appeal. They kissed softly in the darkness, her hands now moving, roving, seeking the folds of their respective duvets. It was then that Dirk could contain his reserve no longer and came to her fumbling assistance, his pulse-rate increasing. She responded in a fervour or released emotions, all her inhibitions abandoned.

They wrestled and intertwined, clasped in a fervour of frenzied searching, but the crisis passed and they clung closely together, their spontaneous euphoria spent, until Dirk, with a shuddering, self-willed control, rolled free. A slow, silent, mental recovery followed in the dark silence, broken only by the sound of deep measured breathing.

Finally Dirk spoke. 'Why?' he asked softly and repeated it. 'Why?'

There was a pause, followed by a sibilant response. 'Because I needed you,' she murmured simply.

'But we are only fellow travellers,' whispered Dirk huskily.

'Yes, two ships that pass in the night, this time one in distress,' she added. 'Don't worry, Dirk, it won't happen again. I was a very frightened child and I needed company, that's all.'

They lay there till dawn, sleeping and waking. When Dirk finally awoke, Catriona had gone. The connecting door was closed. He was alone with his conscience.

By nine they met again for breakfast. It was as though the night had been a dream. Catriona was neither distant, nor was she affable, and Dirk was equally relieved. They passed the day in each other's company with no mention of the night. The day after was the soccer match. Although the visiting English turned out in a variety of strip and a varied array of footwear, to the chagrin of the villagers, they held them to a three-goal draw. Back in the hotel after dinner the teams celebrated with beers and wine in the assembly hall to the rear of the hotel with a mixed audience. Catriona, still apprehensive of such functions, gravitated to a place within talking distance of Dirk, without attaching herself to his group. He smiled at her reassuringly. The event passed off without incident; that is, until the following day.

Dirk awoke next morning feeling like something the cat had dragged in. His mouth felt like the bottom of a bird's cage, dry, rough and gritty. He had to make a dive for the toilets where he realised that he had contracted the dreaded Continental tummy-bug. He confined himself to his quarters, feeling dejected and sorry. Catriona noted his absence and sought him out, thinking that he might be avoiding her. When he explained his predicament she, with professional proficiency, produced the antidote from her room.

'Take two of these now,' she ordered in her professional ward-voice, 'and two before retiring. Avoid fruit and drink only brandy in water until you're normal again.'

Dirk looked at her, admiring her professional efficiency and positive tone.

'Yes, nurse,' he managed to smile, whilst wincing under the griping pains affecting his stomach. She read his thoughts, diagnosed his symptoms and pronounced, 'Cheer up. The first twelve hours are the worst. You will be normal again in twenty four.'

'I feel shocking,' groaned Dirk, writhing with pain, 'and I've got the shivers as well.'

'That's because you're running a temperature,' she announced. 'That will stop in an hour or so as the pills take hold. Best thing you can do is to remain in bed.'

Dirk considered this, concluded she was right and obeyed the instruction without demur. She regarded him with a sympathetic smile and sat on the edge of the bed to take his pulse. Dirk limply subjected himself to her ministrations out of sheer apathy.

'Your pulse is fast,' she announced in a matter of fact tone, and then, placing a cool hand on his forehead she said, 'get some sleep if you can.' She then drew the window curtains and departed.

Dirk came to several hours later, feeling drained of energy, having to make a mad dash for the toilet. He felt as though someone had kicked him in the stomach where there was now a dull ache, but the pains had subsided. He knew he was dehydrated and needed liquid to replace that lost, so he had to wash and dress to go below. As he tied his tie, he heard the connecting bolt on the door slide back and in came Catriona with a jug of water and a glass.

'Got you some spa water,' she announced cheerfully. 'Drink as much as you can. It will swill you out and replace the lost liquids.'

Dirk murmured his thanks dolefully. He wasn't too sure of his intestinal gymnastics.

'Come on,' she bustled, pouring out a glassful, 'don't look so woebegone. You'll pick up after breakfast.'

Dirk couldn't face food. Even the mention of it revolted him. 'No coffee, mind,' she added. Dirk drank the water, which appeared to have a soothing effect, but he was certainly not ready to face the world at large.

'Some of the others have got it,' Catriona announced. 'I'll bet it was the fruit. It hadn't even been washed. Plums. They're the culprits. Avoid 'em.'

Dirk drank the water thankfully and eased himself back upon the bed. Their respective positions had been reversed. He was now the patient, she the one in charge.

'Just get back into bed and keep warm,' she admonished, 'I'll fetch you something to settle your stomach.' With that she went out and returned later carrying a small glass of clear liquid.

'What's that?' enquired Dirk.

'Kirschwasser," came the reply, 'in other words firewater.'

Dirk downed the proffered drink wrily and as he did so he felt a warm glow percolate the linings of his stomach. He perked up visibly. Catriona smiled. 'That's a good boy,' she pronounced archly.

'Thanks for everything,' intoned Dirk and leaning forward he kissed her on the lips.

'Patients are not permitted to make advances to the nurse,' she warned, now smiling with satisfaction.

The next day Dirk was a new man but tentative as to his eating habits, not wishing to repeat the dose. The days passed speedily and the farewell party was put in hand. Neither Dirk nor Catriona was looking forward with any enthusiasm to the return journey, with its wooden seating, its full carriages and four changes of trains. They made sure, however, that this time they carried water and wine and a luncheon pack which they put together and shared. A weary eighteen hours brought them to London Victora once more. They walked slowly down the platform to the entrance where they stood forlornly, wondering what to say in farewell. 'This is goodbye,' said Dirk, sighing.

'I'm afraid so,' responded Catriona. 'I've no regrets.'

Dirk could not echo her sentiments. Instead he kissed her tenderly, saying tritely, 'Our paths may cross again sometime.'

They looked into each other's eyes plaintively, helplessly. They embraced and exchanged kisses once more.

'Auf wiedersehn,' whispered Dirk.

'Grüs Gott,' came the reply. Dirk gathered his gear, raised his hand in a parting salute and walked away, heading for the Underground and his digs.

11

The remainder of the summer term of 1936 Dirk spent at his home in the Pennines. He renewed former friendships, did familiar things, visited relatives and walked the well-known footpaths which criss-crossed the fields and woodlands which flanked the valley. Nostalgic memories were revived, the whole contributing to a gradual restoration of his energies. Good food, leisurely eaten, congenial company fondly appreciated, social functions of an intimate nature gave healing balm to his erstwhile flagging spirits. Inevitably, in his solitary moments, he headed for the banks of the lake where he spent so much of his rising youth, pitching in pebbles and watching the ripples fade away.

The scene was soothing and soporific. Old thoughts returned, mocking him. He compared the drowsy peace of the countryside with the turbulent, ceaseless bustle of the city suburbs and its artificial ambience. Surely, he mused, there was more to life than the daily round and the common task his working routines offered him. His gaze strayed to the flag irises in the upper shallows, thinking, 'Consider how they grow, they toil not, nor do they spin . . . . What,' thought Dirk, 'was the divine truth behind the text?' The lilies, the trees, the woods, the meadows were eternal and static. He was mobile. He toyed with the word 'mobile', allowing his reveries free rein. 'A rolling stone gathers no moss.' . . . He remembered having to write that for penmanship in the village school exam. Was the saying a stricture on mobility or did it infer that motion produced a polished stone? He plucked a seeding blade of grass from the clump at his side and casually examined it. 'No grass grows on a busy street' passed through his mind. The more he chased these thoughts, the more confused and complicated became the solution to the problem that he knew was gnawing away at his brain. He admitted that he was restless, seeking an aim in life. Indecision ruffled his calm composure. Was there something in his racial memory, handed on in the genes, which was striving to surface past the censor of his conscious mind?

The limpid surface of the water which had hypnotised his ponderings was abruptly broken as a silvery trout leapt high to catch a hovering fly, dropping back with a loud plop and sending out those travelling ripples to fade into nothingness. Was this a sign? The facile beliefs taught him in his formative childhood years regarding divine intervention and predestination surfaced as well. Hamlet's soliloquy followed . . . 'To be or not to be . . .' and Dirk played around with that for a while. He was rudely snatched from his idle reveries by a roll of thunder rumbling round the surrounding hills, presaging the sudden summer storm. He rose and quickly retraced his steps as the first large drops of rain fell from a passing nimbus cloud. He had solved nothing.

The end of his holiday came all too soon. He was not at all keen to return to suburbia and his lonely bedsit. A friend drove him to Manchester and, as he walked up to the departure board on the station complex, he found himself once more in the 'madding crowd . . . and the ignoble strife . . .' He grimaced.

A tap on the shoulder caused him to turn and he found himself looking into a face which was familiar, but to which he could not, at once, put a name. The face spoke, 'Sealand aerodrome, three years ago!' it said. It was Lightbown the rival athlete, dressed in civilian clothes. They exchanged greetings and news. They were travelling to the same destination, Euston. It appeared that Lightbown had served his short term commission in the RAF and was now working in London for a firm of brokers on the Stock Exchange. He had been to visit his fiancée on the Wirral and was contemplating marriage. He had a flat in Knightsbridge. Dirk filled him in as to his own curriculum vitae and the chat turned naturally to athletics and sport in general. During a lull in the conversation, Lightbown suddenly leaned forward and asked in a low tone, 'Have you ever thought of joining the International Brigade?'

Dirk was taken aback. The question echoed a thought that he had flirted and dallied with, but dismissed from his mind as impractical, considering his commitments. He had too many hostages in the hand of fortune . . . his mother, his sister, Naomi and Miriam. After a pregnant pause, during which Lightbown maintained an expectant silence, he said, 'I've toyed with the idea, but never seriously.'

'Think about it,' urged Lightbown. 'Here's my address and phone number. Call me if you're coming up to the City at weekends. We can have a chat about it.'

Dirk agreed he would phone him, but his thoughts were now in a turmoil at this sudden turn of events. He looked at the card he had been given. It said simply Nigel Lightbown, followed by an address and a phone number. They lunched together on the train, remaining in the dining car to pass the time. Not until the train passed Hemel Hempstead did they return to the compartment. They parted at Euston with a promise to meet on the third Saturday in September, outside the Cumberland Hotel near Hyde Park Corner.

Dirk returned to the teaching routines. He put the encounter with Lightbown to the back of his mind as the pressures of the school day and evening commitments took over. The numbers attending his keep-fit classes never seemed to dwindle so that his sole relaxation was the weekly outing with Naomi and Miriam, who was now happily attending the local high school and becoming a much more self-confident young lady. When the pressures became overwhelming and depression tended to get in, he chided himself by thinking of how his mother had coped with problems much graver and this screwed his courage to its sticking place with renewed resolve to carry on.

It was in one of these fits of despair that he set forth to meet Lightbown at the Cumberland. Nigel was there, propping up the bar. He could see that Nigel was anxious to impart some tremendous news, which soon came pouring out. He had been in touch with the Spanish Embassy and offered his services as a pilot. He put it to Dirk that he should accompany him as a navigator and observer. Dirk laughed at the idea. He knew nothing about navigation and said so.

'No problem,' said Nigel, 'I'll teach you all you need to know. There's no great hurry yet. I've a few things to sort out.'

His enthusiasm infected Dirk. If he complied he would have to send in his notice by the end of September to leave at Christmas or he would be breaching his contract. He explained this to Nigel.

'No problem,' countered his friend, 'we can leave it until Christmas. Come to think of it that will suit me better. I've some problems to sort out too.'

Dirk promised to give it some serious thought over the next week and they went through to the luncheon room. After a light lunch Nigel produced two complimentary tickets for the first house at the Palladium. 'We can have a stroll through Hyde Park first and spend an hour at Speakers' Corner for a laugh, followed by a spot of tea and then go to the show.'

This they did and parted in the late evening, Nigel his customary bubbling self and Dirk in sombre contemplative mood.

In the tube train to Wood Green Dirk wondered whether this was the tide in his affairs of which he should take advantage at its flood. He resolved to sleep on it and in chapel the following day to ask divine guidance as to the decisions he faced. Strangely coincidental, the Sunday sermon was about sacrifice and dedication to causes. As the minister, a chaplain in the Territorial Division, developed his theme, Dirk felt his mind clearing, the clouds of his doubt lifting and his resolve refining. That noon he sat down at the table in his bedsit and wrote three letters, one to Nigel, one to his mother, which took a long and heart-searching time, and a third tendering his resignation to the Education Authority. He felt guilty about all three. Posting them that evening, Dirk knew that he had now burnt his boats. He had reached the point of no return.

12

Dirk broke the news of his decision to Naomi when next they met. She was quite calm about it. They had already discussed Dirk's impressions of Hitler's Germany and agreed that the situation was becoming ominous. The reports from the Olympic Games had already demonstrated the arrogance of the Führer and latterly Jew-baiting was not only becoming overt in Bavaria but quite widespread. More and more of Naomi's race were moving out to avoid humiliation. The decision Dirk had made brought them closer in spirit and they resolved to make the most of their time together before the end of the year. Nigel spent hours with Dirk, coaching him in astro-navigation, and in the finer points of aviation. Several times they flew from a private aerodrome to put theory into practice and Dirk soon had sufficient flying hours in, as a solo flyer, to take his pilot's licence. Before this happened they went gliding on Dunstable Downs on appropriate weekends to give Dirk the feel of flying and the use of thermals. His sensitive touch on the controls and the intense thrill of being airborne as an integral part of a machine without power was magnificent. A new and exciting world was opening up for him in which he felt he was at one with the birds of the air. The silence of the upper air was soothing, the sweeps and lifts on the thermals exhilarating. By December he was ready to take his test for his wings by flying a Gladiator plane solo and putting it through all the manoeuvres required. They all celebrated his success on the run up to Christmas by dining at an intimate restaurant in the Strand and rounding off the evening at the Savoy Theatre.

By the penultimate day of the year Nigel and Dirk had packed all their requisite gear and said their farewells. In Naomi's case it was a very tearful and emotional parting. After receiving final instructions from the Spanish Embassy they caught a train to Falmouth where they boarded a trawler which left within the hour for the Channel Islands. The sea proved lively. Dirk was violently sick. But by the time they had anchored in Jersey Harbour, Dirk had acquired his sea legs and was taking nourishment and a lively interest in things nautical again. Nigel kept him up to scratch with revisionary instruction on the finer points of flying as they coasted down the west of France to lie at anchor off Arcachon. Here the radio crackled into life, seeking instructions for running the blockade. The skipper was impatient to proceed, but it was three days before the anchor was once more weighed at dusk. Meanwhile, they had existed on short commons and had resorted to fish for their main meals.

There was to be a fast night run to the Spanish port of Ribadasella, under cover of darkness. At five a.m. tensions rose. Dirk could sense a nervousness as the crew paced the decks and kept a sharp lookout all round for patrols. The hold was full of guns and ammunition and could not bear inspection. As they neared the harbour the engines were cut down from a noisy pulsing throb to half-speed, and finally, to a dull phut-phut as the outline of the fairway loomed up. A patrol boat off the harbour entrance zoomed up to investigate. The loud hailer was activated and recognition calls exchanged. As the launch came alongside, Nigel and Dirk disappeared into the forepeak locker where all the sailing gear and cables were stowed. They had already donned seamen's rig as a precaution and would have been coiling ropes in the locker had anyone boarded for inspection but the launch sheered away, satisfied of the boat's bonafides, and everyone relaxed. The course was then set for the harbour mole and RB 3506 slipped in, past the light on the breakwater, to make fast on the inner mole just before dawn. The sudden silence as the engine cut out, the soothing lap-lap of the water against the boat's side, the iodine smell of seaweed, the pleasant aroma of tarred rope, assailed Dirk's sensitive nostrils. Lying on the lockers down below, he passed the time by identifying the several mingled smells until they were called to embark on the next stage of their journey.

It soon came. They were transferred to a tavern where a meal had been prepared and where they ate and drank their fill. Dirk had never tasted tuna steaks before and the gourmet experience presented by the *dueña* of the tavern, washed down with copious draughts of red wine, left little to be desired. Chopped fresh vegetables with lemon juice and herbs revived their flagging spirits. When the coffee was served, together with a small glass of anis and a tumbler of water to sip, they felt replete. Lifting his glass of anis, the skipper of the boat, in his hearty gruff voice, called, 'Good for the digestion,' and tossed the tot down with one throw of his grizzled head. Nigel produced English cigarettes and passed them around. Everyone relaxed in easy chairs or on the long settee which flanked the cooking stove, fuelled by the billets of wood that were stacked nearby. The warm smells of cooking mingled with woodsmoke proved more than soporofic as the inmates dozed off, slumped in curious postures. Dirk, as usual, slept heavily but was rudely awakened by being shaken by the shoulder.

'Wake up, time to go,' called a harsh voice. Dirk roused himself, unsure of his bearings. He needed a toilet and could do with a wash and said so. He was directed to a place at the rear of the tavern where the offices were quite primitive, but he managed a cat-lick of his face and hands. Returning, he learned that a lorry, belching out diesel fumes, awaited them. Nigel, Dirk and two strange Spaniards they had not seen before piled into the rear and sat on a heap of sacking, backs to the driving cab. A flurry of sea-rain spattered them. The two Spaniards showed them how to use the sacks to make a hood, placing another over their knees. Off they trundled along the rutted streets, full of potholes, causing them to jolt and jerk constantly as they progressed. Soon they were climbing up some steep roads into the mountains to the rear of the town. Dirk's geography came into play. Turning to Nigel he remarked, 'We're going up the Cantabrian Mountains, they're called *Los Picos de Europa.*'

One of the Spaniards, hearing the remark, echoed his words, *'Si señores, Los Picos de Europa,'* and pointed with his thumb in the direction the lorry was taking. As they trundled on, the scenery was magnificent. Above the cloudline vast forests appeared, shrouded in dank curling mists. The sun's heat was welcome. They crossed bridges where torrents of foaming white water tumbled and every so often they stopped to allow the engine to cool. Dirk snatched the opportunity to wash in the stream from which everyone drank with cupped hands. The water was cold, refreshing and crystal clear.

They passed through tiny, remote villages of huddling houses, clinging to the steep hillsides with shuttered windows and doors made of crudely-cut planking, weathered and warped. Eventually they stopped at a farm in a high mountain clearing. It was evident they were expected, for a table had been set for them and a full post midday meal prepared. Dirk was always ready to eat and the smells from the kitchen were inviting and mouthwatering, reminding him of Naomi. Bottles of home-made cider, a savoury vegetable soup laced with herbs, rabbit pie accompanied by an array of chopped vegetables, followed by ripe plums and cream and what purported to be a home-made cherry liqueur, all of which were supplied from the farmlands and its environs, more than appeased their hunger. Outside, in the full glare of the hot afternoon sun with the cool mountain breezes fanning their faces, they slept. The altitude gave the air a crisp freshness, almost as heady as the cider. The sounds of Nature enveloped them, coming from a wealth of wild life. Was it an eagle that Dirk spotted as he gazed heavenwards to a spot where a bird with a huge wing-span quartered the blue vault? Suddenly it plunged with folded wing like a pointed projectile steeply down, disappearing behind the trees to rise again, bearing in its drooping legs and talons some unfortunate prey. Dirk recalled his favourite place, the Echostones, and the kestrels of the valley. Soon he might be like that bird, only a mechanical one, as he headed for the mesetas where history was being once more written in blood.

Dimly, in the distant uplands, Dirk's ears detected the faint tinkling of bells. As he concentrated on the direction from which the sound was coming, his eyes scanned the tree-clad slopes behind the farm. Several well-marked footpaths led upwards to the belt of trees and shrubs and disappeared within. From the various sounds which assailed his ears, he could pick out that tap-tap-tapping of the woodpecker, the cooing of doves, the clucking of nearby poultry, the bark of a dog and the trilling of a variety of birdlife and still the tinkling of bells came nearer. How idyllic and peaceful it all seemed for a country engaged in civil war. Then, out from the treeline, leading a flock of plaintive goats and a few sheep, came a girlish figure. Her red embroidered bolero caught the eye, partially revealing a snow white blouse and sleeves, below which flared a plaid skirt and high leather boots to knee-level. The straggling procession fanned out down the slope as she led the way to a group of corrals away to the right, swinging a leather thong which Dirk guessed might be a sling with which to throw stones to redirect the wanderers or the stragglers when in the high mountains. The gate of the corral swung open and the flock of goats filed in without demur. Through a second gate went the sheep with docile familiarity. Dirk was fascinated, remembering the rounding up of the unruly lonks on the slopes of the Pennine hills at home. There, the dogs ruled, and drove the sheep. Here the sheep were led by a lissom human figure, and a bellwether. With a graceful twirl of her flared woollen skirt, the girl swung to the hurdle which penned the flocks and marched towards the rear entrance to the farm. In his imagination Dirk could visualise her on the rocky mountain slopes, fitting the stones in her sling and swinging it to direct the projectile at some recalcitrant stray, wandering into danger. Only a casual glance did the girl throw in the direction of the sprawling menfolk on the grass before she disappeared from view.

Dirk rose and stretched himself to disperse the torpor caused by relaxation in the sun, which was now declining towards the distant peaks. The pungent smell of resinous pines, the fragrance of bruised grasses and the woodsmoke which drifted across the clearing from the curiously shaped stone chimney leaning against the timbers of the farm had a soporific effect inducing a pleasant lethargy, welcome after the long and varied journeys.

Suddenly, the staccato crackle of rifle fire shattered the peace and set the birds and rooks in chattering flight. The sound came from the east and not too far away at that. The men had risen precipitately and were rushing towards the farm, galvanised into headlong activity. Dirk roused Nigel and they followed at the double. Once inside a babble of voices assailed their ears, all of it unintelligible. Rifles appeared from nowhere. Small boxes of ammunition were flung on the table and men were stuffing them into their pockets and shouldering bandoliers gleaming with bullets. Rifles were thrust into the hands of the two Englishmen with a significant nodding towards the boxes on the table. Dirk, alert to the situation, began to stuff loose ammunition into his pockets, followed by Nigel who said, 'Ever used one of these before, Dirk?'

'No, but I had an air rifle as a kid and know how to use that,' came the response.

'OK,' rapped out Nigel, 'now's the time to learn, and learn fast.'

He began pushing shells into the breach and told Dirk to copy him. His first fumbling attempts were a failure so Nigel exchanged weapons and loaded the second.

'Grab some more ammo,' he ordered, 'as much as you can comfortably carry.' That done, they followed their comrades at a brisk run across the clearing to the belt of trees to the west.

'At least,' commented Nigel, 'we shall have the sun at our backs and be higher.'

Dirk did not reply. He was too busy with his ungainly load and a passing thought as to the girl. He stumbled and fell, dropping his rifle, and as he turned to retrieve it, he caught sight of the girl leaving the farm, two bandoliers across her breast, carrying a rifle and a pack. She broke into a lively trot as a shot rang out from across the clearing. Hearing it she began to zig-zag.

'Come on,' shouted Nigel, 'get a jildi on. Run for the trees. We'll cover her from there. She'll be all right. The range is too long for any accuracy yet.'

Dirk obeyed and running, they reached cover together, Nigel lying down and taking aim. No further shot was heard and the girl made cover away to the left. Turning, Nigel said, 'Work to the right at forty five degrees towards the girl and keep to the scrubland.' They pushed on weaving in and out of dense tangles. As they went, several shots whistled through the air and slashed through the dense scrub. Eventually they reached an outcrop of rock with a commanding view of the clearing below.

'This'll do,' panted Nigel. 'I'm not in such good nick as I thought.'

'I'm OK,' responded Dirk, 'but I'm worried about the girl.'

'To hell with the girl,' barked Nigel. 'She knows the terrain like the back of her hand. Come on, we'll have to take cover.'

Again Dirk complied, still unsure of his role. He scouted the area for a good pitch and was not at all happy with what he saw. 'This place is no good Nigel,' he called. 'There's no way out except over the drop here. We'd be picked off.'

They both looked down over a steep drop at the jagged pinnacle below. 'You're right,' murmured Nigel, 'we'll have to go up higher,' and as one man, they began once more to scale the heights with increased zeal. The firing had ceased, a fact which could either be advantageous or ominous, nor did they know the size of the pursuing force nor its capabilities. They therefore climbed the more speedily and with increased agility. A low whistle to the right halted them and a voice called, *'Aquí! aquí!'* Dirk looked in the direction of the sound and glimpsed a flash of red. 'It's the girl,' he said panting heavily. They traversed in the direction of the sound until they spotted her a little higher up the slopes. *'Prisa, prisa,'* she urged, signalling with her arm to hurry. They put on speed with difficulty and on following in her wake had difficulty keeping pace.

'She's like a chamois,' panted Nigel. 'I don't think I can keep this up.'

Dirk had already passed the pain barrier of his breathing and laughed. 'Pretty smart mover, what?' he called. He now had his equipment better balanced. 'Let's catch her up.'

Nigel grunted as they put on an extra turn of speed. The distance between them decreased but she, on turning to look, increased hers still more and they, with a mutual grunt of appraisal, agreed to call it a day and just follow. They were following scarcely visible goat-tracks winding through the scrubland and the rocks. Eventually she stopped and they caught up with her. With her free arm she pointed to a defile ahead to which she began to walk swiftly, saying, '*Vamos* . . . queekly.' They reached the defile which was a narrow pass through steep rocks on either side. Reaching a bend she turned and said, 'OK, now!' Round the corner, in a tiny open space, they saw their former companions together with the men from the farmstead.

'*Holà,* Lolita,' exclaimed the heavily-built bewhiskered man, festooned with bandoliers, '*los ingleses no tienen balas?*'

'You 'ave no bullets?' queried Lolita.

'Yeah, *si, si* . . . we have,' and Dirk pulled a handful from his bulging pockets.

'*Muy bien,* OK,' grunted the old one, who seemed to be the boss-man, and turning, he motioned them all to follow with a circular motion of his free arm. He led them behind some huge rocks, where, pulling away some dead bushes and scrub, he revealed the mouth of a cave no bigger than was possible to squeeze through when bent double, but which led into a cavern much larger than what one would have expected to find. The last through closed the aperture by pulling on a rope attached to the shrubbery which had been dragged aside. The grizzled leader switched on a torch and indicated lamps which the others lit. They then proceeded single file along a low passage which eventually led upward by means of roughly cut steps to a hole at the surface. Emerging into the light and extinguishing the lamps, Dirk saw that they were in a kind of redoubt which overlooked the terrain below and which was protected on all sides by a precipitous drop whilst backing onto the mountain wall, an ideal place to defend, given the necessary weapons. Two of the men moved a smaller rock over the aperture which led below and the leader, after making sure that all was in order, began to introduce the assembled band. He called himself Domingo, the others being Vincente, Pepe, Largo, Juan and Chico. Angel and Lolita were twins of whom Domingo, the father, seemed very proud. His growling voice and craggy appearance belied the affection which shone in his eyes whenever he spoke to them and it was obvious that they in turn idolised him. They spread themselves out around the perimeter of the natural redoubt and began to check the motley array of weaponry which consisted of hunting rifles and a few double barrelled bird-guns, mighty useful at close quarters. Nigel, anxious about Dirk's knowledge on weaponry, went over the details of loading and reloading and indicated the approximate ranges from the redoubt towards the edge of the timber line. He was anxious not to waste any ammunition and the old monition, which Dirk had heard many times from a previous generation, was trotted out, 'Wait until you can see the whites of their eyes.'

Domingo went to a corner of the parapet where, under a cache of small rocks, he unearthed a box containing dynamite sticks with short fuses inserted and in another section, under an overhanging rock beneath more shrubbery, a case of hand grenades. Meanwhile Lolita, who had carried a large rucksack as well as rifle and ammunition up the mountain, began to open her bundle to reveal and distribute an array of comestibles. Two others unslung wineskins from their shoulders and Dirk noted that Domingo also had one. Apparently they were well organised and had left little to chance, despite the brevity of the warning. The question was, where was the enemy? This was a mystery to Nigel and Dirk. Domingo finally came over to them and with a broad grin which revealed a full set of tobacco-stained teeth under bristly moustaches and two day's growth of beard, exclaimed, *'Bienvenida amigos, ahora pronto impieza la corrida!'*

Dirk, dredging his mind for the equivalent in Portuguese, translated, 'Welcome friends, now for the bullfight.'

Nigel laughed. 'Some bullfight,' he countered, 'we didn't reckon on this. I'd sooner be up there,' he continued, pointing to a buzzard circling overhead.

They switched their gaze aloft to watch the graceful quartering of the bird scarcely a hundred feet above, marvelling in its slow sweeps and its superb grace.

'The prefect glider,' added Nigel, 'silent, stately and self-assured.'

His poetic utterance was quickly switched as Lolita's voice cried, *'Mira, allá.'*

They all gazed in the direction in which she was pointing, her eagle eyes had noted some movement along the treeline, some 300 yards away. Within seconds a group of figures broke cover and were filing up by the goat tracks below them. The watchers checked their rifles and settled themselves to wait. Lolita came across and spoke to Nigel and Dirk, 'My father, he say, no shoot,' and she accompanied this with a stern face and a warning finger waved from side to side, adding, *'Silencio, todos!'*

They watched the laboured climb of the oncoming group, counting twelve heads, as they began to traverse the slope from left to right across the line of fire, gradually shortening the range. The seconds dragged by. You could feel the tension in the silence. As they reached a given point, Domingo struck a match and lit a fuse. The initial hiss as the flame travelled, gradually faded until Domingo called, *Cuidado!'* and Lolita called, 'Down!' to the Englishmen.

All crouched behind the parapet. A tremendous explosion rent the air, followed by a rumble of rocks falling, as in an avalanche. Looking over the parapet after Domingo had risen, it appeared that the mountain to the right had begun to slide towards the oncoming men who, now in disarray, were leaping and bounding in a vain effort to dodge the oncoming tide. Hypnotised, Dirk watched the futility of their efforts as the hurtling debris quickly engulfed the group. Shouts and screams were eliminated and a pall of silence descended. Dirk looked up. The buzzard had gone. He then looked towards Domingo, who was lining up his rifle along with others in case anyone had survived the avalanche. Nigel, leaning over the parapet, his rifle at the ready, laughed. 'If it moves, shoot it.' His remark broke Dirk's tension.

'Do you think anyone will survive that?' he asked, appalled.

'They might,' replied Nigel laconically. Seconds ticked by. Finally a figure stirred amongst the murrain of rocks. Domingo lined up his sights, as did others. He fired and the man fell. Nonchalantly he reloaded and lined up his sights again. There was no further movement. Domingo growled at Vicente who extracted a Biretta from a holster at his hip and together with Pepe and Juan they removed the rock from over the hole and disappeared. Moments passed and eventually they were seen cautiously approaching the killing ground, Vicente first, with the two others covering him with their rifles. Reaching the murrain, Vicente bent down. A shot was discharged. He rose and moved along. Another shot echoed as he used his Biretta.

'Putting them out of their misery,' murmured Nigel out of the corner of his mouth.

Finally Vicente signalled with downcast arms, the 'none left' sign, and they retraced their steps. Everyone relaxed and stood down except for Domingo who kept his aim and stance on the parapet until the three reappeared in the redoubt. Only then did he turn and remark, *'Que se mueren así todos los feos!'*

Nigel raised his eyebrows and looked at Dirk questioningly. Dirk shook his head and said, 'Something about, "Thus may the hideous die", I think . . . I couldn't be sure.'

Everyone put down their guns and Lolita handed round the food. Little comment ensued as the wineskin passed round. Finally Domingo gave a loud 'Brrrurp!' at the same time breaking wind. Everyone laughed. The tension was broken. Lolita said something to her father which wasn't complimentary; he replied with laughter and great warmth of displayed affection as she blushed and glanced towards the two English. They pretended they hadn't heard but Dirk heard Nigel say, 'Better out than in,' and turned away. Domingo then spoke aloud, *'Cuando puesta el sol, marchamos.'* Dirk recognised the meaning and repeated it. 'We leave at sunset.' Lolita came over and also said, 'At sunset we march, *entienden?'* Dirk nodded and said, *'Si, comprendo señorita!'*

Everyone relaxed and made themselves comfortable whilst eating and drinking. They laughed at the efforts of the English with the wineskins. They then busied themselves with restoring the redoubt to its former innocuous-looking self by hiding the ammunition there stored, camouflaging it and retreating down the long passage of the cave into the open again. As the sun dipped behind the high peaks they rose and trekked up the mountain towards the south, keeping the sun on the right, Domingo leading, Lolita at his heels and Nigel and Dirk in line behind with the rest bringing up the rear in Indian style. For two hours they plodded upwards, resting every half hour or so to draw breath. The air was becoming crisp and cold as darkness descended, but the track was well defined in the afterglow of the sun. Little was said and soon they reached the summit of their laborious climb to where a mountain cabin stood, offering relief and welcome shelter.

They entered and lit lamps already there, revealing tiered bunks with slatted boards for sleeping upon. Paco, who seemed to know his way about, went out and brought in sticks and logs for a fire. Domingo, on shedding his pack, which was considerable, unloosed his wineskin and directed a jet of the red liquid down his gullet and straightaway placed himself in the horizontal on one of the bunks, signalling with his hand to the two English and saying, *'Cama . . . duerme.'* His words needed no translation. Lolita handed them another wineskin from which they drank, holding it as near to their mouths as was safe. The thin jet of wine was welcome to the palate and inducive of sleep.

13

Everyone lay down and soon some were snoring heavily. Came the dawn. Lolita, inexhaustible as ever, was already up and bringing in water in a large pan which she placed over the revived embers of the fire, slung from a hook in the wide chimney. She made strong black coffee, adding sugar which she then poured into mugs and handed round. They drank the scalding brew slowly for the night had chilled their bodies. She then indicated bread and butter with a carton of what appeared to be honey on the table. Dirk had seen some hives under the treeline at the outback of the farmstead. The honey took the bitterness away from the coffee. Lolita, it appeared, had forgotten little. There was cheese and raw cured ham, the latter rather strange to Dirk and Nigel, but it went down nevertheless to assuage the hunger which assailed them. One by one the men disappeared outside to wash at the stream which tumbled its way down the steep slope to the valley below. Later all packed and the bothy left ship-shape and tidy, they shouldered their respective loads and gathered outside in the grey dawn.

'Arriba!' exclaimed Domingo, pointing upwards, *'Nieve!'* Lolita translated. 'Snow, up there.'

Off they trudged once more in marching order. They soon came to the snowline, where they stopped. Far below them in the valley they could discern a village with houses, from the chimneys of which smoke was curling upwards. The men strapped on gaiters. Domingo looked at the English a little perplexed, but Nigel anticipated him by taking out his flying boots from the pack and telling Dirk to follow suit. Domingo nodded approval and, all re-equipped, off they set, crunching over the snows. A line of poles which Dirk had noticed whilst climbing now revealed their use as markers of the hidden track they followed. Rests became more frequent as the gradients increased. The sun came up to shed its welcome warmth and they could see the pass opening up ahead. Once through the defile the descent was easier, still marked by the long line of poles. As the treeline once more approached and the snow diminished, Domingo signalled a halt and they removed their leggings and boots to begin a descent through the pines on cushions of pine needles. Through a gap in the trees they glimpsed a bowl-shaped valley below, a cluster of huddled buildings, bathed in morning sunlight. Trudging down towards it, Domingo stopped as the treeline ended and, putting his fingers to his mouth, gave a long, low undulating whistle, repeated three times. A figure appeared at the door and gazed upwards in the direction of the sound. Lolita took off her yellow scarf and waved it to focus the watcher's attention, upon which he gave a beckoning sign with his right arm and Domingo grunted, *'Vamonos!'*

They descended towards the farm where cries of greeting, followed by many embraces, ensued. The welcome was obvious and turning to Nigel and Dirk, Domingo introduced them to the lady of the house, saying to Dirk and Nigel with consummate pride and generous gestures, *'Mi hermana, señores.'* Lolita butted in with, 'My father's sister, my aunt,' at which the babel of noise resumed, deafening after the silence of the trek. The fire was kicked into flame and logs added. Coffee laced with brandy appeared and by the odours emanating from the kitchen an English breakfast was on the way. The smell of ham cut from the shanks which festooned the wooden rafters and the faint familiar noise of sizzling fat lifted Dirk's spirits. He strolled to the window which gave on to the steep valley falling away to the south, now bathed in yellow light etched by long shadows, magnifying the greens and golds and browns of a fascinating landscape. Whoever had originally chosen this spot to build certainly appreciated beauty and entertained a feeling for Nature at one with his own. Dirk drank in the vista. Lolita, noting his concentration, came to stand at his side.

'Hermosa la vista, verdad?' she commented. Dirk's Latin dredged from the deeper portions of his brain translated.

'Truly beautiful,' he murmured without turning, adding, 'splendid, *sí sí.'*

Lolita's eyes lit up, *'Sí, esplendida,'* continuing in broken English, 'you have a leetle Spanish, yes?'

'No, no,' countered Dirk, turning to face her. 'I have Latin and a little Portuguese.'

'Bueno, bueno,' cried Lolita, clapping her hands together, 'we talk a little yes?' she added. Dirk looked at her face, her bright eyes, her trim figure, her appropriate dress, and his eyes softened as he took in the line of her form. He inwardly marvelled at her energy, her endurance, her resourcefulness and cool efficiency under adverse circumstances. She must have noted the tenderness in his eyes and turning, remarked, *'Ahora voy a la cocina . . .* the kitchen, yes?' And pointing to the door from which the mouthwatering odours were percolating, she tripped with a swirl of skirts towards it. Dirk was amazed at her vitality after her previous day's work with the goats, the overnight trail and the weight she had carried. She returned soon afterwards leading two other young ladies, introducing them as Josefina and Maruja. Dirk shook hands with them, pointing to himself and saying, 'Dirk' and then pointing to his companion saying, 'Nigel,' but Nigel was busy with the coffee and the brandy bottle. When he turned and acknowledged they all laughed, obviously pleased and excited at this novel turn of events in their daily routine. Speech being limited, they returned to the kitchen to assist in the chores.

After the first flush of greetings and family chatter was over the menfolk drifted outside to sit on benches in the sun, rolling cigarettes and sucking, exchanging views with much gesticulation and verve. Dirk felt the genuine warmth and friendship which the ties of family and blood evoked. These ties were durable and sustaining, reliable and supportive in times of stress. The easy way the men spoke and the reaction of their womenfolk, the friendly banter, the demonstrative affection were all touching and as he thought on these things and gazed at the enthralling scenery which spread out around and below him he began to sense the first pangs of homesickness and uncertainty, and the question gnawed at his brain. Had he made the right decisions? His reverie was broken by a gentle hand placed upon his shoulder, it was Nigel offering him a glass of wine with a thick slice of heavily buttered toast on a salver.

'Come on Dirk. Snap out of it. The die is cast. Make the most of the present.'

He must have read his thoughts as Dirk struggled to switch his attention. He took the salver and placed it on a bench nearby, where they stood eating, and discussed the events so far. Soon they were summoned by the girls to breakfast proper and they all filed indoors to seat themselves at the family table, white with years of scrubbing and application of lye. The log fire had grown into a crackling blaze which cast flickering lights upon the white painted walls and ceilings from the thick wooden beams of which hung pans, weapons, bundles of herbs, shanks of cured hams and strings of garlic and onions. The food, the laughter, the general bonhomie, the musical cacophony of voices, lifted Dirk from his momentary plunge into the pit of depression as he attacked the savoury victuals placed before him to appease his genuine hunger.

He gathered that they must stay there for several nights. Lolita explained in a series of broken English phrases, supplemented by a little French, that they must await an arrangement of transport. Dirk and Nigel did not mind the delay. Good victuals, good company, idyllic surroundings . . . what more could one ask? They actually stayed several nights and during the day assisted with the chores around the farm. Dirk taught Nigel how to milk cows and they even tackled the goats. They had never before seen sheep milked and this proved to be an interesting sight as the girls demonstrated and took the pannikins away to make cheese. The two sawed and chopped timber from the fallen trees in the forest, trundling it on sleds back to the farm and stacking it below the eaves. They cleaned shippons and byres, fed chickens and collected eggs. Dirk taught Nigel how to discover whether a hen was laying eggs by first catching it and laying three fingers across the pelvis. If the gap between the bones was only two fingers wide, or less, the hen had ceased laying and, if old, was ready for the pot. All the skills he had acquired in his youth found a ready use here. The farm girls were delighted with his facility in animal husbandry and agreeably surprised, such that he became a focus of their attention. Nigel was tentative about approaching pigs for they jostled him noisily in a threatening manner as he entered the sty so Dirk showed him how to place himself and the bucket when emptying the swills into the troughs. One day in the forest Dirk came across some eggs from a hen which was laying away. Taking them to the stream he showed Nigel how to test for soundness. If they floated they were bad; if they sank slowly they were too far gone to eat, but if they sank quickly and did not turn point down they were edible.

'You might need this knowledge before you're much older,' admonished Dirk.

Nigel was fascinated with this country life which had never been his lot to experience. He in turn kept Dirk up to scratch as regards air skills, navigation and weaponry until the time arrived to move on.

It was with a sense of loss that Dirk prepared to depart. A truck was ready and waiting in the valley below. Nigel, Dirk, Lolita, Vicente and Paco were to proceed, the rest, including Domingo, were to return to the home farm. There were tearful farewells, strong embraces, kissing of cheeks and admonition on all sides. They left at dusk fully caparisoned and equipped for their onward journey. This time Lolita led, her knowledge of the terrain was accepted, her skills unquestioned, as she set a cracking pace in the fading light. An hour later it was dark enough to use the main dirt road and they filed down it until they reached a small clearing, of which there were many, originally used to quarry stone for the road surfaces. The lorry was parked there, the driver asleep. Their soft-footed approach was unheard and Lolita chaffed him for his lack of vigilance. She climbed into the cab beside him, the rest into the back where full and empty drums were lashed together and sacks were to be found. As the lorry jolted over the potholed roads the din from the empty bounding drums was deafening, advertising the lorry's passage through every village and tiny hamlet. On the other hand the noise could prove that there was nothing sinister afoot.

They progressed slowly, the driver stopping before reaching every hamlet with one of the men going forward to ascertain if there was any difficulty of passage. Before they reached the lower levels of the valley they stopped at a road junction where they pulled off the road behind some trees to try to get a little sleep. As dawn broke, they stirred, a little stiff and cold, and began jumping up and down and flapping their arms to restore the circulation. One collected pine cones and dry twigs and lit a fire surrounding it with stones. A pan was produced from inside the cab and filled with water from a nearby stream and set to boil over the flames. Lolita made coffee of a sort which, when laced with brandy, went down well, inducing a warm glow to spread through the stomach. As it became lighter Dirk could see the scenery around. It was magnificent. Dense forest lined the valleys down which the foaming rivers tumbled, fed by the snows above. They went down to sluice their faces and have a cursory wash. The water was ice-cold, no good for shaving. They had a two day growth of beard and were beginning to look a little sinister.

Visibility increased and Lolita made signs to proceed. They gathered their belongings kicked out the fire and doused it, scattering the stones, and boarded the lorry once more. An hour later they approached the town of Riano, halting at the distant sight of buildings. Lolita descended and came round the side, conversing with Paco and Vicente in Spanish, then, looking up at the two English, she tried to explain in broken English that there was danger up ahead.

'Town . . . Riano,' she began, 'three kilometros . . . *requetes . . . soldados,* soldiers, *entendeis . . . nationalistas* . . . boom, boom!' And she raised her arms as though aiming a rifle. After a further word to Paco, a case was opened from the back of the lorry and rifles extracted and shared around, followed by ammunition from a smaller box. Nigel looked at the rifles and said, 'Lee Enfields . . . that's more like it. Ever used one of these, Dirk?'

Dirk shook his head and Nigel withdrew the bolt and shot it home. 'British,' he continued, 'First World War vintage, long range but a bit dated.' He demonstrated to Dirk how to load and adjust the sights. The other three were similarly engaged and Nigel went over to help them, miming the finer points of adjustment. They all piled into the lorry and began covering the boxes with sacking and shielding them with the drums. That done, Lolita spoke again, '*Soldados* . . . soldiers, stop us, maybe.' Then, putting a finger to her eye, she said, '*Cuidado . . . peligro* . . . danger.'

Dirk turned to Nigel saying, 'Soldiers up front. Keep our eyes open, she says.'

'Yeah, I gathered that,' commented Nigel, still examining his rifle, which was a bit greasy. 'This lot need cleaning.' And he looked down the barrel. Riflings a bit worn too,' he went on dolefully, 'reduces accuracy. Someone's sold them some junk.'

Lolita returned and said, 'When see *soldados,* run to trees,' and pointing to the ammunition, she said, 'take . . . carry,' and pointed to the forest. Nigel nodded, understanding, and added, '*Si,* chop, chop, run like hell, *pronto, jildi, gleich* and all that.'

Lolita appeared nonplussed at the outburst from the customarily silent Nigel but Dirk laughed and said, '*Comprende*, Lolita, when we see *soldados* run to trees *lleva balas, si?*'

'*Si, si, eso es,*' she exclaimed with relief and her face wreathed in smiles.

They restarted the engine and proceeded slowly along the road towards Riano. At every corner they slowed to a crawl. The stretches of road became longer, but as the valley flattened out, Vicente and Paco stood up to lean over the driver's cab, rifles in hand. The two aviators followed suit. The driver switched off the engine and they coasted along, the sudden quiet broken only by the crunch of tyres on gravel and rumble and boom of the empty drums as they bounced and rocked in response to the potholes. Dirk noted that the birds were numerous, flitting across their path as they advanced. Approaching the next bend, the driver put the lorry into gear and restarted the engine, applying the brakes immediately after it fired. They crept round an S-bend in the road, finally levelling out along a half-mile clear length of roadway. The driver stopped and, descending with a pair of binoculars in his hands, he surveyed the distant stretch ahead. In a low voice he addressed Lolita and climbed back into his cab. Releasing the brake the lorry rolled forward down the slight slope for some fifty yards before he turned off into a roadside clearing where stone had been quarried for the roads. Here they dismounted and at a signal faded into the trees, some to attend to wants of nature, after which Paco, Vicente and the driver sloped off in the direction of the town, keeping to the trees. Lolita tried to explain to the English that there was a road block ahead. *'Carretera está cortada,'* were the words she used, after which she added hesitatingly, 'road cut . . . *soldados . . . requetes . . . nacionalistas.'*

After some time the three Spaniards returned and reported. A consultation ensued after which they motioned to the English to follow. They made a detour on foot through the trees until Lolita put her fingers to her lips and hissed, *'Silencio! . . . Quieto!'* From there on they advanced carefully, footsteps muffled by the soft leaf-mould until they came within sight of a small cabin flanking the road, in front of which was a barricade of logs and barbed wire. Vicente felt in his jacket pocket and produced a wire with two handles either end, showing it to Nigel. 'Garotte!' whispered Nigel. Vicente nodded and pointed to the cabin. They approached within ten yards of it and a signal to fan out was given. As they lay in the scrub a soldier came from the front of the cabin and proceeded to relieve himself in the ditch behind it. Nigel was nearest and Vicente pointed to his own rifle butt and jerked his elbow to simulate the move. Nigel rose and crept up to the man's rear. 'Pssst!' hissed Nigel. The soldier turned as Nigel swung the butt and struck him full on the jaw, grabbing him as he fell and lowering him to the ground slowly with little noise. They all advanced to the hut. Any noise now and they would think it was their companion returning. They waited outside the front ends until Paco and Lolita had crossed the road and lay in the ditch, ready to cover the door with cross fire. Vicente, having donned the red beret, passed in front of the window, glancing inside and raising four fingers to indicate the number of occupants. He halted by the door and shuffled his feet, noisily moving on to the corner and waiting, coughing as if choking. The door opened and a figure appeared calling, 'Fernando? *Que pasa contigo?*'

'Nada,' grunted Vicente just around the corner, who then circled the hut, coming upon the unsuspecting victim from behind as he reached the corner. Using the garotte and coughing again to cover any untoward sound, he gently lowered the body to the ground and turned once more. Dirk moved up, having put on the second beret and he and Vicente, rifles at the ready, opened the door and leapt inside, the others running in behind them. Inside a meal had been in progress, coffee, bread, butter, plates, knives and cups scattered about the table. Three soldiers on stools were still chewing, startled in mid-mouthful. *'Manos arriba!'* barked out Vicente, sticking his rifle into the ribs of the nearest. A tap on the window distracted the gaze of the other two as Lolita aimed her rifle at them through it. Realising that resistance was hopeless they raised their hands in surrender. Dirk collected their rifles and ammunition. Lolita entered and after a few words with Vicente he ordered the men to strip. She already had the jackets and trousers of the two dead outside and staggered Dirk by the speed and verve of her initiative. Paco was sent back to the lorry with the spare rifles and ammo with instructions to bring back ropes. Meanwhile, with their prisoners seated on the floor in their underwear, Lolita proceeded to wash the cups and make coffee on the spirit stove and produced bread and cheese from the wall cupboard. *'Comeis amigos,'* she exclaimed, 'eat . . . *mangez.'* Paco soon returned and he too sat down to eat as each kept watch outside. The others took the prisoners into the wood, sitting

them against young saplings, Vicente demonstrating how to tie them, feet bound first, then the hands behind the tree with a length of rope around the neck and down to the hands, so that if they struggled they choked themselves. He laughed as he worked and checked each prisoner's bonds, then, returning to the hut, he brought back blankets from the bunks to rap around them. Then he stood up and saluted them saying, *'Adios amigos, vayan con Dios.'* Dirk translated for Nigel, 'Goodbye and may God be with you.'

The driver meantime had gone to bring the lorry. When it arrived they all piled in and rumbled off towards the town, through streets unhindered, their red berets evident for anyone to see. Once out on the southern side, they approached a similar road block. The noise of the oncoming vehicle attracted the occupants of this second cabin, who spilled out across the road with rifles at the ready to halt them. Vicente, leaning over the driver's cab, pulled back the bolt and rammed a round up the spout, the others alongside him followed suit. The driver put his foot down on the accelerator and the lorry surged forward at speed. A shot rang out, followed by a salvo from the lorry. The vibration and jolting caused the shots to go wide, but it caused the opposition to cut for cover as they crashed through the barrier, shooting as they went and using the drums for cover once through. A few random shots pursued them, ricochetting off the drums and whining past overhead. Reaching a bend the driver pulled up. Lolita poked her head out of the cab and shouted, 'Vicente, *telefonos . . . cortalos.'* And she pointed to the wires by the roadside. Vicente got down and heaved a coil of rope over the wires, motioning to the others to help. Bringing the two ends together they heaved on the rope and severed the wires. Back on board Nigel commented, 'Good thinking that!' as they proceeded at a breakneck pace away from the town, conscious that the gunfire must have alerted some of the populace. Coming to a road junction to the left, where a sign said Pedroso del Rey, they decided to take it and after some eight kilometres another town loomed up.

By common consent as they were going through doubtful

territory, they then discarded the red berets but they passed through without incident except from a few street-corner loungers who cast enquiring glances in their direction. Next, the driver turned along a forked road signed Vellila del Rio Carrion. This traced the course of a river, where long, fairly straight stretches of road lay, and from thence drove to Garda over barren meseta. The driver stopped to fill up with diesel from one of the drums in the back and everyone took the opportunity to relieve themselves. Before reaching Saldano they stopped again at the entrances to the town. Lolita discarded her armoury, put on a knitted gaily-coloured tam o'shanter and strolled off into the town. Meanwhile the men dismounted, moved to the blind side of the vehicle from the road and rolled cigarettes, later producing wineskins from the cab and slaking their thirst. After what seemed an eternity Lolita returned. A brief conversation ensued with the men after which they all climbed back into the lorry and, within a few minutes, pulled up before a secluded tavern where Lolita indicated she had ordered a meal. Leaving Vicente and Paco to keep an eye on the lorry and give warning, should anything untoward occur, the rest ate and drank and exchanged places with those outside. All fed, Lolita paid the bill at which Dirk wondered who was supplying all the cash. Their own supply, acquired in London was still intact.

Back on the lorry once more, thankful for the break, they negotiated the town's streets and continued down a fairly good highway. Well beyond Salsano, they took a country road which led east. It was in bad repair, potholed and crumbling in parts, making progress slow. At the next stop, Dirk ventured a question to Lolita.

'Where are we going?' he asked. She replied, 'Burgos,' and then added, 'not know where *enemigos* are.' And holding up her red beret she said, *'Enemigos . . . requetes . . . monarchistas . . . por todas partes.'* And waved her arm to indicate the surrounding terrain. Dirk turned to Nigel. 'Get that?' he asked. 'Enemy territory . . . red berets . . . monarchists.'

Nigel pondered the information, then remarked casually, 'We appear to be up against liquorice allsorts, Dirk. Basques, monarchists, nationalists . . . it's all a bit confusing, what?' He then added after a pause, 'Ask her when we will reach any aerodrome with planes to fly?'

Dirk marshalled his few words of Spanish and asked, *'Aviones, donde?'*

'A Burgos,' she replied, *'probablemente.'*

Nigel, who was listening intently chipped in. 'How far Burgos?'

'Sesenta o setenta kilometros,' she replied, holding up six then seven fingers.

'Sixty or seventy,' prompted Dirk, 'that means another three hours at this slow rate.'

However, at Osorno just up the road a way, they joined a better highway and put on speed. The wineskins, which had been replenished at the last stop, were passed around together with freshly baked bread and eventually they slowed to a halt outside the grim-looking walls of Burgos itself. Again Lolita made the usual reconnoitre into the city to test the atmosphere there prevailing, returning later to give the OK after which they passed over the bridge and through the archways leading into the city.

Whilst Lolita was gone the ammunition boxes were once more covered and the drums placed on top. The three Spaniards, after locking the cab, wandered off, whilst Lolita signalled to the two British to follow her. She led them down winding alleyways along narrow streets between tall forbidding buildings and eventually to a hostal where she indicated they would spend the night. She introduced them to the owner as two English journalists who were going to cover the Civil War, and turning to Dirk, explained the change of role, which Dirk relayed to Nigel. On hearing this Nigel's face lit up and he said, 'Rightho! If we are to be reporters let's phone a report back home.'

'About what and where to?' asked Dirk in surprise at his outburst.

'Why? Home of course! Let someone know where we are. We can only try,' laughed Nigel.

Dirk thereupon approached Lolita, who was deep in

conversation with their hosts. *'Telefono . . . Inglaterra,'* he ventured.

The three Spanish looked at each other with concern and astonishment, following which a heated discussion took place which Dirk could not follow. Eventually Lolita turned to Dirk and said, 'Not from here . . . *mas tarde* . . . later, I take you.'

They were all three given rooms and shown the ablutions and services. The communal bathroom contained two cubicles with baths, two showers adjacent and opposite three toilets, one of which had the picture of a lady on the door as had one each of the other facilities.

'No segregation of sexes here,' commented Nigel, 'but I could do with a shower.'

Fitting deed to word they both showered in turn, Nigel first. Dirk, on completing his ablutions, emerged from the cubicle just as Lolita was coming out of the bathroom. They both hesitated, Dirk feeling and showing some embarrassment, but Lolita laughed and remarked, *'Tengo dos hermanos,* I have two brothers.' With that, holding her towel tight with both hands she tiptoed up and kissed Dirk on the lips. He, with his towel tucked in his waistline, took her shoulders and drew her close. She did not resist but footsteps down the corridor caused them to part and she retreated into her cubicle again. Dirk walked out past an incoming guest and returned to their room where Nigel was stretched out on his bed feigning sleep. He too assumed the horizontal under the covers and after musing upon the recent encounter sought the realms of sleep.

A loud knock on the door awakened them. Nigel, already awake, opened the door and there stood Lolita dressed for the street. She said, 'Come . . . see the city.' Dirk quickly dressed and they met her in the tiny lounge. She led them to a restaurant which overlooked the river which skirted the city walls, where she ordered cups of chocolate and some biscuit-type crunchies named *churros* which she dunked in her chocolate and ate. They followed suit and savoured the novel taste. Meanwhile she tried to chat in a mixture of languages accompanied by descriptive gestures which added meaning to the flow. She concluded her efforts with: 'We *mangere* at nine and a half hours tonight.' That was clear enough.

'Where?' Dirk queried.

'Al hostal,' she replied, 'not be late *verdad!'*

The difficulties encountered in intelligent conversation were growing and talk soon petered out by common consent. They paid the bill and strolled through the city streets, dim and dour under sparse lighting. The group aroused no curious eyes as Lolita finally took them inside the fortress-like cathedral, where, on entering she dipped her fingers in the font, crossed herself and genuflected to the distant high altar, leading them round the perimeter of the spiralling Teutonic pillars to the front of the choir stalls. Leaving them to the left of the reredos, she broke away and went to kneel in prayer in one of the rows of the nave. The two men moved on behind the high altar, conversing in low tones and admiring the reliquaries, returning to the main massive entrance doors where Lolita awaited them. Without remarks they passed into the night heading for supper. The meal over Lolita reminded them of the phone call. Once more in the street she pointed out a kiosk where, having obtained the numerals from Nigel she dialled, spoke and eventually handed the phone to Nigel. She and Dirk left the booth, slipping her hand through Dirk's arm as they drew away. Dirk felt the warmth of her body as she clung closely, looking into her eyes, but Nigel soon came from the phone and they parted once more.

'How was it?' asked Dirk.

'Pretty good,' rejoined Nigel, 'some crackling but I spoke to Dad before they cut us off. The money must have run out.'

The trio then sought the shelter of a secluded café and rounded off the late evening hours, playing poker dice which Lolita obtained from the waiter. She ordered anis and water, which they found palatable if strong. At midnight they reached their hostel which was locked. Clapping her hands loudly, a sound which echoed round the tall buildings, a uniformed watchman soon appeared carrying a large bunch of keys, with one of which he opened the door. Lolita tipped him. Dirk saw that he carried a short spear, and being curious asked why. Lolita stammered a little before replying. 'Eet is called a *chuzo,'* she said, 'for defence against *ladrones* . . . how you say, thieves.'

Dirk was satisfied but wondered at her unaccustomed hesitation. Bidding each other *'Buenas noches,'* they drifted to their various rooms and some eagerly welcome sleep. It had been a long, long trek.

Rudely awakened by the energetic knocks of Lolita some hours later, they breakfasted on coffee, rolls and jam, a sparse enough meal by English standards, but one to which they had grown accustomed, after which, all necessary ablutions dealt with, they once more sought out the lorry and were on their way. It was soon evident that Lolita had already been to the open market, the bakers, and bought supplies for the journey. Leaving the city by the same gateway and bridge by which they had entered, they turned north towards Miranda del Ebro which they reached after an hour. Accommodation for the two English was found and they were left with the knowledge that they were in a Republican town and that Lolita would return eventually, after excusing a somewhat hasty leave-taking.

Bidding farewell to their erstwhile companions-in-arms, they shook hands all round, embracing them after the custom of the country and regretfully, with some sense of loss, they watched the lorry roll away into the distance. A kind of desolation descended upon the pair who, after settling into their new abode, ventured out to stroll around the town. They made for a pavement café and sat in the window seats to watch the world go by, drinking coffee and cognac. They chatted and reminisced over the events of the past days until Nigel, never very sure that Dirk was at ease in his mind, ventured, 'Do you still have any regrets about coming?'

Dirk pondered the reply, gazing with unseeing eyes out beyond the windows. 'I get the feeling that I don't know what we're here fighting for,' he replied. 'Vicente and Paco seem to know. They are all for the elected government. Now, these *requetes* guys, they seem, from what I have gathered to be fighting for a restoration of the monarchy. Then there are the Basques who are fighting for independence largely. I get the feeling that I don't know who I am for or who I am supposed to be against.'

A pregnant silence followed until Nigel felt it was his turn to chip in. 'Well I'm for Nigel, that's for sure. Next I'm here to fly planes and put my training to use. I don't like Hitler and Mussolini and to me, Franco falls into the category. I don't complicate matters beyond that. I'm content to do the job to hand without the complications of politics.'

They pondered for a while until the silence between them was broken by a voice which said, 'Are you chaps British?' Startled from their reveries, they turned to see a tall middle-aged fellow standing expectantly by the table. Nigel spoke first, 'Yes, we're British,' he remarked.

'Ah, well my name's Carter, Ralph Carter. May I join you?' he continued.

'By all means,' replied Nigel, 'take a pew.' When the chap was seated he added, 'What brings you to these parts?'

'Ah, that's a long story,' countered Carter. 'I actually live in Spain and at the moment I'm heading for Barcelona. I'm an aero-engine technician currently engaged in importing engines.'

'The devil you are,' said Nigel, 'that's very interesting. We're . . .'

Dirk jumped in quick, before Nigel was able to say more. 'We're journalists covering the war for the British press,' he confided. 'He represents the *Mail* and I, the *Manchester Guardian.'*

Nigel's face registered all kinds of expressions but finally one of dawning realisation as to why Dirk had cut across his lines. So he added hastily, coming to Dirk's rescue, 'Yes we're especially assigned to cover the aerial activities, bombings and all that.'

'I can help you there,' offered the newcomer. 'There's an aerodrome beyond the town where planes are ferried from France for the Republican side for onward staging to battle zones. I could show you if you wished.'

'That's kind of you,' Dirk replied, 'but we already have a guide who is organising our assignments.'

'A Spanish press agent, I presume?' he continued.

'No, a commercial traveller,' chipped in Nigel, 'deals in mechanical ploughs, hails from Bilbao area,' he lied.

'Is he here with you in town?' Carter persisted.

Nigel was becoming irritated. 'No! Not now,' he said. 'Gone off peddling agricultural implements no doubt.'

'Care for a cognac?' asked Dirk in an attempt to switch the talk.

'Most kind of you, yes,' replied Carter. The cognacs brought, the conversation was switched to other matters. Eventually Dirk saw Lolita appear, coming up the street, her long strides and gay beret bobbing amongst the passers-by. She spotted them, made to cross, then seemed to change her mind and steered clear, coming to sit at a table to the rear of the café. Dirk waited a few minutes longer, then clapped his hands for the waiter and standing, paid the bill. They bade goodbye to Carter, exchanging trite remarks, and then left the building walking slowly.

'What did you make of that chap?' asked Nigel

'A bit nosey wasn't he?' asked Dirk.

'Too nosey if you ask me,' replied Nigel.

At the hostel Lolita caught up with them and promptly asked them to her room. They complied and once within and seated on the bed, she spoke.

'The man at the table is *espia* . . . a spy, yes?' she began. 'You must avoid him and tell him nothing.'

Her English was improving, thought Dirk. She then went to the case on a stand and extracting a piece of paper, made a drawing, which she presented to them saying, 'You stay in hostal *hasta* . . . until persons come and say *"cigueña",'* and pointing to the drawing she said, 'It is *cigueña.'* Nigel gazed at it and said, 'Ah a crane!'

'Nothing of the kind,' said Dirk, 'it's a stork, like those we saw on the meseta.'

'Same difference,' laughed Nigel, 'only smaller, mine.'

'Different colour,' argued Dirk, who prided himself on his

ornithology.

Turning to Lolita he said, 'And *tu, qué haces tu?*'

She raised her eyebrows and said, 'I go to General Rojo, *amigo de mi padre para ayudarle* . . . help him.'

Dirk's face showed its alarm and in French blurted out, *'A la guerre comme soldat?'*

'No, no,' she countered, '*escribire, ecrire,* write letters, courier, travel *por acqui y allá.'*

Dirk was suddenly aware that they were about to part from her. During their all too brief acquaintance much had happened and there had sprung up a camaraderie by which he set much store. His alarm showed in his face and she extended a hand to his cheek and murmured, '*No te preoccupes conmigo hombre* . . . not worry for me . . . I am *mujer . . . es mi pasaporte . . . mi salvo conducto.'*

Dirk at this, became a little agitated. Turning to Nigel he exclaimed, 'She says she's going to be courier to some General Rojo or other . . . sort of messenger crossing the battle lines. That's too damned dangerous for a woman, don't you think?'

Nigel leaned forward towards her and taking both her hands in his he raised them alternately to his lips and said, 'God go with you and *muchísimas gracias* for everything.'

A tear came into her eyes at this show of affection, but she shook her head to stem the rising tide of emotions and rapped out. 'We have much to discuss before we go,' and turning, opened the door and motioned them out, at the same time repeating, 'not to speak with Englishman . . . he is *malo* . . . dangerous for me, *comprendes?'*

They could not easily explain that they had told him they were journalists and put him off the scent as they did not have enough of the language, so they promised to watch out for him in future.

The following day Dirk found a bookshop and bought a Spanish-English dictionary, determined to master the language. Daily he studied with the help of a grammar lent him by Lolita. On the third day she bade them both goodbye and departed, after kissing and embracing them both. 'Great kid that,' exclaimed Nigel after she had gone, 'wish she were my sister. She's got guts and initiative. Good luck to her.'

Dirk did not comment. He felt empty and drained of enthusiasm for the task. They daily visited the restaurant but Carter never returned to accost them although they spotted him once or twice in the town. On the fifth day after Lolita's departure, whilst sitting sipping coffee in the café, the waiter brought them a folded piece of paper. Nigel opened it and read it, passing it to Dirk. There were four words in English 'THE STORKS ARE FLYING'. They glanced around but could see no-one who was interested in them. 'Strange!' commented Nigel.

'Curiouser and curiouser said Alice,' was Dirk's remark.

Dirk clapped his hands and the waiter came.

'Quien?' he asked.

The waiter looked cautiously up and down the street and around before motioning them to follow him. He led them through the café to a staircase by the kitchens and pointing upwards said, *'Arriba!'*

They mounted the stairs cautiously, coming to a corridor at the end of which was an open door. A disembodied voice of light quality called, 'Come in!' They entered to discover a very attractive lady seated at a desk. Nigel assumed her to be about in her mid-thirties. 'I am La Cigueña,' she began, 'and you are English airmen, yes? Which of you is Nigel?'

Nigel merely said, 'I am,'

'So you must be Dirk, then?' she remarked.

Dirk nodded assent.

'Very well. Tomorrow a car will call at your hotel at eleven a.m. promptly. You must be packed and ready in the foyer. Your account at the hostel will have been paid. You will recognise the driver by a patch over his left eye which he will remove on entering the hotel. You will then load your luggage into the car boot and sit in the car awaiting the driver, who will arrive five minutes later. Is that clear?'

'Perfectly,' remarked Nigel. Dirk repeated the details and ended with a question. 'Where will we be taken?'

'You will be taken to the Madrid front by a circuitous route.

That is all I can safely tell you,' she informed him. 'Now you must leave here but by the rear entrance because there is a man across the street who shadows you.'

Nigel arose and moved over to the entrance window and gazed out. 'It's that guy Carter again,' he remarked.

'Exactly,' confirmed the lady. 'Tomorrow he is due to meet with an accident which will take him out of circulation for a long time.'

With that she rose, a tall attractive elegant figure, saying, 'Follow me, I will show you the way to go.'

They shook hands. Dirk did not presume to ask her name which she had not proffered. Impressed by the authority in her voice and her calm demeanour they merely obeyed her behest, noting that in spite of her command of English she was betrayed by a slight accent and strange lilt.

14

Everything occurred as she stated and the morrow found them bowling along a road in filthy weather of rain, sleet and even snow towards Lograno and Zaragoza, following the course of a muddy river in spate, and thence by circuitous roads towards the outskirts of Madrid, approaching the city from the east. The terrain they covered was largely bleak and barren, a high meseta scrubland which extended until they reached a series of huge lakes, and which despite the intense cold which descended, afforded attractive woodland scenery and intensely breathtaking views. Despite the rough roads and the mud churned up by the wheels, they soon reached the town of Guadalajara, where the driver stopped for petrol, oil and water. Here the weather improved and a further short run brought them to an aerodrome a few kilometres north of Madrid at a place called Alcalà de Henares, Henares being the river which they had seen from the escarpment to the east.

They were received by a French air force officer who welcomed them and at the same time took them to the mess where they ate and drank. Next he conducted them to their quarters, which were spartan in the extreme with scrubbed floors, whitewashed walls, truckle beds and a narrow wardrobe and tiny desk with drawers. In the gathering dusk he showed them the assembly rooms, the different flight mustering points, and allocated them to their particular flights. Last he took them to the bar where he bought drinks and chatted to them in fairly good English about their assignments in the immediate future.

'Tomorrow you will meet the other pilots in your squadron.

In the meantime you must familiarise yourself with your bearings,' he concluded. He then left them to their own devices.

The following morning they walked out on to the aerodrome where there were dozens of planes scattered about the perimeter. Nigel pointed out the various types. There were Boeing Y16 fighters, Cartier Y15s with Natachas bombers spreadeagled in the waiting lanes. Spanish planes called Chatas and Ratas arrived from distant airfields to the south and west and soon the roads leading to and around the runways were thick with planes. As fuel was at a premium the two English got short shrift in practice flights in the Rata fighters before they were sent up on recces over enemy lines to the north and east with strict instructions not to engage enemy planes but merely to observe movements and report back. These flights gave them ample time to familiarise themselves with the handling of these craft. From conversations with other pilots and official personnel on the base, Dirk learned that in the course of a few days they would be required to assist in the repulse of a Nationalist advance towards Guadalajara which was being mounted by a concentration of Italian troops flanked by Spanish regulars and trained militia along the three roads flanking the railway and rivers, the main one of which was the River Henares. The objective was to cut the road between Madrid and Zaragoza. This had to be stopped at all costs.

Flight formations were allotted and instructions given by commanders of groups as to the modes of attack and the requisite signals. Maps were studied and the enemy positions and lines of advance indicated. The terrain was one of the wildest in Spain, a plateau of barren scrubland dotted with low deciduous oaks in parts, which gave little cover to armament and troops. The weather in the north towards Almazan and Soria where the Nationalist planes were now sited had seriously deteriorated, with heavy rains followed by sleet and snow, such that all but a few of their fighters and none of their bombers, consisting of Junkers and Savoias, could become airborne. Not so near Madrid, some thousand feet lower in altitude, where bombers were taking off regularly, escorted by Chatas and Ratas, to strafe the enemy airstrips practically unopposed. This was the signal to press back the mistimed and ill-planned Italian three-pronged attack towards Brihuega and Jadraque.

Came the day when Nigel and Dirk swept down the runway in company with four other fighters with pilots from the international brigade, one French, two Belgian and a Hungarian. They formed a skein of one-two-three as they flew east by north. In twenty minutes they were approaching the target. The river Henares, which was in spate because of the rains, gleamed white below, guiding them towards the three river valleys beyond Guadalajara. Here the two Belgians peeled off towards Jadraque, a manoeuvre repeated by Nigel and Dirk at the road junction which led toward Brihuega. The flight leader with the Hungarian followed the main road north eastwards to Almadrones. The two English were now on their own, Nigel leading. They reached Brihuega and the river Tajuna which ran parallel to the road and which wound like a serpent through the valley, making flying difficult with the tight twists and turns of the ravine. Sighting the lines of enemy armament strung out along the roads Nigel signalled a shallow dive towards the massed targets. It was bitterly cold. Dirk's hands were numbing and he found it difficult enough to keep his plane on course without having to release the small bombs under the wings and perhaps strafe at the same time. He knew the Boeings were following with their heavier bombs. Their own job was to cause havoc at the head of the columns and hinder the movement of vehicles and tanks and present the bombers with sitting targets. Dirk saw Nigel release his first rack of bombs and pull out of the ravine in a flanking upwards twist. Dirk lined up his craft and seeing a short stretch of road on which several tanks were spaced, he too released his first rack and pulled upwards in a steep roll as the mountain side approached. Clearing the summit, he gazed around the skies for Nigel but Nigel, anticipating Dirk's moves, had lined himself up on Dirk's tail and, when passing, signalled a second run, this time down the valley. They came in low, jinking along the twists in the upper valley until they spotted the tail of the convoy below. They released their second racks which they hoped would do enough damage to make any attempt at retreat by the ground forces difficult. Streaming out at the road junction, having glanced at the damage at the lower end of the column, Nigel pointed to the bombers coming in to effect a heavier drop. They were unescorted, by which Dirk assumed that enemy fighters could not take off. Nigel signalled a third run, circling wide to follow the Boeings in. They dropped their loads from high levels so as not to have the problem of the valley twists. Nigel, seeing the results of the drop, flew low and commenced strafing, Dirk following him down. The heavy bombs had created havoc among the vehicles both on and off the road, where personnel were running around like ants, black in the snow which had fallen.

They turned as before to reverse the run, repeating the strafing as they followed the curvatures of the roads. A glance at the fuel gauges showed Dirk that it was time to head for home. They came in to land after circling the airfield with the fuel gauges almost touching zero. The ground crews rushed up as they climbed out of the cockpits to report to the base commander. The rest of their flight straggled back like homing pigeons, the two Belgians showing signs of flak along wings and fuselage. Their reports induced a flutter of activity as they reported no opposition in the air. Within two hours and following other mounted raids they were in the air again, this time to a specified target along the main highway N.11, where the Italian armour seemed to be concentrated. The results were most effective as Dirk observed the chaos below, coupled with the severe weather conditions prevailing and taking into account the reports of their sparse clothing, entirely unsuitable for the sudden deterioration in the climate. They were sitting ducks with no air cover.

Plans were laid for the following day to press home this fortuitous advantage. Additional planes were committed to the attack but by this time the enemy below had mounted anti-aircraft weapons and several of the Republican planes were shot down. Moreover, one or two Messerschmidt fighters had appeared and were joining the air circus and taking their toll. Plans to bomb their bases, which were still waterlogged, and grounding their bombers were mounted with disastrous results for the Nationalists. Meanwhile the ground troops went into action to add to the discomfiture upon the roads and to capture as many of the enemy vehicles as possible. General Beimler, commanding the International Brigades, took every advantage of the enemy's distress and gradually the Italians abandoned their advance and retreated leaving armament, ammunition, artillery and guns in plenty. What had begun as a determined advance upon Guadalajara had become a rout. It was evident that the Italians were unaccustomed to the dreadful conditions and had become trapped by their own folly. The attack on their retreating forces continued relentlessly for almost two weeks, during which the Italian armour was decimated. The temperature fell to two degrees below zero and blizzards added to the confusion, blotting out landmarks for planes and no doubt giving a slight respite to the enemy on the ground, who must have been perishing with cold and frostbite, with no protection against the bitter weather and wearing clothing totally unsuited to the ravages of winter. Dirk had seen them, whilst engaged in low-level strafing, clad in the same gear they had worn all the summer long. Prisoners were coming in wearing rope-soled shoes with canvas uppers, cotton uniforms almost threadbare, and little else. The Italian contingents were slightly better attired than the Spanish infantry, but grovelling and digging-in in the snows to escape the destruction which rained down on them from above must have been scarifying. By 7th January Teruel had surrendered and a considerable bulge had pushed forward into the enemy positions.

During the lull which followed the rout of the Italians and Nationalists Nigel and Dirk were given leave, which they spent in Barcelona where they were fêted by the local populace. Returning from leave, they were continuously engaged in recces over enemy lines and in escorting bombers, attacking

Franco's lines and airstrips. This involved them in skirmishes and dog-fights with enemy Heinkels and Messerschmidts and Dirk had to learn his craft at the business end. Nigel revelled in the aerial combats, throwing his plane around the skies with professional skill. He accounted for many enemy losses whilst Dirk was more concerned with keeping his plane intact and avoiding engagements than seeking trouble by attacks. As the weather improved and the visibility extended he could not avoid the attentions of the pursuit planes and he too, like Nigel, executed a successions of unorthodox aerobatics which not only caused him to black out but caused him to break out into cold sweats.

It was not long before Franco mounted a counter-attack against the Republicans to the north of Teruel around Alfambre and Vivel del Rio. The Republican troops were now on the defensive, fighting a costly retaining action which crumbled before the regulars who were flung in to regain their previously lost ground. Their air support was now most active and Nigel and Dirk spent much time engaging fighter cover for enemy bomber raids and mounting dog-fights against enemy planes strafing the ground forces. Although Dirk now threw his plane about the skies with the skill of a veteran, the enemy were just as skilful. Twice Dirk's plane was crippled, limping home on a coughing engine and a prayer. On another occasion he had to bring all his gliding techniques into play as his engine cut out, stuttered, then died and he found the earth rushing up to meet him. Choosing what appeared to be a long straight stretch of road ahead, he adjusted his quickly falling approach and praying that the road was not full of deep pot-holes, as were many of the Spanish highways, he dived towards it, pulling up the nose at the last minute to execute a hard and very bumpy landing, which caused the plane to shudder as it rolled along the uneven surface. Half way along the wing caught a roadside tree, which spun the plane round and pitched it nose down in the roadside ditch, Dirk executing a neat parabola into the prickly scrub beyond. He landed heavily on his shoulder, his face lacerated by the prickly spines of the low hedges into which he had dived. With a whoosh and a roar his plane leapt into flames, from the sudden heat of which Dirk made a painful but hasty retreat. A pall of dense black smoke arose and drifted eastwards. Dirk limped away down the road and sat on a rock out of range. A plane dived out of the skies towards the burning wreck to tilt and veer away with a deafening surge of power. As it passed the pilot waved. It was Nigel, who banked and made a slower run at low level, waving and pointing towards the east. Dirk interpreted the meaning as having been spotted and that help would be on its way, but as for walking eastwards, Dirk, with a twisted knee and useless shoulder, thought it better to stay put. As he sat, he brooded on the fact that they had lost thirty planes in the last few days. They would soon be well outnumbered in the air. After resting an hour he decided to try to limp along the verges which he managed to do with frequent rests. Eventually a car approached in the distance and rolled to a stop beside him. A Spanish infantry officer dressed in uniform shouted, 'Get in!' Dirk obeyed with difficulty. The officer reversed his car and set off back along the highway. Dirk spoke first, '*Muchísimas gracias!*' he exclaimed.

'That's OK cobber,' came the response. 'No need to speak the lingo. I'm an Aussie.'

'How do you come to have picked me up?' queried Dirk.

'Telephone message,' barked out the Aussie, 'from some pilot johnny.'

'Must have been Nigel,' mused Dirk.

'Who's Nigel?' asked the Aussie.

'My side-kick . . . he's a pilot too in our outfit . . . spotted me go down an hour or so ago. Must have used his head for once,' added Dirk smiling and wincing.

During the drive they discussed the war. 'We're losing this round, mate,' commented the Aussie. 'I'm with Vicente Rojo, one of the commanders of the International Brigade. I'm one of his aides. Name of Predergast . . . our HQ is about five miles down this road. That's where I'm taking you. You'll be picked up and taken back from there.'

'My name's Waldron,' replied Dirk, 'English schoolmaster turned pilot.'

'You seem to be in pain,' observed the Aussie.

'I am. I've busted my shoulder I think, probably the collar bone by the symptoms, and I've a twisted knee and a badly bruised ankle, too.'

'What about those cuts and scratches on your face?' asked the Aussie.

'Got thrown out when it pitched and I landed in the thorn bushes . . . very unpleasant spines those bushes have.'

'We'll fix you up temporarily at HQ. We boast a jolly good quack . . . a Scotsman. Likes his liquor . . . man after my own heart,' laughed Predergast.

They soon reached HQ.

'Place is called Allepuz . . . some nice country round here too when the weather is good,' commented the Aussie, waving a hand towards some wooded hillsides. 'Here's the sick-bay, chum,' and he pulled up in front of a villa set in ornamental gardens. Dirk descended painfully, holding on to his useless arm and limping towards the steps to the main entrance, the Aussie, preceding him to open the door.

'I'll whistle up the doc,' he called as he proceeded down the corridor, waving Dirk towards a vacant armchair in a side room. Dirk lowered himself into it, feeling sadly worse for wear and not a little sick. The doctor arrived and pulling up a stand-chair sat opposite.

'What can we do for you?' he asked gently.

Dirk explained what had happened and what was amiss with his torso. The doc rose and asked Dirk to follow him to the surgery where, when Dirk had stripped off, he placed a pad under his damaged arm and strapped it to his side. He next treated the cuts and scratches on Dirk's face, examined his knee and ankle and bandaged those too. That done he produced a bottle of brandy, pouring out a stiff shot some three fingers in depth into a tumbler.

'Here, put yourself outside that till we find you some food. Are you hungry?'

'Well,' said Dirk, 'I'd make short shrift of a Lancashire

hotpot, but I don't think you'll have that on the menu.'

'Better than that,' replied the Scot, 'how about some pork chops, with apple sauce, chips and mixed veg?'

'You're kidding,' laughed Dirk. 'I haven't seen a decent meal for a month.'

Sure enough, the meal appeared as described within the hour and Dirk wolfed it down as though it might be his last for some time. Red wine, cheese, French bread, coffee and more brandy rounded it off. Dirk expressed his gratitude. 'Now,' said the doctor, 'we're going to give you a thorough examination with X-rays and a few injections. One for tetanus, one for typhoid, which I don't think you've had so far, and one to knock you out for a time.'

'That's cheerful,' remarked Dirk, grinning a little painfully now that his face was stiffening up, 'and how long do I remain here? I have a job to do, you know.'

'Answer to first, not very long. Answer to second part, you won't be flying for some considerable time yet. Inside a few weeks you should be back on form.'

Dirk submitted to the treatment and before blacking out for the second time that day, he thanked the doctor for his help and hospitality.

'There's an ambulance coming for you and you'll wake up near your airstrip. I've written the details down for delivery to the squadron medics so you need have no further worries.'

Dirk felt the voice fade, saw the lights dim and blacked out once more.

He awoke in strange surroundings to see Nigel sitting by his bed, cheerful as ever. He listened whilst Nigel related all that had happened whilst Dirk had been unconscious. 'We lost fifty planes yesterday, some shot down, some ditched in enemy territory and many returned shot up and unfit for service for some time . . . so you won't be required to fly in any case; we haven't enough planes to share amongst the remaining pilots.'

'How did you come to lose so many?' asked Dirk.

'Between you and me and the bedpost a lot of the new

intake are too inexperienced. It's sheer suicide sending them up,' he muttered through his teeth, at the same time looking around to see if anyone was overhearing, 'and it's bad for the ground troops, having inadequate cover.'

They discussed the battle and Dirk could sense the misgivings which Nigel had about the conduct of the war . . . . His words proved to be prophetic, for within six weeks or so, when Dirk was almost ready to fly again, they pulled out of the Alfambra front and retreated to the north. Teruel fell on 18th February, leaving the way to the Mediterranean coast wide open for Franco to attack the coastal cities. What the Republican forces had gained when putting the Italian army to flight, they had subsequently lost, with disastrous consequences for the outcome of the war.

The remaining ground troops retreated north of the Ebro river where they were going to make a stand. The river offered a natural line of defence and all the remaining ten divisions, the cavalry, the tanks and batteries, together with a goodly supply of planes from all other sources within range were deployed.

Franco did not seem to be in any great hurry to engage as it was patently obvious that he had the advantage. The weakness of the Republicans was in the lack of continuity of supplies of every description. Franco, as a professional, had systematically captured, in various parts of the country, the armament factories, the supply lines by both land and sea. Moreover he was assured of a plentiful supply of planes from both Germany and Italy. The democratic countries were now blowing cold as to support of the Government side for even Dirk and Nigel could see that there was considerable disunity amongst the Republicans about the aims in view. Boats, brought from Barcelona, were massed on the banks of the Ebro in preparation for a swift decisive counter-attack. By the end of July all appeared to be in readiness. The recces by fighter planes had given the generals the full picture of the enemy deployment but they had also reported the massing of aircraft by Franco.

On 25th July, under cover of darkness, the Ebro was

crossed. The surprise attack disconcerted the enemy for a time and a deep but narrow penetration was effected, supported in the daytime by fighter and bomber. The two English pilots were kept busy, but they were told to break off any dog-fights because of the deficiencies of aircraft and the lack of future replacements. To their disgust, Nigel and Dirk had to cut and run on sighting the approach of enemy fighters with the result that the ground forces were left to the untender mercies of the enemy bombing might. The position of Guadalajara was now reversed for it was fairly obvious to Nigel that they would not be able to hold such a narrow salient, as they had failed to fan out after crossing the Ebro. The infantry was caught between the jaws of a vice beyond the river. Franco allowed the penetration, knowing full well that he could stop it by the simple device of opening the sluices further up the river and thus preventing any reinforcements from crossing to aid those already in his noose. Rojo, the brilliant Spanish general of the Republican forces, urged that a diversionary landing down the coast at Motril might detach and deflect considerable opposing forces thither. The strategy was brilliantly conceived and if implemented might have had the desired effect and changed the odds, but the civilian War Minister did not sanction the plan and thus passed up the one chance of saving Cataluña from falling into Nationalist hands. Added to all this the International Brigade, realising that, apart from a miracle, the war was lost, began to disperse and fade away, sickened also by the demoralisation setting in amongst the Spanish conscripts, who were little more than boys, totally untrained. Attacks were beginning to be pressed home half-heartedly and counter-attacks were met with a resistance. Moreover, desertions were becoming more frequent and punishments meted out for misdemeanours were growing severe. Casualties of infantry were heavy and by December, so close to the Pyrenees, the weather was closing in. One could feel the general malaise of demoralisation creeping up and round and in, like a relentless tide.

Meanwhile Tarragona fell to the Nationalists, followed in January by Barcelona, the principal supply base in Spain.

Many Republican generals and commanders, particularly those of Spanish rank, sensing the end quite near, fled to France. Franco's northern armies cut all supply routes this side of the Pyrenees. The few remaining planes were kept in the air by cannibalising the damaged ones and were totally outnumbered and no match for the overwhelming opposition of Cadernas, Fiats and Heinkels thrown into the battle by Franco. There followed a shortening of the front by a general retreat to the Pyrenees where they were boxed in. It was at this stage that Nigel and Dirk resolved that enough was enough. Putting their heads together, they resolved to hijack one of the planes and fly it to Perpignan where they knew there was an aerodrome which had been used as a staging post for delivery of French fighters.

15

Once the Minister for War in Madrid had vetoed the plan of General Rojo to mount a diversionary invasion on the Mediterranean coast to draw off Franco's forces from the northern front, the battle was virtually lost and defeat inevitable. Apart from a holding action and some desperate isolated forays into enemy held territory, few knew who was organising what, and for what purpose. Nigel's scheme to hijack a plane and pull out was forestalled, however, when the English pilots and the French and Belgians were summoned to military HQ for briefing, at the behest of Rojo himself. Rojo, as everyone knew had fought a brilliant war against organised trained troops with little else except a conscript army and the International Brigades. His political superiors had ignored the expert advice with the result that he was now forced to fight a battle which he knew he could not win. He frankly stated his reasons for ending the strife, well knowing his superiors in Madrid were about to sue for peace. So as not to cause a general alarm and confusion he resolved to stay with his troops to the last, but in that event he needed planes to stand by to evacuate his principal officers in the field and his staff to France. He enquired if Nigel had ever flown bombers or transport planes and got an affirmative. Dirk had no such training and said so. The other foreign pilots stated their skills and plans were drawn up to fly out to Perpignan with the consent of the French authorities when the moment for departure arrived.

The moment arrived earlier than expected, but the planes were already serviced and ready to fly. Dirk was to help give fighter cover. Nigel was to fly transport bombers with personnel and baggage. Staff cars began to roll into the airstrip with officers from all parts of the front. Dirk strolled past these to his Rata ready to take the air. As he buttoned up his flying suit and checked his maps, a voice from alongside one of the cars hailed him by name. He turned to look. It was Lolita in totally unfamiliar uniform. She ran towards him and they involuntarily embraced. There were tears in her eyes when Dirk announced, *'C'est fini . . . terminado la guerra.'*

'Es una lástima,' she sobbed. 'I go to France . . . *je suis desolée.'*

Dirk put his free arm around her shoulders to comfort her. *'Somos vivos, verdad?'* he encouraged, *'ánimo, chica!'*

'Ah you now speak Spanish, yes?' she cried. *'Me alegro.'*

'Sí, ahora sí. He tenido que apprender. Muchas frases y palabras,' he added.

'Very good,' she smiled through her tears, 'after war you come to *finca* . . . to farm, yes? I go there some day, *no sé cuando* . . . not know when.'

'I too am going to France . . . *me voy a Francia ahora mismito con vosotros.'*

'This minute?' she echoed,' with us? *Que suerte* . . . what luck!'

'Nigel . . . he fly transport,' and he pointed out the bomber on the runway. 'I protect him from enemy.'

Lolita clapped her hands in ecstasy.

He had no further time to spare for with a roar and a screaming dive the enemy planes punctuated his final words just in time to fling Lolita to the ground and unceremoniously roll her under the nearest car. Two fighters from the farther runway took off in pursuit, followed by two more and soon the sky was streaked with ribbons of vapour trails which dispersed into arching spiral loops. A snarling dog-fight developed with the crescendo and diminuendo of whining, over-strained engines. A Heinkel III streaked by, chased by a couple of Chatas. A Fiat dived to assist the Heinkel, spitting raking fire which splattered the runway. As each stalked the other with loops and turns the enemy dived for ground cover and disengaged. To the west a Rata was harrassing a bomber from which smoke was pouring. You could hear the short, quick rattle of machine gun fire.

The sudden attack was over and Dirk gazed round to survey the damage. Two of the bombers in the waiting area were burning. They would have to be replaced. One or two of the fighters on the perimeter were leaning over drunkenly. Lolita slowy got to her feet.

'Time your boss got out of here,' said Dirk in English.

She failed to understand and Dirk could make her no wiser as he ran to inspect his own craft for damage. The raid had been costly but his plane was intact, ready to roll. Normally the fighters would have been patrolling over the base and on the approaches but the chronic lack of fuel prevented even this simple precaution.

Personnel began to spill out of the buildings into the cars directed by ground staff to waiting planes to board. Nigel had his engines warming up. Dirk climbed aboard and flashed up his own, checking the dials and flaps. Anxious to be off, he looked back to see if Nigel was moving. They were closing the doors and he was rolling forwards to the runway. His would be a long take-off. His supply of fuel was minimal, sufficient only for the flight, with a margin for emergencies. He wondered which plane would carry Lolita.

Four bombers rumbled down the flight path with a deep sonorous roar, followed by eight fighters which, when airborne splayed out to guard the flanks. They all converged over the coast and took up flight formation, fighters above and below, quartering the skies like ranging dogs. Dirk sat on the tails of the transports which turned to port on leaving the coast, and set course for the airstrip at Perpignan. The flight was brief and he was soon following the heavies down to cover their landing pulling away and soaring skywards when he saw the last one safely grounded. The fighters then formed a line ahead and with tight precision dived for the now clear runway, zooming in with practised artistry, mainly to impress the French reception party. Ground staff signalled them to the waiting lanes on the far perimeter opposite the control tower.

Three cars pulled up to take them in as Dirk retrieved his precious cargo of confidential papers to hand to Rojo. As a gesture of farewell Dirk gave his fighter a pat on the fuselage, a pat of gratitude and congratulations for services rendered and together with his squadron leader climbed into the jeep alongside. 'Now for a long period of internment,' thought Dirk.

No word was spoken. There were too many mixed emotions. Dirk's fears proved groundless, however, for as Pierre got out of the car a high ranking French Air Force officer rushed forward to embrace him, kissing him on both cheeks, uttering cries of welcome as though he were a long-lost brother. 'Probably he is,' mused Dirk.

The driver prompted Dirk towards a low brick building and as he too approached the entrance a figure ran out to embrace him also. It was Lolita. Weighted down as he was with parachute and the precious cargo he carried, he was unable to reciprocate, so he dropped his load and held her close as though afraid she would disappear. Disentangling at last, they entered the building where a reception party was in full flow. Dirk looked around for Nigel. The crowd was dense and milling about, the noise of the chatter almost deafening.

'Where is Nigel?' shouted Dirk above the din.

'*No sé. . .* don't know,' replied Lolita.

'*Estara con las botellas, yo juro,*' laughed Dirk, 'with the bottles.'

They elbowed their way towards the bar on the far side and there he was, sure enough, the bottle to his lips and waving it about in between as if in ecstasy. They crept up on him and Dirk slapped him on the back, causing him to choke. Nigel turned, coughing and spluttering, and on recognising his assailants threw his arms around them, bottle and all, and executed a jig. Before releasing them he began singing in off-pitch tones:

'Allons enfants de la Patrie
la bloody guerre est terminée'

Out of deference to Lolita who was now an exile he did not pursue the theme but lifted her up and placed her on the bar, thrusting into her hand a spare glass and pouring the contents of a bottle into it. *'Brindes!'* he called, swinging his own bottle. 'May your shadow never grow less.' Putting down his bottle he picked her off the counter and swung her round, until she begged to be put down. They spoke inanities in their relief at being on neutral ground.

After the Lord Mayor's Show, however, the realities of life began once more to emerge. Documentation, passports, details of currency, allocation of accommodation, transport, escorts and all the paraphernalia of diplomatic jargon and ritual. Their baggage began to be brought in from the bombers. Dirk and Nigel collected theirs. The customs search was informal and nominal, just a check for arms and ammunition. Nigel, as usual with malice aforethought, had secreted a Biretta in his flying boot and ammunition for it in the other. Being English they received preferential treatment. The pilots were then mustered in one corner where a Spanish paymaster dealt out wads of paper money in lieu of paying them off, adding a few French franc notes for immediate use. Nigel wondered whether the Spanish money would be accepted as legal tender, so he desisted the temptation to count it and stuffed the notes in his breast pocket. He still had a wad of English fivers stowed away in the lining of his flying jacket. Dirk examined his blood-money and decided that they had been over-generous. They returned to the bar, ordering more drinks, Nigel saying, 'Eat, drink and be merry, for tomorrow, who knows?' It was typical of Nigel's philosophy, the carefree Bohemian type, mostly unflappable.

Lolita had been whisked away with the Spaniards. The French pilots and mercenaries were free to leave after documentation. They could go home wherever that was in France. As for the other nationalities, they were transferred to hotels in town.

The following day was scorching hot. They discarded their uniforms for less formal wear. Dirk then realised that his waistline was thicker, much to his disgust. The question about their future came up in the conversation. Nigel had obviously already pondered it. 'I'll phone the old man to transfer some cash out here to a local bank,' he announced as an opening gambit. 'After that we can make definite plans.'

Matching deed to word he despatched a cablegram and they awaited results. Three days later the money came, £500 worth in francs.

'See?' laughed Nigel waving the notes aloft, 'pennies from heaven. We're laughing old chap.'

'Yeah, that's OK,' chipped in Dirk, 'but I've only that Spanish rubbish and a few quid besides.'

'Not to worry, old chap! I got you into this, I'll get you out. Half of this is yours, I insist . . . a loan if you like it better that way,' he hastily added as he read Dirk's face.

'OK, a loan it is. How about getting back to the UK? Any ideas?'

'Hitch hike, old boy, hitch hike. See the country *en route.* Sleep under the stars like the gipsies. Spring's here, warm weather and all that. *Nil desperandum.* Give us a smile!'

Dirk grinned. 'You're incorrigible, Nigel,' he said.

After a week's open detention the French authorities gave them the necessary papers to enable them to travel home. They held the promised council to decide the moves. Nigel's opening remarks stunned Dirk.

'What about our Lolita?' said Nigel in measured tones.

'What about Lolita?' echoed Dirk.

'Well, we owe her, you know, and we ought to help.'

'You surprise me, Nigel. Didn't think you cared so much.'

'Oh, I've a soft spot for that young lady, Dirk. She has got guts and talent. She's not just a pretty shepherdess of Dresden china.'

'How can we help her now?' deprecated Dirk.

'Two suggestions, my moonstruck friend. One, her repatriation. Two, take her with us.'

'But General Rojo will see her right. He is a personal friend of old Domingo her father, remember. They were once comrades-in-arms.'

'Ah! But Rojo did not come to France with us. He decided at the last minute to stay to supervise the surrender of his men. A good soldier, that one.'

'Then we have no choice. We must act.'

'I thought you'd say that,' said Nigel. 'Right. The question arises, how?'

'Four options,' proffered Dirk,'road, rail, air or sea.'

'Let's analyse your theses,' pontificated Nigel, all banter gone and the true Nigel surfacing. 'Our names will soon be known to the Nationalists and could be on lists already at the frontiers. That makes road and rail a high risk. By air is practically impossible, unless we can nick a seaplane, and they are as plentiful as snowflakes in hell. So we are left with the sea. What do you know about the sea?'

'Damn all,' grunted Dirk. 'River craft, yes, but the briny, not a sausage.'

'Let us then ponder upon the subject of canoes,' suggested Nigel archly.

'I don't see any point in discussing canoes in this regard,' countered Dirk. 'She lives up in the mountains behind Ribadesella, remember, and that part is some eighty miles along the coast of northern Spain from France.'

'And what separates Irun at the other end of the Pyrenees from Hendaye in France, my dear friend?' pursued Nigel.

'A river . . . a fast flowing river with a tricky tideway, if I remember my geography,' hedged Dirk.

'And how wide do you imagine that river is?' pressed Nigel.

'I don't really know, do you?' replied Dirk.

'Yes I do. Went there for a holiday. Swam there as a boy. Could stand up in the water most of the way across at low tide.' A silence followed this piece of information.

'How do we know that she will want to go home just now?'

'We don't. We assume it, knowing her character and resilience.'

'Where do we get canoes, then?'

'No problem. We could "half-inch" them. They are two a

penny there. Most kids use them in the tideway.'

'Suppose the Frogs refuse to release her from restrictive parole here?'

'They won't.'

'Why do you say that?'

'She's a woman, a very attractive woman, and the French have a soft spot for a damsel in distress, especially where romance is concerned.'

'You've lost me,' chipped in Dirk.

'You haven't, you know, because you have the answer. You will make it widely known that you are her fiancé and you wish to marry her. That way she becomes a British citizen and, hey presto, she's released.'

'Hold on, hold on, Nigel, who said anything about marriage? There's Naomi, you know. How do you get around that snag?'

'Two solutions. One, you can say you were married in Spain and the documents are lost. Or, we can forge a marriage certificate, given time. Or, we can fake a marriage.'

'Your imagination is running away with you, Nigel,' Dirk commented. 'Too much cognac and a highly induced euphoria.'

'No! Seriously, Dirk. If you don't do it, I will. I hardly think you'll agree to that. Look, seriously, we can explain it all to Lolita. We either fake a wedding or forge a certificate. If you ask me, the first is easier.'

'You win, Nigel . . . so let's get down the nitty-gritty, the nuts and bolts.'

'Now you're talking. The Frog squadron leader will help us I feel sure. Leave that to me.'

16

Nigel ferreted out the French pilot and explained the dilemma to him. He was sold on the idea; thought it a huge joke. He suggested a doddery old priest in charge of a village church. They could grease his palm. Lolita was taken into their confidence and after much delicate persuasion, for she wasn't altogether happy about the scheme, she complied. Nigel found an interpreter who concocted the passionate love story and permission to arrange a marriage was granted. They conned the old priest to show them the necessary documents and, having plied him with cognac, whilst his back was turned, pinched one. They found a wedding dress for Lolita and borrowed a suit for Dirk. The whole thing had to look genuine. They strolled to the church and once there explained to the priest that the wedding had been called off. He was too old to mind and as Nigel had seen to it that the priest had been well oiled in stomach and palm, he even got him to sign a receipt for the fees. With his signature they completed the already filled-in marriage certificate with the help of the squadron leader who, with Nigel, signed as a witness, and the certificate, once presented and accepted by the authorities, Lolita was acknowledged a British citizen by them and released from restricted parole.

They cleared the town the same day just in case anything untoward occurred and caught a bus as far as Pau, and the following day to Hendaye-plage. There, once accommodation had been found, they studied the French holidaymakers boating, surfing and canoeing in the river's tideway. They then acquired a list of the tides, explored boat-hire possibilities, bought charts, studied the phases of the moon, listened intently to weather forecasts. Finally, having sifted the data, they picked on a date for a night crossing. They christened it 'Operation Moonlighter'. Nigel eventually came up with a better plan. Why not get one of the local fishermen to take them and their canoes as far as the fishing grounds off the Spanish coast near Bermeo, it having a sheer, rocky coastline and a headland with a lighthouse for a leading light? Nigel conned a fisherman, spinning, through an interpreter, the usual romantic yarn about thwarted love, and he agreed to cooperate. He even made suggestions as to the best night, for he informed them that the Spanish fisherfolk seldom fished from midday Saturdays to afternoon on the Sunday and, as the night was only about four hours long at that time of year, they would need a passage free of shipping. He promised to take them in as near as he dare inside the three mile limit. Meanwhile, they exercised in acquired canoes, planned the supplies and necessary gear, bought inflatable life-jackets, fishing lines and hooks, a powerful torch and two smaller ones for signalling and Nigel even called his father for more funds, which came.

On the longest day of the year they put to sea in the drifter at high tide and sailed out into Biscay, the canoes under wraps on the deck. The afternoon sky was cloudless. They sailed over a blue sea lifting with a slight swell, a heat haze over the water. The skipper said he would make eight knots and Nigel calculated that they would be in position to launch the canoes by sunset. Everything went according to plan and midnight saw them paddling steadily without undue fuss towards the light on Cape Machichaco.

They paddled in line abreast so as to keep each other in sight. Their paddles flashed fluorescent in the water. Every quarter of an hour they rested for five minutes and listened out for other craft. None was heard. They had a clear run. By 0130 hours they were under the beetling cliffs and passing the lighthouse, paddling westwards in line ahead, Nigel leading, Dirk as tail-end Charlie and Lolita in between. Dirk occasionally directed his powerful torch against the cliff sides and ahead to avoid any outcrop of rocks. As the dawn came up they moved in closer to the cliffs to gain cover and in the broad light of a Sunday dawn reached Grecho, where they beached. They hauled their canoes above the high water mark, made a fire of driftwood and ate a cold breakfast washed down with wine. There they slept until noon with the warm sun soothing their tired muscles.

They were awakened by Sunday trippers, some of which were curious about the canoes. Lolita, using the regional dialect of Asturias, explained they were going to a canoeing competition and engaged them in conversation to dispel any suspicions they might have harboured. Fires on the beaches and picnics at weekends were common anyway. The men feigned sleep. In the late afternoon a few yachts put to sea and fishermen left harbour. Launching their craft once more they proceeded towards Urdiales as agreed, having studied the maps. They were hailed occasionally by pedaloes and the dinghy types, but Lolita used her dialect and no suspicions arose.

They arrived at their destination by sunset, having rested and eaten along the route. Once more they found a sheltered spot and dragged their craft up the beach above high water mark. They caught some sleep in the warm sand dunes and after the picnickers and all retreated, they took to the sea once more, hugging the coast and eventually reached the fishing port of Noja on an isolated stretch of coast. Here they held a conference. They needed better food to maintain their strength. As of old, Lolita volunteered to reconnoitre and discovered a dockside tavern where they could eat. Nigel volunteered to stay with the boats whilst she and Dirk dined and later the two men would change places until Nigel had been fed. Their luck was being stretched to breaking point and once all back at the canoes, Lolita suggested that in view of the fact that the shipping might be denser on their next planned leg, which was across Santander Bay, they might consider another plan she had in mind. She would attempt to find a lorry or van to take them and their gear to Unquerra some fifty miles along the coast, on the pretext that they were competing in a regatta and they had been delayed. They all approved and a van was eventually found, the driver of which, for a consideration, would take them as far as Unquerra. There Lolita was on home ground, for she directed the driver to a farmstead to the rear of the town where she knew the owners and they could obtain further assistance. The driver was paid off and dismissed.

Some thirty-odd miles now separated Lolita from home. Another consultation was necessary. To walk or not to walk, that was the question. The Picos de Europa reared high above their heads. To cross them was another matter. Lolita's home lay on the other valley to the west. To go by main road was risky. Los Picos were as familiar to Lolita as the Pennines were to Dirk. It was high summer. They could live off the land, game and fish in plenty. Bread for three days, subsequent supplies from isolated farms, Nigel's Biretta, three wineskins yet to purchase . . . no problem, and a minimum of suitable clothing. With these they could survive, moving along the high ground out of sight. One snag was the *Guardias* who patrolled those upper regions. Lolita gave a warning piece of advice. If anyone asked the two men where they were going, they were to say only one word, 'Covadonga' and nothing else. Covadonga, she explained, was a place of holy pilgrimage near her home. If pressed, Lolita would say that they were on a pilgrimage and that the two men had sworn a vow of silence until they reached the shrine.

They slept that night in the hay of the barn, washing at the stream at dawn. It was like old times. After an hour of daylight they were under way, once more stepping out with a brisk stride. For seven miles they followed the river bed, then turned right on a country lane at a road junction which ran parallel to the coast along the lower slopes of the mountains. The weather was warm. They were in no great hurry. They kept for the most part in the shadows of the trees ready to take to the timber should they meet any difficulties. They caught trout in the streams and Lolita showed the men how to grill them by skewering them lengthwise on a peeled stick plunged into the ground, close to the glowing embers of a log fire. She demonstrated how to stalk the rabbits when they came out to feed and how to snare them with a noose of fishing line near the hole, on an anchored stick. She skinned and roasted them in a manner similar to the fish but over the fire on a spit. They slept in caves and shepherd's bothies which were to be found along the higher slopes in sheltered corries where flocks could be penned. With bracken and heather for a mattress and scented herbs and grasses for a pillow, who could wish for more?

Nigel was delighted and Dirk was adding daily to his store of country lore. The air was like wine, the atmosphere was crystal clear. They collected berries from shrubs and cherries from trees. They even smoked-out a wild hive and dug out the honeycombs. They watched the red squirrels at play, searching for their hidden caches of nuts and having found them, Lolita raided the store, selecting the most edible. At the lonely farmstead and in the tiny clustered hamlets clinging to the ravines and gorges she bought freshly baked bread and milk and cheeses.

The men never ceased to wonder at her ingenuity. She in turn quizzed Dirk as to his Pennine hills and their regional dishes. He told her about Lancashire hot-pot, stew-and-hard, tripe and onions, black puddings etc., etc. It took a long time to make her understand and they had many a laugh around the camp fires but it whiled away the time. At the description of black puddings, her face lit up and the next day she disappeared for a time, returning with a couple of black puddings in the shape of a large horseshoe. Dirk couldn't believe it. She sliced it across and skewered the pieces and grilled them like fish, handing the sticks when done to each one. '*Morcillas,*' she announced, 'we have in Asturias also.' Dirk tasted them. There was a suspicion of garlic but the effect was great. His verdict was 'excellent'. By now neither Dirk nor Nigel cared how long it took to reach the farm. They were enjoying the simple life and the oneness with Nature.

The following day, however, they changed their tune. They awoke to a deafening peal of thunder and crisscross flashes of forked lightning repeated every few minutes. The explosions were ear-splitting and the air smelt of brimstone. Blue flashes lit up the bothy and the resultant explosion shook the very foundations. The rain came down like stair rods, pounding the earth into a squelching mass of pulp with runnels of water swirling down the slopes. Jagged spears of fire seemed to pierce the earth and somewhere amidst all the turmoil the thudding of trees falling shuddered the earth. Crouched in the leaking bothy, paralysed by the cataclysmic power of Nature, they tensed to every roll of thunder, helpless before the angry wrath of the elements. Even Lolita was kneeling in prayer. Eventually its rumblings died away and shafts of sunlight pierced the gloom. A brilliant rainbow hung in the sky as the mist of clouds rolled away and steam arose from the ground warm from the summer sun. It was like a Turkish bath as the sun's power increased and the mists drifted silently like ghostly wraiths cut newly from the tombs of earth. The experience was awful, yet majestic and magnificent; the fear, a grim reality. Nature was at once beautiful yet cruel, peaceful yet prone to violence, gentle yet possessed of latent power. It was a much subdued trio which squelched off from the bothy on the next leg of their trek.

They arrived at Covadonga, a mountain village, above which stood the shrine, a place of pilgrimage for devout souls who gave credence to the recent revelations of the appearance of the Holy Virgin. They joined the pilgrims from the village to the shrine. Lolita halted them as they approached and she went on alone. They saw her kneel in prayer, making the sign of the cross. It seemed to them like an eternity before she returned to continue their journey. They were attracting attention, dressed as they were in unfamiliar garb, their height singling them out from the groups of sight-seers and devotees. Once moving they felt more at ease, for from Covadonga to the farmstead was but a spit-and-a-stride compared with the distance they had already covered hitherto.

It was with soaring spirits and lighter hearts that they dropped down through the forest towards the River Sella and took the road to Oseja de Sajamore passing the village far up within the treeline with Lolita as guide. On reaching the clearing in which the farm stood, they paused involuntarily to survey the familiar scene. The tears welled up in Lolita's eyes and trickled slowly down her cheeks. Words were superfluous. She suddenly turned and threw her arms around Nigel, kissing him on both cheeks, then, swinging round to Dirk, she held his face in her hands and kissed him on the lips sobbing, *'No puedo agradecirte bastante, amigo, ni a Nigel tampoco.'*

She tried to brush the tears away from her eyes and raising two fingers to her lips she gave the same low undulating whistle they had heard her father give over the other side of the pass. They waited. She repeated the sounds. A figure appeared from under the parra at the entrance to the farmstead. It limped painfully as it raised a hand to shield the eyes and gaze along the treeline. Lolita took off her bandana and waved it to and fro to focus attention. Dirk knew it was Domingo from the set of his shoulders, now a little stooped, his grizzly appearance unmistakeable. Lolita tripped down the goat track across the clearing as he hobbled jerkily towards her. The two men stood fast, hypnotised by the scene before them. Once locked in a protective paternal embrace, they perceived others running from the farm, with loud cries of joy. It broke the spell and Dirk and Nigel walked forward towards the tiny knot of milling folk. Vicente, Paco, Juan, Domingo, Dona Inez the mother and even Angel were all there, tears falling from brave men. The embraces were firm yet silent, none capable of coherent speech. It was Domingo who spoke aloud in his familiar deep gutteral tones. *'En hora buena, amigos. Vamonos a casa,'* he growled. They all filed back to the house in twos and threes with arms encircling shoulders. Comrades in arms; nothing appeared to have changed.

It was Dirk who addressed himself to Domingo first. *'Porque, señor, es usted cojo?'* he asked. 'Why are you limping?'

'Ach es nada,' growled Domingo, *'una bala en la pierna aquí, nada mas,'* and he pointed to where a bullet had entered his leg. *'Vamonos, sentaos todos,'* he barked, waving everyone to be seated. *'Hay que celebrar. Mi hija ha llegada. Traiga la botella de Carlos Primero, mujer. Hoy es fiesta!'*

They all sat, Angel on the arm of his sister's chair. Dirk's emotions almost gained the upper hand, but he managed to suppress the tears. The quality of the simple welcome, the genuine emotion and bonds of kinship, the overwhelming pride and happiness which lit up the grizzled face, the tears of the men and the faintly detected hint of sorrow at losing the struggle, all crowded in upon his personal feelings. Nigel put his arm around the returning mother as she came from the kitchen, now smiling between her tears of joy. Typically, he relieved her of the bottle and the few glasses that she carried and as she turned to retrieve more from the sideboard he uncorked the bottle and poured . . . a mite too generous, Dirk thought. The glasses were handed round. All served, Domingo eased himself erect.

'A mi hija, Lolita,' he said, raising his glass in a toast. They all repeated Lolita's name. Then without a pause he added, *'A nuestros amigos, los ingleses.'*

At this a cheer went up from the men who then drank. *Y por fin,'* continued Domingo, *'que se mueren los feos!'* after which the room became a babel of sounds, most of which was so fast that it was unintelligible to the two pilots. They quietly and unobtrusively withdrew to the doorstep, so as not to intrude upon so intimate a scene. Gradually the noise subsided. Lolita came out and led them back.

'Now we eat,' she announced, *'jamón, morcillas, huevos, con patatas fritas, y chapan sidra, verdad.'*

Dirk turned to Nigel, 'We are to eat. Ham, black pudding, eggs, chips washed down with champagne cider . . . how does that strike you, Nigel?'

Nigel gazed at him quizzically. 'Perfect, except for your black puddings. Can't say I'm enamoured of them.'

Dirk laughed loudly as they joined the family circle.

They stayed three days. They had no wish to offend by a precipitate departure, nor did they wish to outstay their welcome. There was work to be done on the farm and the most difficult part of their operation lay ahead. They had to get out of Spain. Lolita saw them with their heads together, talking earnestly and poring over maps. She crossed over, exclaiming, 'You are going?'

'Si, eso es Lolita. Hay que marcharnos . . . we have to go!' said Dirk sadly.

Her face fell, then cleared and she smiled wanly, 'I not like see you go,' she said, 'you want see England, yes?'

'Yes,' said Dirk.

'I help you go,' she stated and turned away to seek her father who, after a brief talk, called Vicente, when a long discussion ensued. At length they seemed to agree on something and Lolita returned.

'We think you go fishing again . . . *pescar en el mar* . . . when you arrive here.'

'Un barco de pescar que nos llevó desde Inglaterra?' queried Dirk.

'Si, lo mismo, the same boat, yes?'

Nigel looked at Dirk for information. Dirk explained. 'Hey presto, problem solved. We go fishing. Told you there's always a solution to any problem if you study it hard enough. When do we go?'

'Cuando?' asked Dirk of Lolita.

'No sé . . . pasado mañana, maybe . . . or when ready the boat.'

They waited for over a week, during which they weighed in with the chores around the farm to pay their way, for Domingo would hear no talk of money. Lolita began where she left off with the herd of goats and the sheep going up the mountain carrying her sling and returning before dusk.

Nigel confided in Dirk, 'I could stay here for ever, you know, except I miss the bright lights.'

'Yes, that's our civilised Achilles heel,' agreed Dirk, 'this place is too remote. They should really have some transport, even a donkey or a horse would do.'

Gradually they began to anticipate the return home. A lorry arrived. It was the same which had originally transported them. Fond farewells were said with a few tears from the womenfolk and a long, lingering embrace from Lolita. A lump rose in Dirk's throat, making speech impossible. Nigel said, 'We'll come back for the canoes next year, all right?' He joked and laughed to ease the tension building up. They donned fishermen's gear, boarded the lorry and eventually reached the dockside at dusk, just as the drifters and trawlers were leaving harbour for the night's fishing. They quickly boarded their vessel, the same familiar trawler used for deep-sea fishing. Underneath Nigel's trousers were his flying boots and in those boots the Biretta and ammunition in case of accidents. The trawler immediately cast off and made for the open sea. Once clear of the harbour the skipper called them to the bridge and cheerfully welcomed them aboard. *'Anda y vuelta!'* he laughed, 'single and return.' He then explained that he had arranged to fish off Ireland and was setting a fast course for Ushant. In the case of foul weather he would have to seek shelter off the French coast. In the event the passage was remarkably smooth. A heat haze covered the sea on which was a long oily swell. During the day the flying fish leapt aboard the boat and slithered along the deck. They occupied their time by helping the crew and streaming lines for fresh fish to eat. The second day they left Ushant to starboard and headed for Falmouth across the Channel. They anchored in the roads the following afternoon and a picket boat from the Customs came alongside. Nigel met the officer as he climbed aboard.

'Flight Lieutenant Lightbown escaping from Spain,' he announced abruptly, leaving the officer a little nonplussed. He continued, 'This is Pilot Officer Waldron, also escaping from Spain. Our passports are in order. The Spanish skipper of this craft has risked his neck to assist us and wishes to depart for the fishing off Ireland. I trust you will allow him to sail forthwith.'

The customs officer examined their papers. Nigel showed him their French and Spanish money, gave him his father's telephone number and said that if he required further proof of identity he could phone the Air Ministry who would vouch that he was on the RAF Reserve list. The officer demurred, such a case was unusual. He seemed a little out of his depth. He requested them to stay put until he had reported to his superiors. He left and returned after some two hours. Permission to land was given and for the boat to depart. They both embraced the skipper. Nigel pulled out from his pocket the wad of Spanish money thrusting it in the skipper's hand and urged Dirk to follow suit, adding, 'It's no good to us now.'

The skipper looked at the notes in disbelief, then saluted, saying, *'Muchísimas gracias, Vayan ustedes con Dios!'* Another embrace and a shaking of hands with the crew and they stepped into the launch which sped across the anchorage with Nigel and Dirk standing in the sternsheets watching the trawler flash up his diesels and getting under way. They stepped out on to the jetty. Nigel turned to Dirk saying, 'It wasn't so bad after all, was it Dirk?'

'No, I'm glad I took your advice. I feel I've got something out of my system.'

'Now old chap, let's put something into our systems,' laughed Nigel. 'Where's the nearest pub, officer?'

'At the end of the jetty but we have to ask you a few questions first.'

'The hell you don't,' cried Nigel. 'You'll find us at the bar. Bring your boss and his notebook there,' and with that he stalked off down the jetty, Dirk in tow, calling back, 'we won't run away. We're thirsty and from what I remember of your beer down here, it's lousy.'

The customs wallah was at a loss what to do. He followed on behind.

'What shall we use for money?' asked Dirk as they arrived at the bar. Nigel bent down, removed his flying boot, from out of which fell the Biretta, which he stuffed in his belt just before the customs johnny arrived. Reaching down to the inside sole, he drew forth a flat wad of fivers.

'A bit sweaty no doubt old chap, but they're legal tender and we've still got Froggie-francs we can exchange. Two pints of your best bitter landlord and two double whiskies,' he ordered, 'and another for the two-ringer here,' pointing to the approaching customs guy. They sat on bar stools and Nigel peeled off six fivers giving them to Dirk.

'That's in lieu of the Spanish money you lost to the skipper,' he said. He added, after drinking down the pint without stopping, except to burp, 'I'll phone the old man for more in case these get done.'

The customs fellow was dumbfounded and sat there listening and watching the fivers roll. After the whisky, Nigel excused himself and went to phone his father. On returning he announced, 'The old man's sending us on a banker's order tomorrow to Barclays so we can push the boat out tonight.' Dirk obtained some change from the landlord and whilst Nigel regaled the officer and the owner to harrowing tales of their recent exploits, Dirk went off to phone Naomi through directory enquiries, for he had forgotten the number. Naomi's voice came on the line.

'Hello Naomi, this is Dirk speaking,' he said.

He heard a shriek at the other end, followed by, 'Where are you?' in an excited voice.

'I'm in Falmouth, just disembarked from a Spanish trawler,' he said.

'I'd given you up for lost Dirk, darling,' she cried. 'It's wonderful to hear your voice again.'

'I'll be seeing you within a few days, Naomi. I'm practically broke.'

'Never mind the money. I'll see you right when you get here.'

The pips went. 'That's it, Naomi. See you soon,' and the line went blank.

The two men ate their fill in a nearby hotel. They dealt with the customs officer after that. They caught the first train to London in the morning. At Paddington they shook hands and, words failing, they embraced, despite the curious stares of the passers-by.

'Wonder if my flat's OK,' said Nigel tritely. 'Come and see me soon.'

They shook hands with firm grips, reluctant to part and letting the hands speak for them. *'Adios, vaya con Dios!'* said Dirk, and turned for the Underground without looking back.

17

When Dirk and Nigel had exchanged their farewell handshakes on the busy concourse of Paddington station, it was clear that they would have to put their combat experience in the Spanish Civil War behind them. Dirk was undecided what his future should be. Nigel, he knew, would go straight home to his parents in Chelsea and most probably resume his former employment on the Stock Exchange with the family firm. For Dirk the situation was different. All he now possessed were the clothes he stood up in and the few changes of well-worn linen in his rucksack and the fivers which Nigel had given him to replace the pesetas handed to the Spanish trawler skipper in Falmouth. The pay-off as regarded the French francs had already gone in the process of smuggling Lolita back to her home in the mountains behind Ribadesella.

Dirk, turned and watched Nigel disappear into the milling throng of people before wandering across to the phone booth. At last he found Naomi's number and dialled her home. A strange female voice answered and when Dirk queried whether the number was the right one and asked to speak with Mrs Lishman, the voice regretted that she was not at that moment at home and added that she was Mrs Lishman's paying guest and could she take a message? Dirk hesitated before replying in order to collect his thoughts. There were only three rooms in the house for sleeping accommodation and the one he had once occupied was now in use. Eventually he said, 'Just tell Mrs Lishman that Dirk Waldron phoned and was hoping to call but that he will be travelling home for a spell. Got that?'

'Yes, I think so,' she replied and repeated the gist of the message.

Then Dirk added as an afterthought, 'Tell her I will telephone soon.' He put down the phone and leaving the box made for the Underground and Euston station, where, after snatching a hasty meal in the buffet, he boarded a train for Preston, well knowing that from there he could catch a bus home.

Once ensconced in a corner seat back to the engine, he began to muse on the word 'home', placing the *Manchester Guardian* he had bought upon his knee. 'Where is home?' he asked himself. He had given up his North London bedsit to go to Naomi's and that for a short while had been more than a comfortable home, but the voice on the telephone prompted him to revise that opinion and concluded that he could not just pick up the frayed strands of his former life so easily. He could not just appear out of the blue and become an embarrassment to Naomi, much though he knew she would have readjusted the household to accommodate him. It would mean moving Miriam into her mother's room and in any case the menage with a second paying guest would have been awkward to organise, especially taking into account the relationship which existed between Naomi and himself. So, he dismissed any immediate solution of that problem from his mind for the time being and concentrated on catching up with the current news about which he was sadly in ignorance.

He scanned the pages of the *Guardian*, his eyes rapidly taking in all the headline news. He didn't like what he cursorily read. From various journalistic commentaries he gathered that a fragile situation existed in Europe. Hitler had already been condoned in his much vaunted policy of *Lebensraum.* Persecution of Jews was now an overt fact of life. His sabre rattling was alarming the neighbouring states and major powers were becoming apprehensive. As Dirk assimilated the information in print and added to his own recent experiences and the memory of his trip to Germany in

1936 he concluded that a drift towards another war was inevitable. The question was, 'How soon?' He then turned to the sports pages and discovered again that his long absence had put him out of touch with current form in major team games and athletics in general and that many of the names now being highlighted were unfamiliar. He put off the tempting crossword as long as possible and finally, when time and circumstance forced him to turn to it, he had first to get up and grub around in his stained and dirty old rucksack to find an old stub of a pencil he knew was there.

It was then that he became aware that he was being eyed by two of the occupants of the carriage and became conscious of the fact that his appearance must have aroused some curiority. Grubby flannel trousers, a knitted seaman's jersey, a leather flying jacket worse for wear, flying boots with seaboot stockings turned back and a two-day growth of stubble on his face was definitely not *de riguer.* He gave a wry smile to the lady opposite who quickly averted her faintly disapproving gaze, and then nodded to the city gent with the pinstripes in the far corner, who was casting sidelong glances towards him at intermittent intervals. Dirk smiled inwardly as he tackled his crossword. Even its clues were unfamiliar. They contained many oblique references which were in fact not the custom before. Some dealt with current affairs, with which he was completely out of touch. As a result he found his concentration wandering and his gaze shifted to the passing scene, which was in many aspects more familiar.

A perceptible slowing of the train, coupled with an irregular clanking of wheels negotiating a skein of intersecting tracks, told him that they might be approaching Crewe. He put his paper aside to pick out the landmarks and the train slowed to a subdued crawl as it approached the station. Next, the raised voices of porters as the carriages slid gently into the station complex, where loaded trolleys trundled noisily along. Dirk read the familiar signs of the platform buildings, read the anxious glances of people waiting to board, followed by the final squeal of brakes on wheels and loud hiss of escaping steam. Doors clanged and a general hustle ensued. Dirk's long absence in Spain had dulled his senses to these sights and sounds of England. He was undecided whether he was appreciative of the unfamiliar jangling and the pressures of so many people and he felt relieved when, after some five long minutes, the train began once more to roll and the engine wheels to spin under their first initial attempts to pull the scores of tons into motion.

He wasn't in any mood for conversation, nor did he think were his fellow travellers. For once he welcomed the typical British reserve and aloofness which prevailed and which left him to his own private contemplative thoughts. He closed his eyes and pondered on the future's possibilities, casting around for some temporary relief from dependence upon others, but he had no guide lines to follow, no update of current knowledge of the industrial and commercial climate to assist. He would have to wait and see. It was not a very uplifting prospect nor did the uncertainty do anything for his morale.

The train eventually rolled into Preston station, where, gathering his few belongings, he walked slowly towards the ramp leading from the station to the street. Reaching the bus depot, he boarded a waiting bus and an hour later found him striding along the road to his home village in the dusk of evening. Came the problem, should he open the front door and walk in as he had always done when living at home, or should he knock and await his reception? He was not sure of the quality of that, as his letters had been infrequent and, if some had arrived it might have been a miracle. He tapped lightly on the inner vestibule door, tracing with his eye the all too-familiar patterns of the coloured glass which filled the upper hall. Then, opening it, for it was never kept locked, he called down the corridor, 'Anyone at home?'

No-one came. He advanced the few steps to the door of the dining room and repeated the operation, when his mother's voice from the kitchen called, 'I'll not be a minute, I've a pan on the stove!'

He cast off his rucksack and placed it on the sofa and stood in front of the fire, which offered a welcoming glow. His mother came in from the kitchen and, recognising her errant son, gave out a cry of *'Dios mio!'* The embrace which followed told him all. This was his home. This was a haven to which he could always return and where the weary wanderer could find recuperation and rest.

The kisses and welcome over, the talk became sporadic and desultory, a sort of leap-frogging from one subject to another in a vain attempt to extract some cohesive account of Dirk's absence. There was so much to tell that it was difficult to know where to begin, and to marshal the facts in some sort of order was Dirk's biggest problem. He learned that his grandmother had died and that his sister had completed college and was teaching in Liverpool's docklands. They sat in opposite armchairs and talked incessantly, broken only by the call of food, and replenishing of the dying fire, until midnight struck on the chime of the off-pitch clock which had seen its own share of travel. The clock broke the spell and more food and drink was forthcoming in the form of newly-baked bread and a steaming mug of cocoa. To Dirk this tasted like the ambrosia of the gods.

'You can have Janet's bed for tonight,' his mother said, 'she won't be home this weekend. We can make yours up tomorrow. Hers is aired.'

Dirk knew his sister would have to move in with his mother and wondered whether she would be pleased about that. He was the prodigal son and was getting the fatted calf. They eventually retired and the house fell silent, silence only to be found in the country, hypnotic and soporific. Dirk eased himself between the sheets and soon was sunk into a long and dreamless oblivion. He was awakened by his mother standing by the bed holding a cup of tea. He hoisted himself up from the horizontal to a sitting position and took the proffered cup. He could not interpret the expression on his mother's face but it gradually dawned on him that she was appalled by the state of his tatty discoloured vest. He smiled and reading her thoughts said, 'No pyjamas, Mum, those disappeared a long time ago and no laundry either.'

'That I can see,' retorted his mother sharply, 'we'll have to look at your wardrobe.'

'There's no wardrobe Mum,' he murmured, 'and precious little cash either.'

There followed a prolonged dialogue as she sat on the side of his bed and quizzed him still further regarding his true state of affairs.

'I'll have to find some sort of a job pronto,' he stated, 'or it's the dole.'

'You'll find a job,' replied his mum, ever the optimist. 'There are one or two vacancies in the local schools according to the local paper. Phone the Education Offices.

'Give us a chance, Mum. I'm not entirely broke yet and I can still fly planes, you know. Teaching is not very appealing to me after what I've been through. It's a bit prosaic and mundane. If it come to hey-lads-hey, I'll give it a go.'

'Don't forget that it will put bread and butter in your mouth,' warned his mother, ever the canny Scot. 'Meanwhile I'll have a look at yon rucksack.'

Dirk knew it was useless to argue but he grimaced at the thought of what his mother would find and say about the inside of his pack: a threadbare towel, two bits of old soap, underwear soiled and discoloured, a few scruffy shirts, shoes with the soles through, and other nondescript odds and ends. His had been a hand-to-mouth existence and the clandestine trip that he and Nigel had made to get Lolita back to her farmstead home had caused him to abandon his better civilian clothes at the hotel in Hendaye, to be picked up later, if ever. Part of the contents he described to his listening and astounded parent who, for once speechless, shook her head and said in Portuguese, *'Que asco, filho da mei,'* at which Dirk laughed and replied, 'You forgot to add the *"resta parte".'*

At this they both laughed and Dirk felt that his homecoming was complete and that his sins were forgiven, despite his lack of filial support for all the sacrifices she had made. In his eyes she was a saint for he often marvelled at her dour resilience and the courage which she evinced in the face of adversity. She deserved a better deal from him at least.

Eventually Dirk rose and gazed through the rear window at

the familiar plantation of trees, at the recently mown meadow beyond which a herd of Friesians and Ayrshires were grazing peacefully. He lifted his eyes to the woodland beyond and the hills above them, drinking in the truly rural scene. Five years ago he would have been out and running up those slopes in the early morning sunshine, with the dew heavy on the turf and the cries of the wheeling plover and moorbirds around. Spain and the Civil War faded into insignificance before this eternal quality of Nature. The future was the enigma which he had somehow to solve.

He first of all wondered what the reaction of the village folk would be to his return. He knew them all. They might not be so generous as his mother. Village gossip was a fickle jade and could make or mar a reputation. Two and two were oftimes made to make five as fact became distorted and word of mouth turned it into fiction, a fiction which could prove damaging as acerbic comment was bandied about. Dirk went through the habitual motions of his ablutions after paying a long overdue visit to the toilet at the bottom of the back yard. Even that was luxury compared to some of the situations in which he had to attend to natural functions. Holes in floors, sunken oil drums on lonely airfields, trenches with quicklime and planks for seats, holes dug with helving tools and hastily filled in, the cramped loos in ship's holds with tip-up seats and seawater flushing. He selected his better clobber to dress in, such as it was. His mother had dug out some old vests of his and a shirt from a long forgotten corner of a drawer in the mahogany dresser. No doubt there were other mementoes of former years secreted here and there. A pair of shoes appeared, neatly polished if a little cracked on the instep. He remembered those shoes from his schooldays. They still fitted him and within the hour he was looking more presentable than he had been for a long time. He wondered how Nigel had fared for he was in a slightly worse state than Dirk. No doubt his parents had carted him off to Saville Row and had him kitted out with rolled umbrella and bowler hat. He smiled at the thought and what Nigel might have said. They could dress him up as a city slicker but underneath the regulation clobber there was the incorrigible and unpredictable Nigel, an inveterate adventurer, conjuring up some madcap scheme or other kind of hairbrained stunt.

The breakfast laid before Dirk was a piece of nostalgia. Porridge, bacon and eggs, toast and marmalade, washed down with tea made from pure hill-water, reputed to be the best in England. This was a luxury Nigel would not have. Dirk began to shed some of his tenseness as all the familiar household routines pervaded his soul. He found his self-respect and confidence returning and after completing the old remembered household chores he resolved to venture out to greet the village.

His original fears were groundless. Each person he met after their first fleeting surprise at recognition, was most affable. They were pleased to see him back in circulation again. He detected a few curious expressions cloaking the unexpressed queries but these were quickly set aside as familiar conversation ensued. Dirk's spirits mounted with every encounter. He felt that, as always when anything out of the ordinary interrupted village life, it became the subject of gossip for a week, a sort of seven day wonder, and then, as some other event superceded, lapsed into the generally accepted scene.

He went to the one telephone kiosk the village possessed and phoned through to the Education Offices. After stating who he was he gave a general outline of his *curriculum vitae* to date and asked if there was any supply teaching available for such as he. They remembered him from pre-college days and from the tone of voice he detected that there was curiosity as well as surprise at his disclosure of his recent whereabouts.

'Yes', came the eventual reply. They could place him almost immediately if he cared to come to and see them. Dirk left the kiosk and surveyed his makeshift sartorial rig. He must do something about it forthwith. He imparted the welcome news to his mother and caught the next bus to Burnley, where he walked into Burtons the outfitters and blued a fiver on a suit. You could tell by the expression on the assistant's face that he disapproved of what Dirk was currently wearing, but that did not disconcert him. He pitied the poor devil tied to a shop counter day in, day out. Down the street he bought underwear shirts and ties with another of Nigel's fivers and walked into Saxone for a pair of shoes. Back home he transformed himself from a dishevelled looking tramp into a smart tailored man of the world. The relief in his mother's eyes was eloquent as she seized his discarded linen and proceeded to attack them with soap and water. Thence, after a late lunch, to the Education Offices where he was received with some deference and quizzed as to his recent exploits in Spain. He supplied them with the necessary information as to his academic life, gave them two referees, one of which was Nigel, and was requested to start the following week. He walked over the hill back to the village. Halfway there he wished he hadn't, for the new shoes were crucifying his feet. However he pressed on and after a few encounters with acquaintances and contemporaries in the main street he reached home and the ease of more adaptable footwear.

18

Dirk's teaching session was short-lived. After two months the clouds of war were accumulating on the European horizons. Nigel wrote him to announce that he had been called up with the Reserve, a fact which set Dirk thinking, conscious all the while of 'itchy feet'. As a qualified pilot, he knew the Government would have his name on some list or other and it would only be a matter of time before they looked him up and dug him out. He knew that they hadn't his present address so he wrote to Naomi to tell her not to disclose his present whereabouts and to return any official government mail for him unopened. In his own time he had not decided what should be his own role if war broke out. Came the July holidays, extending into August, for which he received no pay not being on the staff, so to raise some cash he hitch-hiked to Southport where he knew that a couple of 'stringbag' planes were taking up holidaymakers on joy rides and where he hoped to obtain temporary employment. He presented himself and his credentials and after a trial flight was taken on on a temporary basis. The pay was fairly good and he was given time off to visit home, which he did, thumbing lifts from cars and lorries.

Towards the end of his stint and before the schools started up again, he received a buff envelope marked OHMS in which he was ordered to report to a recruiting depot at Preston Barracks. There he was asked to give his *curriculum vitae* as to aviation and a full enquiry was made into his exploits in the Spanish Civil War. He was then told that he would be called up for training in the near future, at which he demurred, saying he wished to make his own choice of the Services. At this *contretemps,* the interviewing panel of three-and four-ringed regular officers from the three Services looked somewhat askance with raised eyebrows and, politely and not a little haughtily, told him he would have no choice in the matter. Whereupon Dirk replied that if that were the case, in the interim period he would quietly disappear and take up Portuguese citizenship to which he was entitled having been born in that country. He would fly their civilian planes and if they entered the war he would join their air-strike. This obviously was a turn of events they had not encountered before, and the wind was taken out of their too stiff upper-class sails. They went into a huddle, much to Dirk's amusement, in order to discuss this turn of tables. They returned after a short discussion asking to know which of the Services Dirk might choose. He made a snap decision.

'The Naval Air Service.' he snapped out smartly. On being asked why this choice, Dirk replied, 'I'd rather be on a moving airstrip than a static one because when you come up against snap raids by Messerschmidts and Heinkels some of you would wish you were too.'

Dirk knew that the Air Force officers had no real experience and their haughty attitudes relaxed when he touched their raw spot. They then proceeded to pick his brains regarding his experiences in raids and combat and his advice on the dispersal of planes around airfields in the event of sudden strikes. Dirk was happy to oblige and before long they were listening intently to what he had to say. He was now the instructor and they the pupils, at the end of which he exacted a promise from them to assign him as he wished when the time came. They agreed and each shook his hand as he left the room. Dirk knew that their experience was only simulation and theory whilst he had experienced the real thing.

Some weeks later Dirk received his papers to report for training at a naval air training school in Scotland. On arrival he was kitted out and given two rings as a temporary flight lieutenant. He then wrote to Nigel and Naomi to apprise them of this turn of events in his career. He spent part of his first leave in London. Miriam was now an attractive young teenager, growing in self-confidence and poise. They spent a few days on the Thames in a hired motor-cruiser and savoured the interrupted pleasures of former years. It was as though time had moved back as each fell into the old familiar patterns set by them a few years before. Dirk paid a visit to Nigel's parents for the first time. He was received as a long lost son, fêted, wined and dined, and there he learned of Nigel's assignment over in Canada where he had to train young pilots in the arts of aerial combat. He could picture him in his element, wheeling and diving around the skies and inspiring his eager pupils with zest and enthusiasm for their task ahead, but he knew that when the real thing started Nigel would be champing at the bit like an old warhorse, anxious to get his slice of the action, sympathetic to his predicament and needling him a little as to his current role in Canada. He knew he would be envious of Dirk who had chosen another more exacting type of flying, with the added risks and dangers from the elements and for once he nursed a secret satisfaction that he was perhaps one-up on his friend.

Dirk was attending morning service at the chapel near his former bedsit whilst spending a few days leave with Naomi. The congregation, many of whom he knew, had sung two hymns interspersed with a reading from the Bible. A prayer followed and then another reading which Dirk thought very apt.

'Remember thy Creator in the days of thy youth when the evil days come not nor the years draw nigh when thou shalt say I have no pleasure in them . . . also when they shall be afraid of that which is high and fears shall be in the way . . . .'

At that moment a siren placed upon the roof of a nearby police station began to wail its undulating theme, followed by another in the distance. The effect upon the congregation was electric. The minister, a Territorial Army chaplain of the First World War faltered as he read, then reining in his momentary distraction, continued to the end of the passage. A tenseness was running through the pews and a restless stirring as people stiffened and prepared to face the unknown. A few heads turned this way and that as if seeking a lead for a precipitous escape. The janitor in the rear pew slipped out, presumably to open the doors, as the steady unruffled voice of the preacher droned on. He ended his text quietly and calmly, in a voice devoid of stress or excitement, announced that he would end the service there and suggested that the congregation should leave quietly and either make their way home, or, if they wished, stay quietly in their pews until the 'All Clear'. As was his custom he then walked up the aisle to the main exit to shake hands with all his retiring flock, pausing on the way to reassure a couple of old ladies who seemed distraught and not a little bewildered. Dirk sat still, knowing the moment of truth had arrived. He bowed his head and uttered a mental prayer for the safety of those near and dear to him, picturing them in his mind, in the locations where they might at that moment be. He then rose and made his way to the main doors, extending his hand to the padre, who gripped it strongly. Looking into each others' eyes, acknowledging a mutual empathy, the cleric finally said, 'So it has come at last.'

'Yes,' responded Dirk. 'It was inevitable and it looks like you and I will be quite busy.'

'God bless you my son,' said the minister, giving a final affectionate squeeze and placing his hand on Dirk's uniformed shoulder, added, 'It's up to men like you now.'

'We'll do our best, sir,' countered Dirk. 'We can do no more, but believe me I fear it is going to be rough.'

With that the padre turned to speak to others retiring from the chapel. Dirk ventured out into the street and gazed at the skies above. The sirens had ceased their wail and an uncanny silence prevailed. Figures scurried along pavements with purposeful intent, apart from which Green Lanes seemed singularly denuded of pedestrians. A car swept past with unusual haste, followed by another equally precipitately driven. Dirk strode purposefully down the highway towards Palmers Green and Naomi. He knew she would be upset and distraught. He hopped aboard a passing trolleybus which slowed down as the driver spotted the uniform, an unaccustomed procedure which marked a sudden change in human conduct. With an acknowledging wave to the driver he boarded and quickly reached his destination. As he put the key in the lock and opened the door, the siren wailed the 'All Clear' and Naomi rushed forward and flung her arms about him, trembling with fright. Miriam followed and he placed a reassuring arm around each one, leading them slowly back to the dining room. They sat down on either side of the hearth, Miriam on the arm of his chair facing her mother. Dirk spoke first.

'Well, Naomi, it has begun. Your fears were correct. We have now to adjust to a totally new situation and it is not going to be easy.'

They then discussed the immediate problems. Evacuation was high on the agenda. There was nothing to keep Naomi in London except for Miriam's education and that could be catered for elsewhere. In the depths of his heart Dirk knew that his home village would be an ideal place for the two of them, but he realised that his mother was totally ignorant of this liaison, so he did not touch upon it and lunch intervened. A heaviness accompanied the meal which normally would have been sparkling and cheerful. Even the wine seemed flat and slightly sour. Dirk, however, raised his glass and proposed a toast. 'I give you a toast,' he said, *'Que se mueren los feos!'*

Miriam immediately asked what it meant, and Dirk launched into a long story as to when he first heard the phrase, recalling old Domingo and the farmstead. As they listened the spell of heaviness was broken and the conversation adopted a lighter vein. All three assisted in washing the crockery and cutlery whilst Dirk kept the flow of talk rolling by describing the food that he had used to eat in Spain, but he did not mention Lolita in case Naomi might question him more closely. As he looked at Miriam, however, he knew she now faced a situation similar to that faced by Lolita but failed to picture her shouldering a bandolier and a rifle, let alone roughing it out in the wilds of a forest.

Dirk left that afternoon to catch the night train back to base in Scotland, with nothing resolved for Naomi. He knew that he would have to make the routine patrol flight to the Norwegian coastline to monitor movement of shipping in and out of the Baltic. There had been a routine for a fortnight past, although the times varied in order to confuse the German patrols which they had already observed and reported upon. Much depended on weather conditions for the odds set up by Nature far outweighed the odds of interception by the enemy, which might prove hazardous from now on. Fog, rain, low cloud and gales made flying difficult and provided cover and camouflage for surface vessels against the grey windswept seas. Dirk always flew now with an observer. Previously they had flown unarmed. He expected that the planes would henceforth be tooled up to capacity to deal with all eventualities. His duties consisted in cover for coastal convoys down the Scottish coast, seaward patrols to give advance warning to the Navy of approaching enemy planes, using VHF radio communication with the escorts. Meanwhile training was given in landing on pseudo flight decks of make-believe carriers. Skuas and Swordfish were the planes in use and although the latter were rather slow they could be thrown about the skies with infinite ease and reliability. Moreover they had long range, whereas the Skuas were planes of shorter duration in flight. Dirk was at ease in the Swordfish, better known as 'stringbags', for he had great confidence in his own ability and in the aerobatic quality of the plane itself, should any of his former German opponents appear within range.

At the end of the course, Dirk received orders to join the aircraft carrier *Ark Royal.* He was highly delighted with the draft. She was a ship capable of thirty knots, and more in an emergency, which made deck take-off and landing easier. The hazard he now had to face was finding that moving landing strip when fuel was running out and the visibility was down to zero. He would have to rely upon the capabilities of his observer. The ship might be on an entirely different course from that on which she was sailing when he left and there was the additional nightmare of finding base and then landing on the flight deck in bad weather when the deck was rising and falling some thirty feet. The whole operation not only required a great deal of skill on the part of the captain, but a few risks and many prayers on the part of the pilots. He knew that in extreme cases the safety of the ship was paramount and that he might be left to ditch in the sea with the faint chance of being picked up by an escorting destroyer. There were times when he kicked himself for volunteering for carriers and then he envied Nigel and his circus in Canada.

19

He joined the *Ark* in Scapa Flow. His reception aboard was mixed. His *curriculum vitae* had gone ahead of him and his Spanish interlude placed him as a sort of joker amongst the pack, many of whom were in years his junior. As someone who perhaps knew more than his superiors, he was treated with some reserve and caution. The second ring he had acquired gave him little status except in cabin accommodation and wardroom precedence which proved semi-luxury compared to what he had been meted out before, and a veritable palace to what he had to put up with in Spain. The comfort of his cabin, the sumptuous wardroom fare, the well-stocked bar, were ample compensation for all the risks involved. The younger fry regarded him a little askance whereas the older and more time-served officers treated him at first with caution. They were all affable enough and the frequent high jinks in the wardroom reminded him of college ragging, but it took some time before he was accepted as a crew member. Only the Air Commander who, no doubt, had perused his papers was genial and went out of his way when off duty to engage him in cheerful conversation.

Meanwhile Dirk did all that was required of him without blotting his escutcheon. He did not overstay his airtime, nor did he make any risky or crazy landings. His reports on debriefing were always concise and to the point and his flying log impeccable. He trained his observer to his own ways and soon had a rapport with him when flying. He realised the time was fast approaching when initiative would be required and that rules and regulations might have to be ignored when face to face with the enemy, so, until then, he would play it by the book and keep his nose clean. By the preparations on board and the amount of gear being loaded, Dirk guessed that something big was in the offing, and whatever it was it was imminent.

On 22nd October 1939 *Ark Royal* put to sea in company with *Renown* and a screen of four destroyers steaming west and south. Later that day, Captain Power came on the Tannoy to announce that the next stop would be Freetown, Sierra Leone. Dirk began to wonder where the tropical kit was, as none had been issued. The idea was they should ensure that all shipping in the South Atlantic should pass on its lawful occasions. The *Ark* was to give spotter-cover in mid-ocean and *Renown* was to see off any likely opposition. Rumour had it that *Admiral Scheer,* the pocket battleship, had slipped through into the Western approaches and was now operating in those waters. Dirk and his observer were now constantly in the air on search patrols. Commander 'Air' daily briefed the pilots as to direction and distance and the likely action to be taken should sightings occur. They were roughly four hour stints and exceedingly monotonous at that. Swordfish could stay airborne for four hours, five at a pinch, so the safety margin was always generous, but those dawn patrols meant rising in the small hours and stints were usually twice a day. Everything was highly organised and executed with clockwork precision. The flight deck cowboys, after the fitters brought the planes up the hoist, pushed them down aft and secured them. The wings were then spread and fixed and the engines warmed up. Pilots and observers were next strapped securely in their seats and all operational gear checked by them, with the plane always positioned slightly to port of centre so as to avoid collision with the bridge island on run up to take-off. Next, the Deck Officer Flying checked all ready and gave the thumbs-up sign to the Air Commander in total control on the port wings of the bridge, who himself checked to see that all the radio masts were horizontal. Jets of steam were brought into play among the centre of the flight deck to indicate to the crews when the ship was steaming directly into wind for take-off.

This accomplished, the chocks were removed on signal from the bridge to flight deck and the first aircraft took off, followed by the second and third in rapid succession, requiring all the skills of the various units involved to perform their several roles with alacrity.

The afternoon flights took off at two and had to be back before darkness fell, when again the ship-speed and wind had to be balanced to receive aircraft. The whole manoeuvre was a tense business and had to be accurate to a fine degree. The Landing Control Officer would signal the approaching plane with his 'bats', the plane's hook was then lowered to catch the arrester wires raised athwart the deck and, throttling back and using brakes, the plane was brought to an abrupt standstill, when the pilot released his brake to allow the plane to run back for the hook release. This had to be executed with speedy precision to allow the second and third and others to land in quick succession so that the flight deck 'cowboys' were pushing the planes forward and to the starboard side with wings being folded as their counterparts dealt with the second and so on. Upon this highly skilled cooperation between the various specialist units the very life of the pilots and observers depended, whilst the speed of movement ensured the minimum damage to planes and ship alike. Some planes, when there was a hitch on the flight deck had to circle the ship with rapidly diminishing petrol supplies, until the fault was rectified. During this time the carrier was at its most vulnerable. Its guns could not be fired for obvious reasons: it had to operate away from the main force as wind and sea directed and when all planes had touched down and been secured the ship had to steam at high speed to rejoin the main force. Only the escorting cruiser and the attachment destroyers could cover the carrier during flying on and off.

The Skuas which often relieved the Swordfish had less air duration time and these pilots were often airborne to make dummy attacks upon ships and practice air combat techniques. Dirk's main problem, in addition to all the other factors, was to keep alert over the monotonous drone of the engines when on reconnaissance, for the hours were long and the vast expanse of sea and sky had a soporific effect when the weather was clear and navigation not too difficult. Often in the vast expanse of the Atlantic Ocean nothing was observed but the occasional surfacing whale or a school of fish ruffling the immense unending expanse to the horizon. At such times, in his innermost thoughts, Dirk wondered whether his precipitate choice had been the correct one. Only the sporadic chats with his observer broke the routine quartering of the ocean. He was becoming a little depressed. However, early in November he spotted a ship and radioing back the detached force captured it and it was duly escorted into Freetown. The Force then proceeded south to round the Cape where reports of sinkings were being relayed to them in code. A raider was at work and they were to prevent her doubling back into the Atlantic. The weather below the Cape was very bad and after an abortive search, during which Dirk flew many hair-raising missions and risked his neck in the landings the carrier put into Capetown, where great excitement was generated as her huge bulk entered harbour. The hospitality afforded by the populace to ranks and ratings alike was tremendous, Scarcely a house, hotel or bar lacked generosity to the crews. Everyone felt they deserved a spot of extended leave, but their hopes were very soon dashed. Within forty eight hours they were out at sea again, following a report of sinkings around St Helena. Once more they cruised the South Atlantic to search, patrol and if possible intercept the raider.

On 13th December the pocket battleship *Graf Spee* was engaged by cruisers *Ajax, Exeter* and *Achilles,* and after a gruelling classical sea battle in which the three used all the skills of sea warfare they penned her up in the River Plate and stood off to lick their own wounds and await support. The *Ark* was ordered to proceed to Rio at full power and refuel there, then to proceed south to Montevideo. Excitement was at fever pitch as news of the battle was received by radio and broadcast over the Tannoy. No leave was allowed in Rio so the matelots, long penned-up in the ship, were left to do the 'snowdrop act', leaning over the side of the ship to gaze at the spectators on the quays and the bright neon signs flashing along the waterfront.

She put to sea at twenty five knots heading south, later in company with *Renown,* which was delayed four hours. All planes were serviced and doubly checked ready to roll, the pilots keyed up to combat duty. Dirk's spirits rose as the hours went by. He scented combat at last. The excitement was shortlived, replaced by a ripple of exultation and envy as news came through that the *Graf Spee* had scuttled and Dirk was again robbed of his hour of glory.

Back in Freetown Christmas was hilarious. Leave was vastly overdue and the crews made the most of it. They had crossed the Equator many times and never had the traditional ceremonies been performed. As a result, King Neptune was arrayed in all his glory and paint, lather and ducking was ordered for those who had not experienced the ritual. It was great fun and reminded Dirk of his college rags. He too was a victim as neither rank nor seniority were respected in the roughing-up which was meted out. It was the Skua pilots who were champing at the bit for they had not yet been able to fulfil their true role. However, the *Ark* was overdue for a refit and in February sailed for home waters, when leave was given to the crew.

Dirk went home for the first week and from thence to London to see Naomi. From there he phoned Nigel's father to discover that Nigel was also on leave and at home. They all met for a reunion at the Savoy to chat and reminisce. Dirk sensed that Nigel was not his usual self. The three rings he sported on his sleeve were small compensation for his absence from combat. Dirk tried to appease him by describing how monotonous were the recces that he had to perform day after day and how boring some of the routines could become, but Nigel did not seem to be mollified.

Back aboard the *Ark*, they sailed for the Med. Three squadrons of Swordfish were housed on board, the idea being to carry out night reconnaissances over the western deserts of North Africa. On reaching Alexandria they were shore-based to effect training and were kept busy flying incessantly, but all these efforts were nullified when *Ark* received orders to sail for home waters once again in response to Germany's invasion of Norway. They were back to the old familiar ground but this time the prospect was deemed more hazardous. One assignment was to give air-cover to the troops who were making landings. This was not the kind of operation for which Skuas and Swordfish were designed and they were sadly disadvantaged against the now land-based enemy air power. Added to which, the weather conditions were not always suitable for flying. The Skuas, which had been dying to get to grips with Jerry, did show their paces off Namsos where significant landings took place. Although outnumbered and outdistanced they fought like eagles and by their skill and youthful tenacity reduced the numbers of German aircraft considerably. Junkers, Dorniers and Heinkels were all grist to their mill. They shot them down with unfailing regularity, put them to flight when attacking and caused them to jettison their bombs in the sea to make their getaway. Even when the Skuas ran out of ammunition they made dummy attacks and such was the respect in which they were held by the *Luftwaffe* that the enemy turned tail and fled before their onslaught.

Dirk was in the thick of it. He had, in conversation with the Air Commander, told some of his experiences against these planes in Spain and had been assigned *pro tem* to the Skua squadrons which were working overtime. In fact he was now so experienced and reliable that they switched him *ad lib* from one to the other. At Andalsnes he shot down the all too familiar Dorniers, whilst later, at Vaernes, he took up Swordfish to bomb the aerodrome an operation all too familiar on the Spanish Front. There was no respite and Dirk was glad to be so occupied for the fleet was coming in for a pounding from enemy attack planes and he would much rather be occupied in the air than down there twiddling his thumbs. His one regret was that Nigel was not there but the rapport he built up with his aircraftmen observers was some compensation for the disrupted friendship. It was like Guadalajara all over again in a vastly different setting, for the scenery around the fjords was glorious. He matched the manoeuvrability of his Swordfish against the faster Heinkels and the fire-power of the Dorniers with consummate skill, thankful for the efficiency and expertise of the fitters and mechanics who kept those planes on top line and serviced them with meticulous care. The campaign was nevertheless hard on the nerves and gruelling and many of the younger newly-fledged pilots never returned. Some landed on Norwegian soil, to be brought out and shipped home by the Norwegian undergound. Others ditched in the sea to be picked up by fishing trawlers and sailed back to destroyers or Scottish ports, reappearing in due course in the mess, their tales of adventure embellished. Others never returned and were unaccounted for.

The *Ark* became number one target for the *Luftwaffe* for her planes had accounted for too many of theirs. Even when the planes were all safely back and down below the ship was harrassed and harried from dawn to dusk whenever spotted by enemy reconnaissance. It meant that the pilots were seldom out of the action. A brief respite was afforded when back in Scapa for refuelling and supplies, but it was all too brief for she was off again to Narvik. It was May and there was no night. Only a dusky glow marked the hour of midnight. The Northern Lights were Nature's contribution to the warlike scenes. Again flying was non-stop for twenty three hours each day. When rough weather came up flying on-and-off was dangerous and sometimes impossible, and even when so-called calmer weather superceded the long heavy swells caused a lift of the flight deck and a corresponding lowering which held its own risks and dangers as to landings aboard. Standing out from the Norwegian coast some hundred miles to minimise attack, her own planes had to fly the intervening distances, which lessened their time over the targets and tested to the fullest extreme the duration of their fuel supply. Many times the cloud cover gave shelter to the Heinkels, which were gradually improving in their combat performance so the effectiveness of the slower Skuas was minimised.

Eventually our troops were evacuated from Norway, the *Ark* and her sister ship *Glorious* giving cover. The operation was so intense that the *Glorious* was attacked and sunk leaving a large gap in the Northern defences. The *Ark* was detached from the home fleet to bomb the *Scharnhorst* in Trodheim fjord. It was June and perpetual daylight and the distance from the ship some 160 miles, giving little time over the target. There could be no element of surprise. Jerry would be ready and waiting. The squadrons of attacking planes sighted the battleship with its escorts of cruisers and destroyers at anchor. As expected they encountered a fierce and intense barrage of anti-aircraft fire both from ship and shore mounted batteries. Messerschmidts came up to the attack, which was so intense that they were forced to break formation. This suited Dirk for he had often argued from experience that formation-attack, unless a surprise one, would lead to heavy casualties. The first wave went in, in ragged formation, followed by the second, flying through a merciless hail of flak. Dirk dived away and came in at sea-level as his experiences had taught him, thereby avoiding the upper flak. As he approached the battleship he pulled up and over to release his load, then diving down over the forward end, headed for the mists on the margins of the fjord which would give him some cover till he could pull up and out over the town. Heading out to sea, he circled to await his colleagues but few appeared as he flew back towards the *Ark* to give his report. Sixteen of his colleagues did not return, their observers with them. Later it was announced that the evacuation of all British and Norwegian troops had been effected and Dirk was left to ponder upon whether the loss of such equipment and skills was really worth it all.

The *Ark* sailed for Gibraltar from where Dirk took part in one of the saddest operations that was his lot to be involved with. The French fleet under Admiral Darlan lay at Oran. The French had capitulated. Negotiations for their immobilisation had been put in hand on a friendly basis and delegations were put ashore to treat with Darlan. The terms put forward by the British were not acceptable to him so the ultimatum to destroy his ships was given. That evening Force-H, with the *Ark* supplying planes, bombed and bombarded the French ships lying in the harbour. Dirk was sent up as a spotter for the big guns whilst others of the squadrons mined the entrance. This sad and grievous task was efficiently yet remorselessly executed. It was the classical rabbit shoot on the grand scale. Before the action was joined however, a small French force of a battlecruiser and her escort, by a dint of superb seamanship, broke out and steamed eastwards along the North Africa coast. Dirk and his colleagues were sent up in pursuit, armed with torpedoes for the first time. He wondered whether his French colleagues in the Spanish War were mixed up in this jungle warfare. The flak they met on approach was not only heavy but accurate, but dusk was falling and Dirk employed an old tactic which he had often explained, of coming in low against the blackening landmass. His squadron was ordered to release their torpedoes outside the destroyer screen and the action proved abortive. The following day they were sent to attack the already crippled units at Oran again with torpedoes to immobilise them below the water line and these raids upon sitting ducks set a new pattern for carrier-based planes and a new role and dimension for Swordfish. Torpedoes were now part of their strategy.

20

Dirk's next assignment was the bombing of the Italian airbase in Sardinia at Elmas. The planes there were a constant menace to the convoys to the Eastern Mediterranean and particularly to Malta. A line ahead formation of attack was ordered and Dirk did not like the idea one bit. The attacks were to be coupled with mining operations at the mouth of the harbour nearby. The *Ark* had shipped new Fulmar fighters and these were to be sent up against the Cants and Savoias. Dirk had fought Cants in Spain and was familiar with their tactics in combat, but he never got the opportunity to engage. Whilst out on a reconnaissance flight they sighted what appeared to be large units of the Italian fleet south of Sardinia and reported two battlewagons, six cruisers and sixteen destroyers. This was the long anticipated sighting and much desired opportunity to engage the Italian fleet in action. As they were well out of range of Force-H, they had to be slowed down to allow Force-H to come within range and engage. The following day, by noon, the air strike spotted the cruisers steaming east and being engaged by the faster units of surface craft sent on ahead to intercept. It was obvious the Italians had, during the night, split into two sections. The battleships were some thirty miles east of the cruisers. Dirk's squadron's objective was to cripple the battleships, now recognised as the *Vittorio Vanetto* and her companion as one of the Cavour class. The attack was pressed home through a heavy barrage of flak and though both ships were damaged, insufficient harm was done to allow *Renown* to come up and engage. On the other hand, the cruiser force turned away heading for the Sardinian coastline. Again it was left to the Swordfish to cripple the cruiser force. One cruiser was badly damaged and Dirk's plane was riddled with flak. Dirk broke away, struggling to keep his plane on course and managed to limp back to the *Ark.* His landing was dodgy and he finished up in collision with the island bridge structure with the cowboys all ducking and scattering for cover. Skuas were sent out to finish off the cruiser but they failed to locate her, due to low cloud. They spotted another three ships heading north and this time the cloud afforded them excellent approach cover as they went in to bomb. Back with Force-H the Italian counter-attack was in progress whilst the *Ark* was busy receiving planes and at her most vulnerable. They straddled her with sticks of heavy bombs but she appeared to bear a magic life for although the huge gouts of water rose flight deck high and splashed the deck, she steamed through unscathed after each attempt.

February saw an attack by the Swordfish on Sardinia's Tirso Dam. The weather was bad with rain and hail and ice forming on the wings. The ack-ack were intensely active against those who went in on the regulation pattern. The squadron led by Dirk went in on his instruction at ground level and escaped the flak until on target. Dirk could never persuade the hierarchy that this mode of approach was the most effective and invoked the least losses. The raid was only a partial success.

There followed attacks on Italian oil installations on the mainland and the cruise took them on the Sunday morning at dawn to stand off Genoa. The bombardment which followed was the traditional duck-shoot and the thunder of the guns and the echo of the explosions must have struck terror into the sleeping populace of that city.

May saw the *Ark* Atlantic-bound in search of the *Bismark* and the *Prince Eugen.* The Malta convoys had been ideal for the fighting Fulmars which had proved their worth, but now the Swordfish came into their own. The loss of the *Hood* in an engagement with these pocket battleships put Force-H on its mettle. The Swordfish pilots wanted a crack at those two. A sighting sent the pilots running to the flight deck anxious to be off. They sighted the *Bismark* and attacked with torpedoes damaging her amidships. During the night she altered course and could not be found, but a Catalina eventually found her heading for Biscay and presumably Brest. Up went the Swordfish to make reconnaissance. Heaving seas made flying off and on very dangerous but it had to be done. Meanwhile the Catalina reported a second sighting some 700 miles west of Brest. Word went out to the prowlers, now almost drained of fuel, to return. Dirk's plane was fitted with extra fuel tanks and sent off to relieve those still airborne and this pattern was continued, to keep her constantly under surveillance. She had the legs of the pursuing fleet, however, and the only way to stop her was to cripple her with a torpedo attack. Many planes returned with scarcely any petrol left. Normally, the conditions prevailing would have cancelled out flying but the urgency of the matter and the importance of the prize was paramount.

The first flight to arrive at what appeared the target area, because of poor visibility and shocking weather conditions, attacked the cruiser *Sheffield,* fortunately missing, and they had to return for more missiles. *Sheffield* had *Bismark* on radar and her information, radioed back, enabled the succeeding attacks to press home. The low cloud and driving rain split up the squadrons and Dirk smiled to himself, knowing that an individual approach was now possible. He broke cloud ahead of the battleship and dived to sea-level for an oblique approach, launching his torpedo at a very low level and close to the ship. He pulled out amid a hail of flak and felt the bullets rip through the wings and fuselage. His left arm felt numb and an ominous wetness was trickling warmly down his thighs. He spoke to his observer, who was slumped forward in his seat, and got no answer. He set course for the *Ark* which was pitching and rolling in heavy seas. His screen ws constantly being swept with flurries of blinding rain and his eyes kept dimming as he felt himself slipping into unconsciousness. He fought to keep alert and to fly the craft steadily against the constant buffeting. Eventually he spotted the mother craft wallowing in troughs of green seas and lined up his plane to approach. The first time he was signalled away and circled the ship. He looked at his petrol gauges. They weren't registering. Probably they had been damaged by flak but then again his tanks may have been holed. At the third circuit he was given permission to fly on. He felt himself slipping away into oblivion but he gritted his teeth and lined up his crate. Down, down he came towards the tilting deck which he hit with an almighty crash, skidding sideways and entangling with the arrester gear. He then blacked out as the plane tipped up on its nose and crumpled over.

He learned much later that the cowboys had cut him free and released his observer, all but dead. They rushed them both to the sick-bay where the waiting surgeons operated on them both. He came to the next day, wondering where he was and seeing others of his squadron in the bunks. He was swathed in bandages like a mummy and feeling very weak. He first asked about his observer and learned that he had died on the operating table. The 'vets'on their rounds gave him details of his condition, adding that they had merely patched him up and that he would be attended to in Gib. hospital very soon. He and several others were so transferred a day later and further surgery was performed. During convalescence they informed him that the tendons in his upper leg and arm had been badly damaged and some lacerated and that he would have to be flown back to UK for physiotherapy or he would be permanently crippled. He stayed in Gib. hospital for several days and was finally flown home in an RAF bomber with others from the Rock. He could walk short distances but very painfully and the torn muscles in his left arm partly immobilised it. An ambulance rushed him and another army officer to a convalescent home in a commandeered country mansion, where specialists in muscular injuries were on tap. The Wren driver rang the bell at the imposing front facade. Two nurses appeared to assist him. One said, 'Hello Dirk. We meet again!' Dirk looked up into her face. It was Catriona, the nurse he had spent the holiday with at Gernsbach.

'Good God, it's Catriona,' he remarked. 'Looks like you've got me where you want me this time,' he added.

She supervised the operation of wheeling him into the house and to the ward, placing him in an armchair next to a bed. Dirk managed to smile above the pain of the movement and once relaxed in the chair, said, 'I knew we'd meet again sometime.'

Catriona chatted to him. He learned that the other denizens of the ward were out and about somewhere. They could be in the lounge, or in the gym, or out in the grounds.

'Are there any other Navy chaps here?' asked Dirk, gritting his teeth to ease himself more comfortably in the chair.

'No, just Army and a few Air Force men at the moment. The last Navy chap left about a month ago. He was a physical wreck when he came, but we soon had him running around,' affirmed Catriona.

'Let's hope you can do that for me?' smiled Dirk.

'First you must have a bath,' Dirk,' Catriona announced. 'Come on, I'll help you. It's just along here.'

Dirk didn't fancy being bathed by a nurse, but he thought he could make an exception in Catriona's case. She seemed to him more mature, more self-possessed than she was six years ago, as she jollied Dirk along and got his reluctant acquiescence. Getting into the bath caused him excrutiating pain, but he suffered it in silence and surrendered to Catriona's administrations. As she dried him off, she remarked upon how fit he seemed and assured him that he was in the very best hands in the country as far as the medics were concerned.

Dirk finally spoke above the level of his pain. 'Had you been anyone else you would have had a very rough time with me in that bath, but with you . . . well, we have a different relationship. Remember those duvets at Gernsbach?'

'Shall I ever forget! I was very young and immature then. I thought we had agreed to put that incident behind us, Dirk,' replied Catriona archly.

'*Touché*,' replied Dirk, 'from here on it is forgotten.'

'The surgeon will be seeing you tomorrow,' she announced, changing the subject. She dressed him in some regulation pyjamas and, bringing a wheelchair, wheeled him back to the ward, easing him back into the chair.

'I have to go now,' she announced, 'we'll talk sometime later. I'll go and send you up some tea. Your ward mates will be back soon.'

Within minutes another nurse was bringing him some sandwiches and a pot of tea which she poured for him. He had just finished the sandwiches and downed the second cup when the others came drifting in. Noting the new arrival, they came over to greet him, some on two sticks, some with one and others in wheelchairs or pushing a zimmer. Finally a wheelchair fairly whizzed round the corner, bowled down the room with its occupant immitating a motor bike. He almost collided with the table in the centre of the room. Spotting the group around the new arrival he revved up and whizzed across, letting out a screech of brakes as he came to a halt at the foot of Dirk's bed.

'My God, it's Dirk, isn't it?' the voice exclaimed. Dirk looked in his direction. It was Nigel, still the high-jinks-incorrigible, despite his disability. They greeted each other warmly as the others crowded around. The rest was a battery of questions and answers on both sides. Nigel had apparently crash-landed a faulty trainer plane and finished up nose down in a ploughed field. They had hauled him out with his legs badly damaged. During the next hour tea was served on the centre table and the conversation continued.

About seven in the evening Catriona returned to the ward. Nigel was at the foot of Dirk's bed, facing Dirk in the armchair. As she passed to deal with Dirk, Nigel grabbed her around the waist and sat her on his knee. 'Enough of that now Lightbown,' she announced in a peremptory voice, 'you'll damage your legs.'

Nigel released her saying, 'Smashing nurse this Dirk, especially on the physio side. You'll like her.'

Catriona retorted sharply, 'I'll have you know, Lightbown, that Dirk and I go back a long way.'

That took the wind out of Nigel's sails and for once he was silenced. Turning to Dirk, he said, 'You dark horse. You never told me anything about Catriona before.'

'Oh, you two know each other too!' exclaimed Catriona.

'Sure we do,' chipped in Nigel. 'We two lost the Spanish Civil War together.'

'And Dirk and I fought against the Germans in 1936, see?' she commented sharply.

A further pause ensued while Nigel chewed on this further piece of information. Dirk remained silent and smiled at the repartee. He looked from one to the other quizzically. At last Nigel spoke. 'Tell me more!' he rapped out. A silence followed, after which he continued, 'Ah! I understand. Subject exhausted. Box closed. Mind your fingers, what?'

'Exactly,' retorted Catriona. 'Now I have other things to attend to without standing gossiping. You must ask Dirk for any further information.'

She began her ward duties at the far end and Nigel watched her go. By the look on his face Dirk knew that Nigel was smitten. Turning to Dirk he said, 'You know how to pick 'em, don't you? She's a real great lass, that one, and I love her Scottish accent. Never gets ruffled, bags of energy, strong as a horse, and a smashing looker too. What more can a chap ask?'

'Do I detect a wistful note in your voice?' enquired Dirk.

'Yes, you do,' responded Nigel quickly, 'I have designs on that one.'

'But didn't you marry the one in the Wirral?'

'No, she found someone else. I've been freelancing ever since.'

'What about the Canadian girls. You were over there long enough.'

'Yeah, there were dozens hanging around with money bags too. Single, married and widowed alike.'

'What stopped you hitching up with one?'

There followed a long serious pause. Dirk gazed at Nigel's sober and withdrawn features. He had gone into a trance. At length he spoke with a very intense and subdued voice. 'When you've known girls like Lolita you measure every other by that yardstick and they all fell far short. Catriona over there is the only one who had ever measured up.'

He continued to look in Catriona's direction. Dirk kept silent. He had never looked at the opposite sex from that standpoint, perhaps because his yardstick was Naomi, who was special. He cast around in his mind for some appropriate remark. 'You're absolutely right, Nigel,' he said tritely, 'Lolita was something special.' A further pregnant silence ensued, broken by Nigel, who heaved a deep sigh. 'How's Naomi and the kid?'

'I don't really know,' replied Dirk, glad to change the subject, 'I haven't had letters in two months. They are probably floating about Gibraltar, so I can't say.'

'There's a phone down the corridor. Want to give her a surprise?' asked Nigel, brightening up.

'I'd love to phone her but I don't think I can walk so far.'

'No problem,' retorted Nigel, back to his normal inventive self. 'Use my chariot whilst I sit on your bed. Don't prang it, mind. I've got it trained.'

They changed places. It felt like old times. Conspiracy and all that. Catriona was busy at the far end of the ward with her back to them. Dirk trundled off down the ward to the phone and dialled Naomi. It was Miriam who answered. She immediately recognised his voice and called out to her mother, holding him in excited conversation. He could picture them standing there sharing the earpiece. He could tell that they were excited. He gave them details of his whereabouts but did not refer to his condition. They wanted to come as soon as possible but he could not tell them the visiting conditions as he had only just arrived. He promised to phone again as soon as he knew, and rang off. He trundled himself back into the ward to where Nigel was being ticked off by Catriona. He silently wheeled up behind her. Nigel had her pinioned by the wrists and was pulling faces like a guilty scolded child. Noting Dirk's arrival he pretended to cry and twisted her so that she sat sideways on the bed. It was then that she saw Dirk and all three burst out into helpless laughter, which echoed down the ward. Other nurses came to see what the hilarity was about and stayed to hear Nigel launch out on one of his salacious exploits in Canada. In the middle of a sentence a sudden hush descended as he broke off. The listening group parted to reveal the matron in all her regal splendour, arms folded menacingly below an ample bosom, gazing imperiously at Nigel.

'Hello, Matron,' he piped up cheerily. 'You're the loveliest lady I've set eyes on today. Come and meet the new arrival. He's a friend of mine. We fought together in the Spanish Civil War. Meet Dirk Waldron. Lovely, isn't she Dirk?'

He spoke in his best far-back accent and with a winning smile which he often turned on when conning the opposition. Matron was seen to relax slightly. She came forward to Dirk and shook his hand saying that she welcomed him to the convalescent home and hoped he would be happy during his stay there. Turning to Nigel she added, 'And I should be careful of the company you keep whilst here, Mr Waldron.' She then turned to address the nurses who had long ago tiptoed away, and Nigel, seeing the disappointment on her face, chirped up. 'My dear sylph-like Titania, your fairies have tiptoed away.'

With a toss of her leonine head she marched towards the corridor in pursuit of them without as much as a backward glance and Nigel, in a gutteral whisper, leaned forward to Dirk and said, *'Que se mueren los feos'* at which Dirk exploded with suppressed laughter, so apt was the expression for the situation.

The remainder of that evening was hilarious with reminiscence and anecdote. The nurses serving meals at table were scarcely able to contain themselves as they listened to the shafts of wit and the repartee. It was an exhausted Dirk who eased himself into bed and immediately fell sound asleep.

The clatter of pots awoke him as early morning tea was being distibuted. He eased himself into a sitting position the better to deal with the proffered cup, held by a smart young nurse. Nigel, two beds down, got up and wheeled himself round.

'Morning Dirk,' he called cheerfully, 'hundred yards hurdles today. Twelve seconds allowed.'

'Hundred yards nothing,' countered Dirk, 'it'll take me five minutes to get to the bogs, if I ever arrive at all. I'm bursting for a strain-off. Where are they by the way?'

'Don't tell me you haven't been since yesterday?' asked Nigel.

'I used a toilet in the bathroom but none since,' came the response.

'You must have had an extra fuel tank fitted,' laughed Nigel.

'Not so,' cried Dirk, 'I've only had two cups of tea since then.'

'By golly we'll remedy that,' retorted Nigel, 'I've some smuggled beer in my locker. How about it Dirk?'

'How do you secrete it then?'

'It's in some lemonade bottles. Just looks like lemonade. Matron can't tell the difference.' Good old Nigel, thought Dirk, incorrigible as ever. Would anything ever suppress him?

'No, I don't want beer first thing in the morning. Just tell me where the bogs are and I'll see if I can get there.'

'No need to walk. Take the chariot. I'll sit on the bed till you get back. It's the first turning on the left down the corridor. It's signed. Can't miss it.'

'I think I ought to try to walk. I'm stiffening up and that's bad.'

'Tell you what. You hang on to the handles of the chariot and I'll propel it slowly. You shuffle on behind and put your weight on them. It'll be the blind leading the blind.'

Dirk laughed. This was the old Nigel. Game for anything out of the ordinary. They set off in fine style, with encouragement from the others. They turned into the corridor and halfway down ran into the 'battleaxe' matron, accompanied by Catriona.

'And what do you two think you are doing?' she piped up imperiously.

'We've just left the apron and are picking up speed for the

take-off,' called Nigel. 'Clear the runway. Tally ho. Bandits, bandits.'

'Stop,' cried Matron bearing down in full sail, 'where do you two think you're going?'

'We're on course for the bogs, Matron. Dirk here has full tanks and it's dangerous to abort his take-off. Tally ho!'

He propelled the wheels and Dirk stumbled after him willy nilly, bursting with suppressed laughter as they pushed on past the battleaxe.

'Bogs ahoy. Port ten,' cried Nigel and Dirk, entering into the spirit of the game called out, 'midships. Steady as you go!'

Nigel pulled up in the toilet space, Dirk shambling after him and as he gave a ninety degree turn, Dirk seemed as though he were about to fall and Catriona rushed forward to catch him.

'You clowns,' she hissed in his ear, 'you shouldn't be up yet. Matron will only take it out of me as the chargehand for the ward.' But the incident passed off. A second wheelchair arrived and Catriona placed it for Dirk as he left the toilets.

'Race you for a fiver,' shouted Nigel.

'You're on,' cried Dirk leaning forward to propel his wheelchair, 'bandits, bandits! Full throttle!'

They coursed down the corridor, Catriona in pursuit, swung into the ward, Dirk suddenly blocked by the tea trolley. Nigel flashed past calling, 'You owe me a fiver!'

21

The days passed into weeks. The therapy courses coupled with the swimming and heat treatment, improved everyone tremendously. Catriona supervised the routines. Dirk wrote letters home and received replies. He followed the exploits of the *Ark* avidly and wrote to his co-pilots aboard her. It was with a deep sense of loss that he heard on the radio that she had been torpedoed and had sunk on 13th and 14th November but happy that all save one had survived. It was like a loss in the family. He straightaway sat down and wrote letters of commiseration to Captain Maund and the Commander Air, well knowing that they would need every sympathy and encouragement.

By the spring of 1944 Dirk was deemed fit enough to be discharged. He went off home to his native village and passed a long, lazy time there. Then, by walking, next jogging, and later, running, he began to feel his old self again. By midsummer he was trotting up to his favourite haunt, the Echostones. The wheel had turned full circle. There above him hovered the kestrel, or at least one of its offspring, still quartering the meadows below. Behind him, the ubiquitous sheep grazed peacefully. He was tempted to whistle but desisted. He walked back down the long track and called at the farm where he had spent many happy days of his childhood. Haymaking was in full swing. He leaned on the old familiar fence to watch. The loaded cart was coming up to the barn, the faithful shire horse straining in the shafts. George was leading it. They hailed each other as though the years had never been and Clara, bringing the tuck-basket back to the house, paused to chat and reminisce. Time retreated. The smell of the hay, the sun glinting on the meadow, the cherries on the trees overhead, the cattle grazing in the pasture, the chickens strutting and pecking upon the cobblestones, the pigeons wheeling overhead, who could ask for more? The war was far away. In his mind's eye the picture before him switched to the farmstead high up in the Cantabrian mountains. It was a contrasting panorama but equally redolent of peace and the eternal processes of Nature. A pang of guilt nudged him that he had not written to Lolita, nor her family. He strolled down the cut-meadow to the lake on the opposite side of which he had often sat. There he gazed at the ducks and a pair of swans. The fish were still leaping and the ripples expanding. As he skirted the banks his thoughts were far away. He walked in a kind of reverie and eventually reached home.

After a month he returned to London to stay with Naomi. Whilst there he was summoned before the Medical Board at Portsmouth who pronounced him fit for light duty. He was posted to a naval air base near Lossiemouth where youngsters from colleges, universities and even grammar schools were being processed. How young and fresh and eager most of them looked! He had in the interim period notched his half ring and sported the ribbon of the DSC for his exploits. His slight remaining limp, which was worse on rainy days than when fine, evoked a healthy respect from his charges. Despite longing to fly combat planes again, he realised that perhaps his acquired expertise and experiences might save the lives of these youngsters if he set about teaching them well. It was a challenge to stand before a class once more and impart knowledge, particularly knowledge of a practical nature which was a matter of life and death. As he looked into their open, eager faces, he recalled his own thoughts at their age. Ten years had now elapsed. An age gap had intervened. Dirk was now twenty nine and these before him but late teenagers and in their early twenties with a sprinkling of older men. Dirk gave them the full benefit of his experience, nor did he keep to the recognised official drills. He explained his own theories for surface attack, of dusk and dawn tactics, about under-belly approach and blind spots. He crammed everything he could into these crash courses and was conscious of his debt to Nigel who had done the same for him.

The months sped by. Naomi and Miriam came up to stay during the summer holidays. Miriam was in her final year at Oxford, reading Modern Greats, and was quite the most attractive twenty-two-year-old. Her presence caused a flutter amongst the young officers and she flirted with them outrageously. Naomi smiled and let her have her head. Wartime had been restrictive enough without additional parental curbs. They discussed her future. Dirk suggested the Diplomatic Service, but Naomi was biased in favour of a business career and executive training. They talked the various options through, more to clarify than to influence. The final choice would be Miriam's. All Naomi and Dirk were interested in was that it should be the right one. They both felt that with Miriam launched upon a career their own problem could be safely solved.

The women returned to London where the doodle-bugs were menacing the city suburbs. Three weeks later Dirk received a telegram from Miriam to say that her mother's house had been demolished by one and Naomi had been killed. Dirk had the utmost difficulty getting compassionate leave as officially Naomi was not a relative, but he managed to attend the funeral in the local synagogue, where he could not sit with Miriam and had, by custom, to wear his hat. Afterwards he met Miriam's relatives for the first time. They discussed Miriam's future plans and he came away assured that her welfare was in secure hands and that she would be well cared for. Taking leave of the tearful and distressed Miriam, he embraced her and made her promise to write to him as often as possible and that if she was in any difficulty whatsoever she should either write, or, failing that, come to him. He himself felt numbed and desolate. An important slice of his personal life had suddenly been excised.

On his return to base a letter from Nigel raised his flagging spirits. He was invited to be the best man at his forthcoming wedding. He had apparently proposed to Catriona and been

14000

accepted. Dirk smiled inwardly as he pictured Nigel on a much shorter rein. When they met, the day before the wedding, Dirk was shaken to see Nigel still on sticks. He didn't enquire too closely as to his condition for he could sense that Nigel was sensitive about it. He consulted Catriona after the nuptials as to his chances of full recovery. She was very optimistic.

'Another year,' she said, 'and I'll have him back to normal, almost.'

That lifted Dirk's spirits tremendously. Nigel's father was delighted that his son was in such excellent nursing care. They welcomed Catriona as a long-lost daughter, which now of course she was. As Dirk took his leave, he kissed her saying, *'Auf weidersehen, gnädige frau.'*

'Grüs Gott,' came the whispered reply, and the squeeze of the hands said the rest. Turning to Nigel he remarked, 'Beat you in the 220s hurdles next year.'

'I'll hold you to that,' came the quick response.

VE day came. Celebrations were in order, but Dirk had no-one with whom to celebrate except his own personal family. His sister was married to an airman and both she and his mother were evacuated with a group of school children in North Wales. Now on extended demob leave, he returned to stay in his home village in his grandfather's home with his aunts. It wasn't the same. Time had passed on. His youth had flown. Another generation had taken its place inthe scheme of things. Dirk cast about in his mind as to his future plans. To go back to teaching would be an anticlimax, a denial of all that he had to date achieved. He pondered long on the matter whilst joining in the village festivities. Then his demob notice came through. He was medically examined, advised to apply for a disability pension as a result of his wounds, given his back-pay and 'blood-money' and departed to collect his demob suit. The doctors had warned him that there was a danger of a recurrence or complications from his injuries and they signed the forms required to be submitted for a pension. He had saved a fair sum during his convalescence and since, and, after paying a visit to his mother, he decided to take a holiday. Packing his old Bergen rucksack, he set off across the Channel to Paris and thence to Hendaye, scene of his former escapades. He then, after a few days, decided to try to cross the Spanish frontier, wondering whether his name would be on their list as *persona non grata.* He walked across the bridge dividing France and Spain quite casually, presenting his new passport which listed him as a teacher. The official glanced through it and after a cursory riffle through the rucksack the customs officers waved him through. He took a taxi to San Sebastian and booked two nights at a pension, spending the next two days perusing timetables of buses and planning his next move. The next stage took him to Santander from there, after a night in a small family-run hostel, he managed to hitch a lift with a commercial traveller who was staying there and was moving on to Gijon the following day. He dropped Dirk off at Ribadasella where he made his way down to the docks and entered the tavern which had first housed them from the Spanish trawler nine years before. The *dueña* remembered him and welcomed him with a cheery embrace. After explaining his destination, she offered to accommodate him for so long as he required to stay. Dirk, however, anxious to move on, asked her to look after the remainder of his gear, after packing his rucksack with the essentials for his mountain journey. The following day he set off for the Picos de Europa, covering ten miles, with frequent rests as far as the foothills, for his leg was playing him up.

He followed the old route as far as he could remember, through the woodlands parallel to the roads, always keeping the highway in sight and within easy reach. A lonely farmstead gave him shelter for the night and provided an evening meal for which he was grateful and paid generously. After an early breakfast of coffee and farmhouse coarse bread, with raw ham, cheese and butter, he struck upwards following the sheep and goat tracks towards the high peaks. He was accosted at an early hour by two officers of the Guardia Civil in their familiar black tricorn hats, who demanded to see his passport. No doubt they were unaccustomed to seeing foreigners off the beaten tracks in those parts. They began to question him about his intentions and his destination but Dirk pretended not to understand them and instead produced a map and with his finger traced out the route which he said he was intending to follow, a route which took him back by a circular track to the coastal town of Unquerra. They let him pass and stood to watch him breast the rise and once more disappear into the trees. He tried not to limp until he was well clear of them and adopted a gentle stroll. Evening saw him high up on the lofty slopes and seeking a place for the night.

The last time Dirk had trodden these mountain tracks had been late winter time. Now it was high summer, but he still remembered the sudden storm which had struck fear into them and he began to feel a little anxious. The forests which had before seemed so enchanting to him were now transformed into a fairyland by the lush flora and fauna which grew in abundance. Flowers were everywhere massed in a kaleidoscopic carpet of ever changing colours. Rainbow tints and hues, bright and vivid colours delighted the eye. He stooped often to examine the strange exotic blooms which strewed his path, flowers he had never before imagined, let alone seen. The busy drone of wasp and bee and the myriad flies, lit by shafts of sunlight percolating through the canopy of branches overhead, hypnotised him. It was a severe temptation to sit down and relax and imbibe this feast so generously provided by Nature. Lilies, lupins, campanulas, violets and exotic orchids bloomed with gay abandon, dappled by sunlit patches on the forest floor. By chance he spotted a tiny mountain farmstead, nestling in a sheltered clearing and he plucked up courage to knock and ask for milk, cheese and bread. The startled peasant lady supplied his needs, gave him cider to drink from a wooden cup filled from a barrel mounted on a still. He felt he could trust her and spoke to her in Spanish, asking the way. He sat underneath the vine-pergola on a bench against the whitewashed wall and slowly savoured the peace of the mountain and the wonders of Nature. As he sat he watched the moths and butterflies with unbelieving concentration. The size of many amazed him whilst their colours delighted the eye. Some as big as a hand and others tiny as a thumbnail, all intricately patterned and weaving undulating rhythms of mobile light. The blue canopy of the sky, the greens and yellows of the trees and shrubs, the glorious bursts of colour from the flowers, the flight of birds and the air like wine, riveted his rapt attention, until it was with reluctance that he paid the paltry sum requested and proceeded on his journey.

As he trudged along the winding tracks which wove their way up the gorge, he heard the cascades of tumbling waters below him, saw it foaming over the rocks and swirling into the deeper pools where the fish lay. Reaching the head of a steep waterfall, he paused to take a breather, leaning silently against a rock his face lifted to the sun. Across from him a lizard appeared from out of the crack of a rock and waddled slowly across a sunlit patch to the ferns beyond, heedless of his presence. Upstream, a young deer stooped to drink at a pool raising its head from time to time to test the air for scent and sound. Whilst Dirk recovered his strength, he savoured the delights of the terrain around him. Never had he seen so much wild life so concentrated in one vast area unsullied by man.

Dirk tore himself away from the magic of the place. He had to find the shepherd's bothy before evening closed in. He was tempted to sleep out but the nights were chilly and heavy with dews. Moreover there were other creatures of the wild roaming the crags and forest which he did not care to meet face to face. There was the wild dog, a few wolves remaining and the Asturian bears were reputed to roam freely. He just had to find the comparative safety of cover. An hour later, from the distant uplands, he heard the faint tinkle of bells and recognised with relief the human presence of a wandering shepherd following his solitary trade. A further climb brought him out of the upper treeline to the grassy heathered slopes and the grazing grounds. In the distance he saw the flock of sheep and goats approaching slowly, the shepherd leaning on his long gnarled stick. Dirk approached him and asked directions to the next bothy on his route, at the same time checking the accuracy of his navigation. The fellow spoke in a gutteral dialect which Dirk had difficulty understanding, but by sign-language and pointing, he was given a direction and a distance in kilometres, so the rest was up to him. As a parting gift the shepherd offered Dirk his wineskin, which he gladly accepted and surprised the shepherd by his acquired skill with the jet held above his mouth. Dirk smiled, murmuring his thanks and, bidding the pastor farewell, he limped off along the new trail.

By late afternoon he spotted the bothy and set about collecting dried twigs, moss and fallen timber for his fire. He drew water from the nearby stream, cut ferns for his bed and set about preparing an evening meal. As the sun declined towards the north-west he stoked up the fire with large pinecones which lay around in profusion, adding the broken branches and stacking others around the edges. The heat made him drowsy and the swig of brandy which the *dueña* of the tavern had pressed upon him induced a heavy sleep. He woke with the bird song at dawn. His watch said three. He wound it as a precaution and, rising, kicked the embers into life, adding the remainder of the wood. He went down to the stream for a wash. The water was ice cold and invigorating. He filled the pannikins and returned to the bothy to brew coffee, lacing it with sugar and brandy, delving into his rations for bread and cheese and strips of raw cured ham. The coffee tasted awful but served to wash down the unaccustomed food. Finally he went down to the stream again to draw water to shave and, his ablutions finished, he poured the surplus liquid on the embers, scattered the ashes and set off along the trail.

The path led along the edges of a deep ravine. Dirk had to pick his way along the narrow ledges, strewn with fallen stones and rocks from higher slopes. Overhead an eagle wheeled, whilst across the ravine upon a promontory higher up a wild goat, longhorned, peered down at him from its rocky pinnacle. His leg was starting to give him pain and he envied the agility of bearded Billy watching him. He pressed on whilst the sun was cooler. He knew it would become searingly hot by noon. He kept to the shadows where possible resting every half-hour to ease his leg. He made good time and eventually reached a gorge which led westwards in the direction he finally wanted to go. Dirk halted to point the little finger of his watch to the sun to obtain the north-south line. He laughed at his own audacity in attempting this difficult task of traversing the peaks. If only Nigel could see him now, he would dissolve into laughter.

The thought cheered him and he pressed on. His acute sense of direction spurred him and told him that he was nearing his ultimate goal. Dirk conserved his strength by frequently resting and restored his energies by eating little and often drinking from the water of the streams.

He reached the clearing as the sun was leaning on the tips of the tall pines on the opposite side. He gazed down at the familiar outlines of the farm and paused to drink in the scene. Putting his fingers to his lips, he imitated the shrill whistle of undulating sound which he had so often heard before. Three times he let it echo across the valley floor, until the farm door opened and a figure stepped out from under the pergola which shaded the porch. Raising hand to eyes the figure scanned the skyline to the west and slowly turning, peered along the edge of the treeline. Dirk could see the familiar plaid skirt, the high leather boots, the yellow scarf upon the white blouse, and pictured the dark curls framing those sunburn features. As she finally turned to gaze in his direction, he extracted his handkerchief and waved it as she had done once before. He extended his arms, holding his discarded Bergen sideways at arms length.

It was then that she began to run up the goat path down which he was now limping towards her. They met upon the slope in a silent but firm embrace. No word was exchanged. The pent-up, hidden emotions of the intervening years flowed through that passionate embrace. Words were superfluous. There they stood in statuesque pose as others appeared from the farmstead door to gaze upwards. They eventually parted, looking into each others' eyes. Dirk kissed her gently on the lips as she clapsed her hands behind his neck.

'I knew you would come back,' she murmured simply. Then she turned and waved to the family grouped below.